TO NAME THOSE LOST

Rohan Wilson

TO NAME THOSE LOST

Europa
editions

Europa Editions
214 West 29th Street
New York, N.Y. 10001
www.europaeditions.com
info@europaeditions.com

Library of Congress Cataloging in Publication Data is available
ISBN 978-1-60945-349-7

Wilson, Rohan   ●
To Name Those Lost

Book design by Emanuele Ragnisco
www.mekkanografici.com

Prepress by Grafica Punto Print – Rome

Printed in the USA

TO NAME THOSE LOST

THE LETTER

Her head hit the floorboards, bounced, and a fog of ash billowed, thrown so by the motion of her spade. She was slight of figure, slim with a quiet softly coloured face. She crashed and the spade rang and the thrown ash found volume then fell on her hair and her faded pinafore. Beside the kitchen's great red-brick hearth Maria looked the size of a child. Her light hair slowly dulled to grey under the raining grit. She lay senseless.

When William Toosey came into the kitchen he did not see his mother lying among the cinders. He had a hessian sack on his shoulder, which he placed on the table. One by one he removed half a dozen beer bottles from inside and lined them up. He looked about nervously. He'd scratched the labels off each bottle but by the caps you could tell where they'd come from. What he hoped was that she'd drink the beer and not ask. Stepping away from the table he saw his mother on the floor and gave a start. He smiled.

I've brought somethin, he said.

Ash drifted. His mother lay as before.

Ma, he said.

He crossed the floor and crouched near her. The coals crunched beneath his knees. Her eyes were closed, her mouth ajar.

Ma, he said.

He wasn't smiling now. He tried to lift her and when he got around behind and pushed her upright she was as slack as a straw toy and fell forward at the waist and rolled.

Ma. Stop it!

He shook his mother by the shoulders. Her head lolled and she gave off a fine cloud of dust that he could taste on his tongue as he breathed. He eased her to the floor and stood. This was stupid. She was shamming. He looked around the kitchen, his fists balled by his sides, and an instant passed where he wanted to hit her. He nudged her with his boot.

Get up for God's sake, he said. There is beer for you.

Then she coughed and winced.

What's the matter? he said.

He brushed the ash from her cheeks. Her throat seemed to be pumping beneath her skin. She turned her head, heaved, and let forth a thick liquid over the floor. Her eyes fluttered open and for a brief time she gaped at the ceiling as if looking through it to the sky, the great blue above, but they closed again and she grew still. William wiped her cheek, her lips, with the sleeve of his shirt. He felt the heat from her brow. For a while he just knelt there. His mother wasn't shamming. She was sick and she needed seeing to. He had to think about that. About what it meant. There was a doctor on Brisbane Street and he thought he might know the house, and that was all he could think of.

He ran. The worn road led into town, flanked by homes of weatherboard and brick. Ahead only the inner streets of Launceston, a stretch of rooves studded with church steeples, the river winding through like a wide leather thread. The dawn sun perching beyond the water was already white with heat. He ran and his pulse thudded in his head. His boots hit the dirt with a puff of grit. A man in a tweed coat walked the road and turned, startled, as William shot by, and called, Ease down, for the love of God! William never even looked back.

The town park filled acres of grassland skirted about by an iron balustrade and planted in a pageant of English willow and oak and pine that was wildly contrary to the sombre gums covering the hills above. He knew every inch of that park. The cubbies, hidey holes, blind switchbacks. The routes in, the routes out. All of it. But today, bundling through the gate with his breath firing in the hot dark of his chest, it seemed made new. He passed the ornate water fountain depicting naked cherubs at play in a pool and felt no cheer for the sight of it. The glass conservatory for the keeping of flowers gave his reflection differently, a huge-eyed boy, hair full of wind. He lowered his head and ran harder.

At the far side of the park he spilled onto Brisbane Street and skidded on the dirt footpath as he changed direction. A gig rolled through the crossing, its lamps still lit from dawn, and he ran into the haze it made. With his eyes pinched and searching he studied the street, the neat white-limed houses for that which belonged to the doctor. Plum trees was all that he remembered: two of them in ceramic pots by the door. Yet many had fruit trees, many had brass plaques, the residences of barristers, of bankers and insurers. He ran along a road that was lined with tall stucco or stone places, sucking back the smokey air of morning and scanning every house he passed, and just at the corner as he saw the doctor's house, the potted trees by the door weighted with blue summer plums, just as he felt that small relief, a pair of constables primly uniformed in black stepped from a side lane into the full sun and looked right at him.

William Toosey!

He stopped. They were crossing the road each dragging his dawn shadow for yards behind, the taller one waving off flies while resting his other hand upon the butt of his billyclub. William breathed hard. This man was called Beatty and the low sun in his eyes made him appear to smile. He'd drawn his long billyclub, black and gleaming like a greasy crowbar, and was tapping his thigh with it. William glanced up at the doctor's house and clenched his jaw.

Lovely mornin, the constable said. Just lovely.

William kept his eyes on the doctor's place.

Wouldn't you say so, William?

Piss off.

Beatty prodded his mate in the chest with the point of his club. This other fellow was young and pale in his freshly pressed uniform. Beatty prodded him and then gestured at William.

Not one of your more helpful sorts, this one, he said to the fellow.

No, sir. Looks a rough one, sir.

Rough? Jesus, man. He's a lad of twelve. You can handle a lad of twelve, can't you, Webster?

Yes, sir. I expect so.

You expect so. Well, God help us.

William looked from one to the other. He looked at the doctor's house.

So, Beatty said. How's about this brewery then. Terrible business.

William backed away.

Don't move. I aint said you could move.

William paused. He was breathing even harder. Mr. Beatty, he said. Me ma is sick.

The constable winced in disgust. What a load of mullock, he said.

She fell down. I was goin in there for the doctor.

But Beatty wasn't listening. Where's Oran Brown? he said. Eh?

Beatty tucked his stick in his armpit. They are shy quite a few cases, he said. Down at the brewery. As you already know.

Mr. Beatty, somethin is wrong with her. She needs a doctor. That's God's truth.

Beatty was grinning but he grew sober as he leaned towards the boy. I have Lally Darby under charge for it, he said.

She never went near the place, William said.

Young Lally is as guilty as a Jew and that is a fact.

It's a slanderous lie. She don't even drink.

Beatty grinned. He turned to his mate. Proper little solicitor, this one.

Yes, sir.

Thin as a lawyer's promise too, Beatty said. Don't your ma feed you?

Get naffed, William said and he reached for the gate. But Beatty was not about to have this. He laid his club upon the point of William's throat and they stood for a time thus strangely counterposed, each staring hard at the other, before William let his hand fall. Beatty shook his head in mock sadness.

Weren't just Lally, he said. She had Oran Brown with her.

Mr. Beatty, I have to have the doctor.

Where is he? Where's young Oran?

She needs help.

Webster, draw your stick, Beatty said.

This Webster hesitated, his fingers hovering over the handle. He looked at Beatty. He raised it from the holder on his belt and brought it about.

Give him a piece of it, Beatty said.

Webster made a small laugh.

There's nothin funny about this. Jesus, man. Hittin a child makes you laugh, does it?

No, sir.

Then belt him. Good and hard, so he knows we aint fartin about.

You want me to hit him?

That's right.

Webster smiled. He frowned. No joke? he said.

No joke, constable. Not a bit.

Webster came forward. He gripped the club in both hands, looking whiter than ever, his absurd moustache twitching. He stood near the boy, who was making himself slight against the paling fence, and he brought it high behind his shoulder and held it there. Where, sir? he said.

Wherever you fancy, constable.

Webster swung a tentative blow that caught the boy across the calf. William jumped. A deep and wounded scowl spread across his face.

Of all the fuckin—I said belt him, man. Belt him. Eh? You hear?

The junior constable looked around the street. Further along merchants at the assorted stores and tea rooms had started placing out signs and some stood on the footpath shielding the sun from their eyes and gazing at the scene unfolding before the doctor's place. This new attention seemed to unsettle him still further. He lifted the club but did not swing.

You want to learn the job, Beatty said, well this is the job. We aint trifles and we aint half-hearts. We do what needs doin.

Sir, he's a child.

Beatty shook his head glumly. I'm as troubled by it as you are, he said. Course I am. But young shortshanks here believes he has the better of us. He wants to withhold what he knows. What do you say to that?

Webster's cheek gave a twitch.

Constable, you are bound to it, Beatty said. Show me the man and I'll show you the law, you ever heard that? So here you are, Mr. Law himself. Stopped dead in his duties by a boy of twelve.

Might we not put him under arrest, sir?

For what? Under arrest. Bleedin hell. Are you a lawman or aint you? All you want is the whereabouts of the boy Oran Brown.

Still Webster did not strike. His eyes in the harsh sun had begun to water. He lowered the club and stepped back. It's not the proper thing, he said.

Well now, Beatty said. Well now this is your first week,

and you are liable to a bit of nerves. No shame in that. None at all.

William stood watching with his mouth drawn tight. He didn't know what to do but the thought of his mother was eating in his chest like spilled vinegar. You'll know a man in small moments was what his father had told him. Here was one such. His own small moment. An appraisal of all his nerve. So he shuffled along the fence line closer to the picket gate and reached for the latch.

Beatty came sharply about. With his long black club he planted a blow across William's back that sprawled him on the dirt and when next William opened his eyes there was the constable, and behind him the sky, and the constable was speaking to him.

What did I tell you? he said.

William stared up at him.

I told you not to move.

He rolled over. He was dizzy and his shoulder hurt. The folk in the street looked away as he climbed to his feet, for there was little to be gained in helping a thing like him and all and sundry knew it. He rubbed his shoulder. The world spun. He concentrated on the task of rubbing. His shirt was an old one of his father's turned in the sleeves and when he looked up at the constable his eyes had grown hard and dark. My pa will hear about this, he said.

Beatty grinned. I'll bet he does, he said. Well-known rogue is Thomas Toosey, he said to Webster. You can see the big dog's nature in the pup. He stood grinning down at the boy from the shade of his peaked cap.

The boy held his gaze. See how you grin when he puts a knife in you, he said.

The mirth fell from Beatty's face. He raised his club with mean intention, a quick action. He whaled the boy about the legs and body in series of two-handed thumps like the axe blows of foresters. William covered his head and curled into a ball but one blow caught on his ribs, drove the wind from his lungs, and another on the bones of his spine caused him to spasm in pain. A rising dread began to fill his thoughts. Beatty would end him here in the dust and sun. With each blow the pressure grew unbearable. Blood rose in his brain in a series of exploding colours.

It was only the coming past of a butcher that caused Beatty to stop. He wheeled by with a barrow of meat cuts covered under a bloody hessian sack, his sleeves rolled to the elbows and stained red, meanly eyeing the constables as he crossed. Beatty turned and watched him pass, his billyclub half raised. See something as upsets you, John? he said.

I can pick a coward, the butcher said.

Oh cowards, Beatty said. Was we cowards last week when your cousin was robbed?

The heavy twined tendons of the butcher's forearms tensed. His mouth worked beneath his mighty beard. He wheeled on. Beatty nodded at him. Soon ripe, soon rotten, John, he said. Better get that meat delivered.

When Beatty turned back his face had taken on a sour look. He rolled his tongue around his cheek as he studied the boy huddling on the dirt and that was all the space William required. He scrambled to his feet and broke for the park at full pace.

Oi! Beatty called.

It was a burst of unqualified terror that propelled him. His legs faltered, deadened and bruised. Every breath hurt his ribs. He stumbled and straightened and ran.

The park stood green and sunlit at the top of the street and he crossed the intersection for the gate, the spread of lawn, and beyond it the deeper glades caulked with black. He did not look back but the pounding sound of their ankle jacks and their calling and swearing came back doubled off the tall stucco homes and he knew they were close. Upon entering the park he hurdled without breaking step a derelict fellow at rest on the grass and he stumbled and steadied himself and bolted for the western edge where close-set trees grew in a thicket bored through with crawl holes. He scrabbled into one such scrub-cave and hid. The constables, each with his stick, were lumbering over the grass for the thicket. They yelled for him to show himself. William bellied deeper into the mess of crawl ways cut by the passing of children.

Boy, you better show out here.

He could hear them clubbing at the brush. He slid through dead leaves, pine needles, keeping low. White light cleaved into the under-dark. All about tiny birds took flight. He pulled and crawled and found the far side that led onto Brisbane Street and here he crouched to assess the likelihood of making the row of houses opposite. He could not see the constables, but he could hear them, hear the brush shattering where they clubbed at it. He looked either way along the empty street, took a breath, and ran.

The houses were huge and well tended and he mounted the first fence he hit, tossed his leg and tumbled after it and lay behind with his steam-hammer heart thudding at the cut grass beneath. They called and called. He put his ear to the palings. A cart rattled by and when it had passed he listened hard. The constables called and it was like the lowing of cattle, yet he knew they had not seen him. He also knew Beatty, the stubborn bastard, would not stop.

He looked around the yard where he'd sheltered. Trimmed apple trees and weeded gardens, a path winding through the shade. He sat up. Standing there in a broad sunhat was a gardener and he was all over burnt black with the sun with a full beard upon his face. He stared back at the boy. He had a broadfork buried into the earth and his foot was cocked on the crossbar where he'd paused in his action. He seemed about to speak when a call came from across the road.

You there.

It was Beatty.

You aint seen a boy come along here, have you?

The gardener looked at William huddled at the base of the fence and he looked at Beatty.

Rough-lookin little bugger, Beatty said.

The gardener yanked up his fork. Soil fell from the tines.

Well? Tell me.

Should rather put out me own eye, he said and drove the fork into the ground.

You what? Beatty banged his club on the fence, giving William a jolt.

The gardener turned another sod and broke it.

I can arrest you for causin obstruction.

Do what you like.

There passed a heavy silence where the gardener worked the rose bed and kept his eyes low. William could see Beatty's hand gripping the fence slat above him, the supple hand of a man who knew no labour. The fingers began to drum.

He's stolen from the brewery, Beatty said.

The gardener shook his head wearily. He turned a sod.

He must've come along here some place, Beatty said.

The fork sank without a sound.

You must've seen the little prick.

You'll have nothin from me, the gardener said.

Beatty slammed his club against the fence slats. I shall be mighty aggravated if I lose him.

Then best you get searchin.

The fingertips grew red with strain. He come along here, Beatty said. He must've.

The gardener levered up a solid lump rife with earthworms. He folded it over.

You hear what I said?

Now the gardener stopped. He leaned on his tool and

looked about the yard, a jaded sort of patience to his grey eyes. No, he said without looking at the constable. You aint hearin me. Arrest me if you like, knock me about, whatever. I'll not sell on a child.

William could hear the out-hiss of breath as Beatty wheeled away, the steadily receding slap of club upon thigh. He sat for a while listening and holding tight to his knees. He watched the gardener kneel to fetch out a stone that had surfaced and toss it among the flowers. He was faced away from William and nor did he look at the boy. The tool sunk with a press of his leg and he lifted a width of dark velvet earth. Rising carefully, William glanced over the fence line to where the constables at some distance scoured the park side of the street, poking their sticks into bits of planted brush and kicking through the shrubs, the pair of them with their sleeves rolled in the manner of sailors, calling for the boy to present. He lowered down.

Get yourself along, the gardener said.

He had stopped work. His hands were cupped upon the point of the handle and his head was bowed so that he seemed to be talking to the very earth.

They'll have me, William said.

I won't harbour thieves.

He was lyin. It wasn't me at the brewery.

I said get.

William took a breath ready to argue but the gardener had lifted his tool and turned.

Get.

I'm going, I'm going, he said. He began to edge away along the fence.

Stay gone.

Yes, sir.

The gardener stopped and stood in a wide stance, the fork braced at his hip.

That was a good thing you done, William said as he edged away.

Thank me by not comin back.

I will. I won't.

As he crossed under the low, harvest-heavy branches of orchard trees he knocked loose some fruit and he cut towards the side fence with it thudding behind him. He topped the palings in a crazed leap, tumbled, and fell into the neighbouring yard. There was a bed of carnations into which he splayed on his back, the wind taken from his chest. He coughed and winced and could not breathe. He went loping across this new yard, heading for the next fence, the next fall. In that fashion, and with a shred of luck, he put some distance on the constables before taking the footpath on Windmill Hill, heading to where he had a view along the road, over the park, and into town. He shaded his eyes with one hand. Beatty and Webster were gone, or at least he could not see them. Wind had slanted the smoke that rose long and lank and grey as drought-plain grass above the rooves. Away in the distance cow fields ran down to where the river shone like wet slate. He sat a moment on the gravel path in thought.

How long did he dare wait? He remembered the ash on his mother's cheeks, the shallowness of her breath. He put his head in his hands and sat considering what to do. There was also the matter of Oran Brown, who'd need warning of what Beatty meant, but that boy might be anywhere and now was not the time. In the end there was little else for it. She must have the doctor. He stood and scanned the park, the road, the stretch of houses that ran away to the mud-fringed river. No sight of the constables. He wasn't sure if that was a good thing or not. Keeping close to the houses along the hill, he set out for the doctor's place. When he crossed the intersection his mouth was dry and his fists were clenched at his sides. But there were only the early risers, the men off to the wharf and the bakeries.

At the doctor's place he unlatched the gate and walked up the path with his head swivelling to survey the street. He took hold of the knocker and was raising it when a fellow stood from out of the garden. He'd been cutting back rose bushes with iron shears, which he was now holding out mid-stroke.

Mrs. Hampson has already taken our bottles, he said.

What?

Yesterday. Returned them to the store.

I aint come about bottles.

The fellow lopped the tip off a stalk. He was concentrating upon this task and seemed to forget the boy was there.

Me mother has taken a spell, William said. She wants a doctor.

The doctor looked up. He seemed puzzled. It's Saturday, he said.

She fell on the floor. She won't get up.

The doctor frowned.

Please, sir, she's not well at all.

He looked around at his roses and then looked at the boy. Does she realise it's Saturday?

She don't realise much about much at the moment.

Can she speak?

No, sir. She's insensible.

How far is it? he said.

Down the hill, down Cimitiere Street.

There's an extra rate payable on Saturdays.

Yes, sir, very well. But you must come. She aint well.

The doctor set aside his shears. Well, come on then. Let's see her.

It was the best part of an hour before he arrived back with the doctor. The doctor was in a coat despite the heat, hair askew in the wind, hauling a carpet bag that must have held his instruments. William went almost at a run. He glanced back in spells to check the doctor was coming. The doctor would jog a few paces and then walk and then wave for him to slow down. At the front of the house William lifted back the latch and held the gate for the doctor. He showed him inside where his mother had fallen before the kitchen fire and the doctor dropped his bag on the table and took one look at Maria and shook his head.

What's the matter with her? William said.

This lady has passed.

Is she sick?

She's dead.

What? William was sweating. It dripped off his nose. Aint you better check? I mean, she looks unwell.

She's blue, the doctor said.

So do somethin.

There's no question. She is past my help.

She's only thirty-eight, and never a day of illness in her life. My boy—

What kind of doctor can't help a healthy woman?

The doctor smiled but his lips were thin and drawn beneath his prim moustache. From the way the wires of his jaw flexed he seemed to want to say more, but he had grace enough to unclip his bag and pull out a bound pad and a pencil, lick the lead and begin to jot.

She can't be, William said. It's a mistake.

He knelt beside her and the moment he touched her forehead he knew it was no mistake. She was cold and eerily still. Not like sleep, not like life. His throat tightened and he felt everywhere a creeping sensation of the skin.

What happened to her? the doctor said.

When William looked up there was no longer anything fretful about him.

Did you see her fall?

No.

Did she hit her head?

I just come in, found her lyin here.

The doctor nodded slowly and without commitment. He studied William, his eyes flicking to the different parts of him, the hair like a sheaf of wheat, the loose and overlong clothes. He nodded and he took from his bag a pair of leather gloves and pulled them on. He came beside Maria and began very carefully to walk his arachnidian fingers around her throat, around her head, and through her pinned-up hair. Last of all he opened her mouth to peer inside.

Where is your father? he said.

William had grown pale. He couldn't speak.

You live alone here with your mother?

After a moment William said, Not no more by the looks.

Do you expect your father home soon? Do you have family or friends who might attend to you?

I don't need no one's help, he said.

The doctor watched him a moment. He stood and retrieved his pad and jotted something else down. His mouth tugged as if he was talking secretly and his pencil moved and made a grazing noise. William looked away out the window where in the neighbouring yard he could see a girl passing sheets through a mangler and he thought his mother ought to be doing her washing too, given the weather, but his mother was dead and he was entirely alone in the world and he felt an utter fool for thinking it.

You must have family or friends, the doctor said. Someone who can attend to you.

I've an aunt and uncle. Cousins.

Where are they?

By the hospital hill. Over west.

Good. That will do.

I aint goin there.

Pardon me?

I'll be right by meself. Like I told you.

The doctor closed his pad. My boy, he said, tapping his pencil. Go to them, or the police will be obliged to put you in the invalid depot.

They won't send me nowhere cause I aint leavin.

You must be in care and the law won't allow otherwise. Surely your father is nearby?

I can take care of meself.

The doctor looked at William and his jaw knotted and unknotted. He tore a sheet off his pad and folded it and placed it on the table. Given your circumstances I'll provide you with fourteen days to pay that, he said.

Pay what? You aint done nothin for her.

Fourteen days, hear me. Not a minute more.

She's as dead as ditches, you bloody crook.

There'll be someone along for her presently. I'll see to it.

The doctor snapped shut his bag. He didn't look at the boy. He strode through the parlour for the door, his bootsoles sounding on the floorboards, then muffling over the possum skin rug, then sounding again as he cleared it.

After the doctor left, William sat and held his mother's hand and wiped her forehead clean of ash. He straightened her collar. He wasn't sure what else to do. In the airing cupboard he found a bed sheet and covered her up to the neck and she stared back as if he'd just delivered some woeful news. After a while he stood and went about making himself a breakfast. There was a little salted ling, a stale heel of rye bread, and some butter for it. Generally it was his mother's job, and he kept expecting her to say something and he'd turn and look but she was ever silent. Her face had changed, slackened. He saw now how the fine shroud of ash she wore picked out the lines at her eyes, her mouth. She'd grown old and he hadn't noticed. He went and took her hand and told her he was sorry. For a long time he sat holding the stiffening fingers, his eyes welling. She stared at the ceiling.

I tried, he said. I'm sorry. I tried.

The doctor must have sent for the cart from the hospital dead-house, for in the early afternoon the driver hove up outside and called from the gate if they had a poor soul inside needed ferrying home. William was sitting with his mother as he had been these last hours. He stood and looked out the window. The fellow saw him and waved. He mounted the verandah, walking respectfully slow. He wore an old felt wideawake, which he doffed and held to his chest. William showed him through the door, through to the kitchen where Maria lay beneath the sheet watching the ceiling.

Oh dear me now, he said.

William could hardly speak. His throat felt stopped up.

Aint she young, though.

Yes, William said.

Least she has come upon it peaceful enough.

William nodded.

Not all of them do, the cart driver said. He fussed with the brim of his hat. Had one a week back, he said. He was a mess. A railways navvy. Been pickin out a blast from a tunnel wall which had missed its fire. Well, you can picture how it went. The thing goes off. Bang. All done.

William looked at him.

We carried the bits of his head back in a kero tin. There was a deal of the poor bugger we never found of course.

There was nothing to say. William watched him quietly.

A deal, yes, the cart driver said. But here, this is a scene of more than ordinary solemnity. This dear woman has met with a visitation from God. No misadventure here and no fool's act. She is taken from us whole.

The fellow was full of emotion and his eyes glistened. An awkward quiet followed. William crossed his arms and uncrossed them.

Give us a hand, the cart driver said.

Now he went about the rites peculiar to his occupation, shaking out a handkerchief and folding a three-inch band, which he placed under Maria's chin and fastened at the top of her head to hold shut her mouth. Over her eyelids he put small pads of wet cotton and he straightened her delicate limbs. She was bound in a bed sheet, wrapped and knotted, and then William took her booted feet under his armpit and they raised her up, the strain turning him a wild shade of red. It was all he could do to hold her. The cart driver watched him battle and nodded. The boy was doing this last and most absolute of acts and said not a word of sorrow. So it was, and so it should be.

In that manner they carried his mother out through the gate, into the street, and lowered her to the footpath. William was feeling the small of his back where he was bruised from Beatty's club when he saw coming up by the town park two municipal policemen. Men he knew. They were at some distance and his best hope was that they'd not yet seen him. The thudding of his heart grew harder. With a count of three they lifted his mother onto the cart, into the sawdust spread in the bed. The driver squinted up at the sky.

She's some summer we're havin.

William watched the constables over the top of the horse standing dead still in the traces. Aint it, he said.

Miserable business, the driver said. Plain droppin dead like that.

Yes.

Best I get her home out of it.

Yes. Thank you.

They threw a rope, tied it off. There were eyebolts placed for that purpose along the flatbed and the driver tensioned the rope with a sheepshank knot while from the edge of his sight William observed the constables. The driver remounted the dead cart bench, huffing in the awful hot weather, and chucked the reins lightly and the whole shoddy concern stumbled forward, his mother joggling, her boots over the tailboard knocking like she'd seen fit to dance to kingdom come. The dead-cart driver made a superstitious sign and spat as the cart trundled off, strange old fool that he was.

Before the cart had drawn away a length William was back inside the house. He found his leather school satchel, unused these last years without his father, and filled it. His coat, a shirt and trousers, a pair of boiled wool socks. In his mother's drawer he found a pound banknote and ten shillings loose, which he pocketed and he stood a time surveying their room, the rusted iron bedhead hard under the window, squares of orange sun cast across the quilt, and he pondered on what he was about to do. They'd clobber colours into his hide that he'd never seen. Bash open his wine-bladder head. Only if they caught him though, only if they caught him.

Beatty banged his club on the door. This is Beatty of the Launceston police house, he said. If William Toosey is in there, I should like to speak with him.

William turned rigid. He could see them cast in cameo on the window curtain. Demented shapes, as disproportioned as shadow puppets. He hooked the bulging satchel over his shoulder and backed away into the kitchen.

William Toosey! Present yourself.

By the kitchen table he paused. There was more he needed. He couldn't leave yet. He stole into the parlour where, among the newspapers his mother kept piled by the rat-chewed arm-chair in which she sat each night, he found a printed biscuit tin and brought it to the light. Inside was her correspondence, sheaves of it, as well as blank paper and envelopes. He crammed this into his satchel. He gripped the bag and ran for the back door.

The yard at the rear was a spread of trampled grass hung across with washing lines. He could still hear the pounding on the door as he hit the fence and he lobbed his bag and threw himself over the palings after it. His high swinging boot heel caught a rope and made him topple but he was on his feet and dragging his satchel about his neck as he ran. The plot of land behind the house had been dug with trench footings for some new place and he leapt these ditches and skidded in the dirt and went on. At road's end was a fringe of wire fence and beyond that unploughed paddocks furred in thin and mousy buttongrass. They would not look for him down there, not these two. He trod down the cross wires and bent himself through the fence.

There was a certain hollow tree he knew on a patch of sand near the riverbank that was long gutted by fire and weathered to a dull black. Leaning distinctly out of true, it reminded him of a figure hunched over a grave. He reached this tree and he sat within the hollow where he could see along the road to the house nestled in the lowering sunlight amongst the many such others. The gate was open. The front yard empty. There was no one below the ink-dark shade of the verandah, no uniformed men with their fearful billyclubs. He withdrew into the depths of the tree.

After a while he pulled his mother's correspondence from the bag. Letters tied with ribbon, fifteen or twenty, all addressed in the same gaunt handwriting as if rather than paper it was a prison wall on which it was etched, dated from three years hence until the last two weeks ago in December. He slipped this latest one from the stack and flipped it over. The return address was simply care of the Deloraine post office. He looked up at a sky ribbed with cloud. A pair of cawing plovers. When they had passed out of sight he pulled a sheet of paper and a pencil and began to write a letter in his own neat schooled hand, and he wrote with great care across the page, his eyes running and his tears punctuating here or there a phrase or smearing out a letter. He dated it January the fifth in the year of our Lord eighteen hundred and seventy four. He wrote and when he was done he signed off, folded the paper into an envelope and on the front he scratched a name that gave him a small thrill of awe even as the pencil spiralled through it:

Mr. Thomas Toosey.

THE SHED

L ate in the night the prisoner Thomas Toosey raised his eyes at the sound of boots to see amber light slanting through the fissures in the siding, light made hard by the weightless dust and growing longer and brighter as the bootsteps loomed. The door swung inward and standing in a hollow of dark was the deadman who had taken him. He was holding a primitive lamp, this deadman, and as he moved inside the shed the shadows wheeled around him. He bobbed beneath a crossbeam and squatted by his prisoner, whistling, not a tune but a kind of birdcall, and he placed down the lamp and tested the bindings that made Toosey fast to the centre post. The lamp was a candle bedded in dried clay, shrouded by a brown beer bottle. Toosey watched it flicker.

I aint the one.

Shut it, the deadman said.

He hitched another knot in the bindings, took up the eerie amber lamp, and walked a turn around the interior. The dark retreating like it was full of life. He looked down upon the prisoner and straightened his hat. The brim was folded back and pinned in place. He waved the lamp a little.

This'll do you.

Listen now, Toosey said.

It's a waste of breath, old mate.

I aint the one they want. I'm tellin you. Listen.

The deadman considered him a time. Then who are you?

Toosey inclined his head to look up. Hard luck, he said.

Oh a hard luck. You're havin a laugh, I see. Very good, very bleedin funny.

You hear me laughin? Toosey said.

The candle flame guttered as the deadman raised the lamp and tapped the amber glass. That's you now, he said pointing at the flame. Caught. Good and proper.

Cut me loose, said Toosey.

Damned if I will.

There's a boy in this. My boy. You'll be makin an orphan of him.

You're off to the constable I'd say.

Toosey shook his head solemnly. The constable, he said. These two don't like constables. They'll hoist me in a tree someplace. With a nice bit of cord.

Will they now.

Believe it.

Forty quids, the deadman said. That's what I believe.

A death on you for the sum of forty quids. You are some kind of saint.

I shall sleep like a lamb, I promise you that.

Stringed grey hair hung past Toosey's shoulders and when he tossed it back there was a quality to his eyes made mean through his hardship. He clicked his tongue. Course I could be wrong, he said.

About what?

The dead man might yet be you.

This seemed to unsettle something in the fellow. He puckered his lips and whistled his low and melancholy birdcall, shook his head, and shaped up to his prisoner like he meant to give him a kicking. He half lifted his boot, turned his hip. But without another word he stepped back and bobbed out past the tools. Toosey leaned against the post and watched the knife-light withdraw through the slats until he was plunged again into cold abyssal dark.

*

There were cows crying somewhere in the night and that was all the company he had until dawn. He sat and waited, his eyes open, his mind burning with thoughts of his boy. The sun was a long time in coming and then a long time ascending and yet he did not sleep but sat with his knees at his chest watching for the first of the sky in the unjoined cladding. In the quiet the cows called and Toosey waited to where the light shot through the wall like sheets of silk, to where he could see by it. Baled hay mouldering in the stall. Articles strung on nails. Piled by the wall were tools for working the soil and tools for working wood. He stood awkwardly by snaking up the post and shuffling his feet closer. Once he was upright he could circle around the post in his tethers. His eyes jumped about for something of use. He would not be kept here. His boy needed him.

Among the straw he spied a hand scythe that had a rusting blade and might have had an edge. He stretched out a leg. If he huddled down he could touch the handle with his toe. He inched it closer with little flicks of his foot and he soon had purchase enough against the dirt floor to drag it under his bootsole level with his thigh and then, heaving, level with his buttocks. He rotated around the post so that his hands would reach and he lowered down and strained hard and he had the coarse wooden handle clutched cigar-like between two fingers when the deadman shouldered the shed door inward. A muzzle-loading rifle over his shoulder, a tin bucket in his elbow. He looked at Toosey and he looked at the scythe. He brought the gun to bear.

That's a pretty trick, he said.

Toosey stood up rigidly. In the band of sun issuing through the doorway the oiled gun barrel shone almost blinding. He did not take his eyes off it.

The bucket sloshed as the deadman set it down, full of milk, a ladle hanging on the rim, and he assessed his prisoner and scratched himself through his waistcoat. Kick it over here, he said.

Toosey didn't move.

Old cock, I will bruise you black. Don't think I won't.

With a flick of the foot, Toosey kicked the scythe towards him. The deadman tossed it among the various tools by the wall and then knelt and filled the ladle from the bucket and held the lip up to Toosey. He drank. The man dipped again and gave him some more. The cream was warm and rich in Toosey's gut. The man lowered the ladle.

They'll be comin this way again today, he said.

Who?

You know who.

Toosey watched him. That Dublin jackeen I suppose, he said.

Aye, and that barmy little man that follows him about.

Toosey gave a snort of contempt. That's no man, he said.

Whatever he is under that flour sack he wears, he gives me the cold horrors.

They aint to be trusted, Toosey said.

Course they aint. Any halfwit can see that.

I'll tell you what I know. There won't be no forty. Not from those two.

The deadman laughed. Gawd deary me.

Your Dublin mate has me mistook for another, Toosey said. That's the truth of it.

The deadman drifted off to lean against the corner brace. He tucked the muzzle-loader under his arm and crossed one boot over the other. Toosey saw how the toe was closed up with roofing nails clinched flat with a hammer. In the rest of his dress he was like most tenants of that district, pants secured by means of a rope, waistcoat festooned with a watchless chain that fooled no one. Every bit of him patched and mended. He idly fingered the gun as he took his ease against the wall. He spoke.

There has been a good deal of talk about the town there has. Bout two men goin up and down chasin some poor fellow. I heard it at Williams' and heard it at the Family and Commercial too. Cause, lord, people will talk now, won't they.

Prone to it yourself I expect, Toosey said.

So when I seen them wander by me fence I knew who they was. They waved me over. I have forty pound for a man called Toosey or Atkinson, says the Irish.

And you believe him?

Forty pound payable upon receipt, he tells me. Know this fellow by his long grey hair and grey whiskers, he tells me. Wearin always a small black billycock.

At that point the man bent down and plucked Toosey's hat from off a straw heap. He tossed it at his prisoner. Now that I seen you, he said, I do believe him.

Toosey studied the hat where it lay upturned, light showing through the crown's holes, a white crust of sweat, and he looked briefly at the man and looked away, as if what he saw was not to his taste.

There came a call from outside, a woman's voice. Jacky . . . Jacky.

Stay out there, the deadman said.

Where are you?

When she appeared in the door she was clutching her skirts in her fist. She was delicate of frame and drawn about the cheeks, or it may just have been the tight coiling back of her hair. She peered into the murk, leaning forward, and said, You in there?

What did I tell you. Stay out of here.

I want to talk to this chap.

She stepped over the worn doorstep and past him into the inner dark, among the bladed light, and on seeing the rope-bound prisoner slumped in the shadows she put her hand to her mouth and stumbled back.

So help me, she said, breathless. I thought he was dead.

He's all right. Aint you, old cock?

Flies squabbled along Toosey's bare weathered arms. He slowly raised his head to look at the woman, the wife most probably.

Don't look like much, does he, she said.

No. Cause he aint much.

What do they want him for?

That aint our concern. Long as I get paid.

The wife crossed through the light slats before him, the sequence lighting the fine hairs of her neck like hot wires. She left the scent of lanolin and soap. He stared at her.

What have you done, mister? she said. Killed someone, have you? Stole a horse? What?

Toosey would not be drawn. He stared at the woman and waited.

He don't look like much to me, she said again.

Well he got this Irishman fired up so I should think he done somethin to warrant it.

You got a name?

Toosey glared back at her.

He's called Toosey or Atkinson or somethin, said the deadman. I know that much.

Cut me loose, said Toosey. Or they'll kill me.

The man sneered. That's more of your lies.

Maybe he aint done nothin, the wife said.

Girl, I swear you are as simple as strikin matches.

How do you know what he done?

Long as I get me forty I don't care if he is king of the queers.

I'm not worth the trouble, Toosey said. Believe me.

Is that right?

Aye.

Then how is it you come to have a price on you? the deadman said.

Ask the Irish. He'll tell you before he strings me up.

The wife crossed back past him, holding her dress off her ankles. Praps we ought not to keep him, she said. We don't want no one killed, do we?

Oh you silly bitch, come here.

Her husband caught her by the arm and hauled her in against his chest, cupping one wide weathered hand about the back of her neck. He said, Give us a kiss fore you flap that stupid tongue again.

They stood clasped to each other with their mouths together. Toosey looked away. When the deadman let her go she staggered a few steps sideward with the suddenness of it, smoothed the hair off her brow and grinned foolishly, her lips red and wet. Her husband leaned down and slapped her on the rump.

Forty quids, he said. That's the buggy you will have wanted, and a fine young mare to pull it.

Would be nice, she said.

Don't say I don't take care of you.

I never said it. Only that you ought to be careful.

Careful, he said. Careful aint got no one rich.

No, I spose not.

Go see about them hens and forget this old loony. It's just him talkin big.

She wandered out into low dawn light that tinged all the fields in bronze, and her husband followed her as far as the path of cobble, where he stood staring into the oblique sun with his morning shadow gaunt upon the ground. He broke off and was heading for the paddocks mumbling a curse when Toosey called from the dark of the shed for him.

You want to know what I done? he called.

A moment of quiet passed before the man cocked his head around the jamb. What you what?

What I done to the Dubliner.

Does it matter?

Matters to you most intimately.

The deadman looked down at Toosey hobbled there among the dark like a malevolent imp. He stepped inside, stood tall above him.

How? the deadman said.

He has offered you a sum, has our man. But he don't have it. He has not more than a few pound.

You're a bloody liar.

Hear me now. He does not have it. I know cause I robbed him of his whole worth.

Like hell you did.

Toosey just stared at him.

The man had jammed his hands into his coat pockets and he stood for a period contemplating his prisoner. He jabbed one finger at Toosey through the coat folds. You're talkin out your arse, he said.

I dropped the money when you presented that gun at me, Toosey said. Two hundred pound, in a pocket pouch. Dropped in the ditch there by the road last night. Go see if it aint.

You dropped two hundred quids in a ditch?

Go see if you don't believe me. No skin off your nose, is it. By the road there where you found me, near the fence.

How old are you, Toosey or Atkinson or whoever you bloody are?

Fifty-nine.

Fifty-nine, the deadman said.

Toosey nodded.

Old man, I don't know how you've lived this long.

All the country air, Toosey said.

I swear. Robbin two hundred off a man as vicious as that Irish.

Me boy is alone. I told you. By himself in that arsehole they call Launceston. I intend to see him safe and sound, whatever comes of it.

I can tell you what will come of it, the deadman said. It's you in a Deloraine cell.

Toosey tossed the hair from his face and sat looking up at the man, one eye asquint in the sun slant that shone through a gap. In the stagnant air the sound of his breath amplified. He held the man's gaze for a good long moment before he spoke. I've knowed the Dubliner half my life, he said. I tell you now. In the sight of God. He will kill me.

The deadman crossed his arms. Will he now.

I may have a prayer if you fetch the money. See it returned to him.

The deadman stood in thought. At length he took up the gun that he'd stood against a crossbrace and he checked the priming and reset the hammer and stuck it over his shoulder. He looked down at his prisoner. The money bloody well better be there, he said. Else I'll be back to kick in your teeth.

It's there. Look in the ditch like I said.

The man crossed and stood in the doorway. Cropped land in belts lay framed in its oblong and beyond it hills rearing in a blue haze where the gum grew like a bristle of dorsal hair. He paused, studying the view towards the road, likely seeking out those two wanderers, the Irish with his hooded ally, but there was neither their figures nor their dust upon that baked and peeling back route. He put along the path towards the road holding the gun levelled at his hip. Toosey then closed his eyes and sought some comfort for his hands and shoulders and his wrists that burned. He dropped his head and in the false dark behind the eyelids all he saw was his boy, the mop of his hair, the thinness of his arms, and he was stirred to a rage.

Some time later the wife came to sort through the tools by the wall. Toosey sat foxing sleep and listening. Within that clamour and contrasted to it was the slight and delicate sound of her skirts. He peered from under his lashes. She was bending over the pile and the shape of her rump had forced the gathers of her dress out flat, and it was a shapely rump at that. The falls of light through the walls marked her back like smelted metal. She tugged a stirrup hoe from the clutter and stood up straight, and as she turned towards the door he lifted his head to address her.

You need a short halter for that greedy horse of yours, he said.

She gave a short sideways step as if startled and brought the hoe up. He aint no horse, she said.

He is draggin you into somethin. By God he is.

She flung the tool out into the daylight where it bounced and rang on the cobble and she squared up to him. There was an agreeableness to her features that at that moment was marred by a tightening of the lips. Whatever you done, mister, she said, whoever you hurt, I hope you get what you got comin.

Funny how men will abandon good sense on the sniff of a few quid, he said.

Oh yes. Funny as a bloody funeral.

Toosey looked her over. Is he back yet?

No, she said.

He continued to watch. I was married once you know.

More's the pity for her I expect.

She would have been near your age when we met, he said and narrowed his eyes. Twenty, twenty-one. Near enough to it.

Where has she gone then? Your girl.

Spose you think I run her off.

She would need to be a saint, wouldn't she. Puttin up with the likes of you.

Toosey smiled. He nodded. That is the truth, he said. The kindest and dearest woman I ever knew. Only God knows why he sent her to me. But she grew sick of my drinking, the many years of it, and turned me out. Since which she has died.

The tears of the tankard, she said. You won't get no pity from me.

I don't want any, he said. What I want is to offer my example. I ought to have valued her while I could. That's the crux of it. If you value your fellow, you will warn him not to cross me.

In the field the cows bayed like wolves. She stood and seemed to consider his words, looking down at him, sucking at her upper lip, but more likely she was giving inward expression to the scorn she held for this bushman. She smoothed back her hair and exited out into the sun, lifting the crusted hoe onto her shoulder and striking out for the crops, and Toosey, his head bowed behind a curtain of hair, was left alone with his life's sorry tales.

Arriving back at the shed some time midmorning the deadman prodded Toosey in the ribs. He was slumped in his tethers like a carcass, mouth agape, limbs slack. He woke in a spasm. The cattledog was there and it pushed to lap at his face and he did not pull away but let the dog taste his whiskers. One eye was dark and the other light as if it had been stitched from the pelts of butchered dead and when the man clicked his fingers the dog fell in alongside him. Now Toosey looked up at the fellow, saw the book-sized wallet tied with lucet cord upon which he was tapping his fingers, saw the grin he was wearing, his considerable teeth bared, and Toosey knew he would soon be with his boy. He wiped the slobber on his shoulder.

What did I tell you, Toosey said.

You're up to your neck now, old cock. Eh? Aint you.

Not by a mile.

Up to your neck in shit I would say.

The Dubliner is goin to want his money when he gets here, Toosey said. And he will soon know who's in possession of it.

I never saw no money.

Toosey breathed hard through his nostrils. He almost laughed. I picked you from the start, he said. The one who dances well when fortune pipes.

The deadman twitched a little at this.

Two hundred is a lot better than forty, Toosey said. That's what you're thinkin. Keep a secret from the Irish. Keep the money. Oh yes. But when you go to the dance, take heed who you take by the hand. For you don't know the first thing about me.

A pissin old bushman due his comeuppance. That's you, I'd say.

Toosey dipped his head. I am due it. But not today. Today I have out-thought you. If you want to keep that money, and I know you do, then it is a simple matter of cuttin me loose.

The man straightened up. He hooked one thumb through his corded belt as his mind worked upon the problem of the bushman.

I'll lay it out for you, Toosey said. Straight as I can. Cut me loose. Keep the money hidden. When the Dubliner arrives you tell him you never saw me.

Is that your fabulous scheme? the deadman said. Give away the money to avoid what you have comin?

That's the first part. The second is comin later.

It was a long and silent moment in which the deadman turned away to pace the shed in a pretence of thought, as if he had a choice that he might otherwise make. He dragged his sleeve across his nose where a sweat had formed upon it. Toosey waited while the man wandered, scuffing his nailed-up boot to make a divot, his eyes on the rutted roadway visible out the door, upon which would soon appear the two ominous figures, the Irishman and his brute. He replaced his hat and pushed on the crown and faced Toosey once more.

All right, you tiresome prick, he said. All right. I'll turn you out. But see now, I want you makin northerly over them hills.

Swear it to me. You meet them micks on the road and it's all our heads.

I have every intention of avoidin them.

Swear it.

Best if I keep meself intact. Aint it?

Then swear.

I swear.

The deadman studied him for a time. He whistled his bird-call tune. He stepped outside.

Among the tools and bits of harness leather littering the floor there lay an axe handle hewn from red-brown myrtle that was coming unsplit in the grain and Toosey was staring at it when the fellow returned, bringing with him the gun. He directed the muzzle at Toosey as he moved around the post, knelt down, and began to uncinch the ropes. Each of Toosey's wrists bore angry welts that showed where the plaiting had bitten. He squeezed his fist to get the blood pulsing. He pulled his sleeves and buttoned the cuffs and sat looking around himself. The man was standing with the gun on him.

Go on, he said. Away with you.

Toosey rolled onto his hands and knees. The dog with its ears raised was watching him. He coughed and stooped into a crouch, coughing and spitting, haggard as he was. Lowering the gun, the man gave a little smile. He started to speak. You need the—he said but then stopped.

It looked like a glowing iron come from a fire, igniting, dousing, igniting as it passed through the sheeted lights in succession, giving off a faint and even hiss, striking the man in the jaw and pitching him over sideways, his arms in a peculiar loose-limbed flail like rag things, the gun spilling, a red spray of blood aflame in the light shears and speckled with shards of teeth and his hat momentarily hanging where he'd been before plummeting with him to the dirt.

Toosey was on his feet and standing over him and he raised

high the axe handle and hammered it down. The deadman scrabbled over the floor making an unholy wail. There was a wild look to him and he screamed out for Toosey to stop but Toosey would not. He swung blow after blow and swung one that took the deadman above the ear, a vicious thing, well aimed, that tore back the scalp to the bone and the deadman sagged and lay insensate among the hay, his fresh blood a brilliant shade on the straw. Toosey tossed aside the handle. He smeared his palms down his shirt. He crouched by the milk bucket and lifted the ladle off the rim and drank. In a corner of thick dark the dog cowered and turned away from him.

As he was dipping for a refill and trying to slow his breathing the light of the doorway filled with someone's shape and a shadow settled over him. He looked around. Here was the wife, hand to her mouth and silent and horror-struck. He replaced the ladle. He nodded.

I give him fair warnin. Give it to you both.

Jacky, she said.

Reckon you better fetch yourself out of here.

What did you do?

I've done for him.

You what?

Best you leave, he said. They'll be here soon.

She turned and bolted. Toosey followed into the white-hot day. She was going full flight among a herd of cattle and she stumbled and corrected herself, her eyes huge as she looked back. Yet it was not the wife fleeing that held his attention there in the noon sun. He pinched up his eyes. Away along the road blew a faint cloud of dust. He waited and he watched. The road cut out of the hills, down through gum stands rising chalk white from a cover of tussock grass, and among that scrub he saw two figures emerge from the trees in a hint of movement. And that was all he needed to see.

Back in the shed he found his faded black hat and planted

it on and stacked in one corner was his swag and his few meagre things, a billytin, a pannikin, turnips, flour, raisins in a gunnysack. These he rolled inside his swag. Flies had begun to gather on the deadman and, squatting there, Toosey rolled the fellow onto his back and opened his waistcoat and removed the pouch of money from an inner pocket. He thumbed through, counting notes quietly to himself, and stuck the book inside his jacket. He took up his swag and settled it across his back, tugged down his hat brim, and stepped outside.

The seekers had advanced somewhat along the roadway and he pressed his hand above his eyes and studied them, two dark nicks against a sand-brown groove, coming only for him. He turned and cut across the field towards the forested hills looming like great unshorn beasts from the farmland, keeping a steady measured pace out through the crops.

Two Seekers

They slogged side by side up the incline where horse carts had traced a pair of thin gutters down from the farmhouse. First came the aged man but in this image he was deceiving for his arms were as thick as derricks contained within a coat tightly buttoned at his wrists. With his hefty walking stick, with the printed neckerchief knotted at his throat, he seemed like some gentleman on tour leisurely viewing his vast ancestral estate. Second came a shorter fellow, spindly armed, and he carried a rolled blanket horseshoed over his left shoulder. Upon his head was drawn a white cotton hood cut with eyeholes. The two shared neither word nor gesture as they laboured up the hill, studying that secluded parcel, two souls avowed in a common aim.

The farmhouse was a crude building in a field of feed oats. They stopped near the cobbled forecourt and looked around themselves. There was no sight of anyone. The wall scantling was hand cut and the planks had buckled for lack of decent nails. Little Sussex hens stepped with theatrical care among the weed and thistle. The traveller propped on his stick and removed his bushman's hat, a limp and sagging thing, with which he waved away the flies. He had on his back a canvas satchel and when he took it off the pots inside clanged in the silence. He moved towards the farmhouse calling out a long cooee. The house listed a foot out of square and a row of props had been placed to counter the mighty lean. Clothes like the quartered dead were pegged on a rope between these braces and he pushed them aside as he bobbed under the poles.

He entered the kitchen, scattering hens. A fire burned in the stove with a pot of water on the plate. He made a slow circuit and found a crate loaded with turnips. A wad of butter on a dish. He picked it up and sniffed and put it down. He went outside again. The hooded man was standing in the shade, leaning on the shed. He crossed past him, came before the shed door and stood staring into the depthless black inside, a blackness cut through with shafts of light. He was craning his neck better to see when a bestial scream came from within.

Mother of fock, he said and staggered back.

There burst from the dark a madwoman. She was wielding a blood-greased axe handle over her head and she caught him by the throat to club him, but the traveller was fit for this game. He broke her grip with a shove and stood facing her, waiting for what would follow. At her side was a stockdog that showed its teeth and growled. Woman and dog looked between those two strangers in a panic.

Careful there, marm, the traveller said.

Get out of it, you bastards!

She swung hard. The traveller stepped aside and watched it sail by. On the backswing he caught the handle and disarmed her. She scrambled out of his reach believing herself in danger, yet the traveller merely examined the point of the handle, frowned at the blood there, tested it with a finger, and threw the gruesome thing to the ground.

You done this, she said. You sent that man.

Oh, he said with a kind of sadness. That man. You'll be meanin Thomas Toosey, I suppose.

She was pressing the heels of her hands to her eyes. Oh my sweet saviour, she said. He's an animal.

He is, aye, he is.

A bloody animal, she screamed.

Where did he go, marm? Can you tell me that now?

You sent him our way.

Where is he, marm?

You killed . . .

The traveller waited for her to finish. What, marm? Killed what?

She had backed up against the layered wooden cladding. A quivering took up in her limbs like the violent shake of a hypothermic and she pressed one hand over her mouth, her eyes pinched and beginning to run, and she collapsed as if struck by something vicious.

At first the traveller seemed unmoved by her display. He watched her shiver and soon stepped away to scan the back paddocks, the thickly covered hills to the east. His eyes searched for sign of the man he'd tracked this last month through scrub stands and fern glades and down trails that ran everyplace across the district, a man he'd seen in his sleep, seen in the black scrags of burnt wattle, seen in the ever-rising dust of the foot roads. But his hooded companion was also watching and the suffering of the farm woman seemed to stir something in him. He moved closer to where she was hunched up, blood on her skirts, blood on her hands, her windblown hair like twine. He hung his arm around her shoulders and rocked with her and smoothed her hair and she collapsed into his shirt folds as if emptied of everything that filled her with life.

The traveller, resting on his staff, observed the scene from a small remove. What a blessed bloody mess, he said.

The woman sobbed. Beside her the hooded man with his stark black eyes sat holding her. That animal, she said through her hands. We was meant to be in town meetin his old grandma today. We was meant to walk into town.

For the love of God, the traveller said, what's goin on here? We've come to find Toosey, not to focking hurt you, begging your pardon. At least let me see if I can't help.

Don't you go near him.

Near who, marm?

She was silent, digging the points of her fingers into her forehead, raking at her own skin.

Can you hear me, marm?

She looked out through her fingers as if from a cage. You're Flynn, aint you? she said.

Aye, Fitheal Flynn, marm.

They talk about you, Flynn. In Deloraine. Mad as a sack of rabbits they say, the two of you.

Fitheal Flynn allowed himself the slight tugging of a smile. In matters of redress, marm, he said, better mad than dull.

Forty blinkin pound, she said. God, you poor silly man.

Is your husband about? he said, but then it all struck him at once.

Stupid, silly man, she screamed.

He glanced around, and his eyes settled upon the shed. He walked to the unlit doorway and peered through. On the ground lay a chap spread in his own blood. Flynn removed his hat. Oh Jaysus, he said.

Inside, the heat was thick enough to cut. A squall of flies covered the bare parts of the fellow stretched out among the straw. His eyes were bloated shut and in the swelter the blood had congealed into a sort of tacky confection. Flynn stood over him, clutching his hat to his chest, chasing flies with his other hand. There was black around the dead man's nose where his wife had tried to bring him around by some burnt rags. His shattered jaw was so misshapen that his lower teeth no longer aligned. The gentleman knelt beside him.

Let's have a wee look at you, he said.

Placing his hat aside, Flynn began to feel through the pockets of the husband, first the inner and outer of the jacket and then down to the waistcoat and pants. He pulled out a watch chain to which no watch was attached. He found a few matches in a box, mostly struck. But he did not find what he was looking for, a sheaf of banknotes written out in ten-pound denominations, stolen from him by the miscreant Toosey.

On winking terms with the devil, is Toosey, he called to the woman. You're not the first he's ruined.

He leaned over the husband's mouth. Still breathing.

He stood and replaced his hat and arranged the droop of the brim so that he could see past it. When he stepped out into the furious sun the wife was watching him through the bars of her fingers. He flicked a thumb at the shed and looked away.

We best be moving him, he said. The flies are eating him up.

He gave a sharp whistle to the hooded man who was perched still with his arm about the wife. The pair of them entered the storeshed and soon returned hauling the husband between them and they swung him into the kitchen and laid him out among the unwashed plates and the enamelled mugs and stubs of candle on the table, showing him no more regard than a side of beef. The fellow groaned and stirred his legs. Flynn stood looking him over, the grotesque lumps of the man's face like cancerous tumours, the lifted flaps of hair thick with gore, and while he was a godless man he nevertheless crossed himself out of sheer superstition.

You'd better be attending to him in here, marm. He has desperate need of you, I should think.

Flynn stepped into the sun before her.

He don't need me no more, she said.

From the noise he's making I wager he wants someone.

She looked sharply up.

Aye, what with the noise and the kicking.

She clambered upright and stumbled towards the house. The kitchen was otherwise furnished with chairs devised out of sassafras still in its bark, and she kicked these aside for some room and reached down a kerosene lantern hung on the crossbeam and lit it and placed it for light. She took a washbowl and a cloth and began to towel the blood from his head wounds.

My blessed saint, she was saying, my blessed saint. He's alive.

By the foot of the table the hooded man waited with his hands upraised as if he dared not touch the battered man but knowing all the same he ought to help. His head inside the hood was swivelling and tilting as he watched the woman at work and in the end he came beside and held the washbowl so she could better reach it. The wife wiped away the foul matter of crusted blood and soil and straw from the fellow laid out there, cleaned up the lumpen jaw and the wide and cruelly split nose, and through it all her husband moaned. The hooded man took the fellow's hand and squeezed it.

Which way did he go? Flynn said. He was standing in the doorway blocking the light.

Please, my husband needs help. He needs the surgeon.

Marm—

He'll come for a shilling. Please, he won't live. He needs help.

No.

You must bring the surgeon. He won't live.

Listen. I should like to fetch the sawbones for you. I should like nothing more, upon my honour. But my companion and I have business with Toosey that will not wait.

Fitheal Flynn nodded towards where the hooded man was waiting by the table gripping the limp hand of the husband. Window sunlight picked out the wealth of stains in the white cotton, old brown blood, rings of dust. Each corner of the hood stood like a dog's ear and his eyes recessed in the shadows were black and dire. A journeyman passed out of some legendary land or a night terror given shape and substance, who could say. He replaced the fellow's hand on the table and stepped back.

She looked from one to the other. Just who are you two? she said.

Farmers is all we are, marm, farmers of the Quamby.

I never saw no farmer get about with a pistol, she said and she pointed at the heavy revolving gun lodged in the band of Flynn's belt. Flynn put his hand on the grip and let it sit there.

Which way did he go? he said.

She was staring at the gun. What? You mean to kill him, do you?

That's the head and tail of it, I suppose, marm.

Then do it without me. I'll have no part of murderin.

She wrung her cloth and set to bathing her husband, nothing more to say.

Tis less the murdering than it is the taking of justice. Don't you see that? Well, and by God, he has all but killed your husband.

She turned fiercely. Him? she said. I'll tell you what I see. I see Jacky lyin here needin the surgeon, and I see you with your gun and your hangman over there, mad as rabbits the pair of you, lettin him die. Who's the murderer? Eh? Who?

Flynn pushed back his hat. If he was bothered he made no demonstration but just narrowed his eyes and nodded. He turned out to the cobbled yard.

A huge wooded range filled the land behind the farmhouse, a field of white and sombre gums studded through with darker wattle that everywhere hewed to the hills and Fitheal Flynn stood for a time in study, looking towards and over the paddocks, searching for some sign of the fugitive. He retrieved his knapsack and drew it over his shoulders and took up his travelling staff as well. An eagle cruised black before the sky's watery blue. For a time Fitheal Flynn stood sipping from a bottle bound around with twine and secured to his bag by a thong, considering the country presented there before him, the bird turning above, the range of mournful gums. When he finally looked away, came about and stoppered his bottle, he saw crouching by the watering trough his oldest child. His daughter Caislin. She had removed her hood and was splashing her forehead with water. She put her hand out to him.

Give us your drink, she said.

A lump swelled in his throat as he looked down at her. Is it hurting? he said.

She splashed herself. Yes, she said.

Oh, my love, he said.

Give us it here.

He unwound the leather thong, passed her the bottle. She plunged it into the trough that was chipped out of a single block of stone fringed with moss from the damp. She plunged the neck and the surface boiled.

We should fetch the surgeon, she said.

His lump tightened. Come on now, he said and it hurt to talk. Come on.

We should.

Cross them hills, you see, and it's clear country the other side. That's where he's gone, isn't it? Cross them hills.

Then let him run, she said and passed the dripping bottle.

No.

We'd be back tomorrow. We'd have that fellow a surgeon.

Give him a day, you might as well give him a year. No. We are close. We shall find him in the valley lands tomorrow or you can hang me from the walls of Derry.

Caislin Flynn dried her hands on her pants, stood, and with the ease of ritual drew the hood over herself and she was, again, that singular man all the world saw. She, his truest blessing, hidden somewhere inside, the illusion of her manliness so complete, so compelling, that even he had taken it to heart and turned it, he believed, to their good. He ought not to have allowed Caislin to follow. She was in pain. She was troubled. Her sisters needed her at home. But how, when she had appeared to him that day he left, dressed in this costume, her arms stiff by her sides with anger, how was he to say no? So here they were on the road together and he was glad for it.

There is them biscuits, she said, if you're hungry.

I'm all right.

You look hungry, she said. You look pale.

Pale never killed nobody.

She fished a bundle from her pocket and unwrapped it, held out to him a pair of hard-looking meal cakes. He took a piece and bit into it, surveying the hills and hills of scrub as he chewed.

What a dour bit of bush, he said around the cake, and, by God, with him in it somewhere.

Flynn moved out into the field of oats that filled the back paddock, and here he paused and took stock of what he saw. For cut through the crop was a trail, snaking out towards the hand-cleared land beyond, the piles of unburned gum and bracken and rows of severed stone-grey stumps. A trail writ plainly in the broken oats, the heavy boot prints of one man. Flynn chewed his biscuit. You are some sort of fool, Thomas Toosey, he said.

Caislin drew up beside him.

See that, he said, and pointed to the divots.

What if he dies? she said. Him back there.

Without another word Flynn set off, adjusting the knapsack on his shoulders, his tin pots ringing. She looked back at the house and she looked at her father hiking through the young oats. She lowered her head and followed after him.

That's our doing, she called.

Flynn walked on.

We might have killed him, she said.

Still Flynn did not stop but spoke across his shoulder as he went. You struck that chap, did you? he said. You beat him three-quarters dead with a focking piece of wood and focking stove his skull and whatnot?

Caislin trod in the tracks he'd made and kept quiet.

Aye, well, and keep your thoughts on what was done, he said. Keep them there. It shall stiffen your arm when the time comes.

He followed the trail towards the wooded range and where it led into wild land unwalked by common folk, the preserve of absconders and bushrangers. The sun grazed a barren sky above. They crossed into bracken taking hold at the scrub's edge, formed up close together, father and daughter, and entered the bush among the racket of cicadas and the desiccant heat. They laboured up a rise that was loosely scrubbed with blackwood and great sallow swamp gum, Flynn leaning into his stick and scouring the trail, beside him his daughter lifting her boots over the rearing stones and setting them heavily down.

Stiffen your arm, he said, as if he'd been considering it this short while. Stiffen your heart too. For that time is coming and we must not flinch.

Liffey Valley

In the early evening dark among the man ferns of the damp hill's foreslope Toosey unbundled his bedroll and sat watching his backtrack and waiting. He built no fire and took no tea but sat on the blankets peeling a turnip with his knife, passing slices to his lips. A bone-splinter moon rose wondrous within the overspread of stars, the dark below the gums deepening into blue and then black, but still no one appeared upon the slope. Had he eluded them? There was no way to know. He shaved a long shining slice, curved like the very moon above, and ate.

When it was full dark he unwound some wire snares from his coat pocket and spread them on his swagroll. Wallaby runs cut here and there through the brush and he walked out and planted stakes and hung the snares with a four-inch loop across the hollows. He made his bed by a ridge where the warmth of the day gave off the stone and where he was hidden as if in a pair of jaws. He settled back and after a time he pulled a crumpled envelope from his pocket. It was addressed to him, care of the Deloraine post office. He slipped the paper out and unfolded it. There wasn't moon enough to read but he knew it by heart.

My deer Mother is dead. I have been turned out of Home. I have nothing at all Deer Father I wish you wood come back. There is no home for me with out you. I have only You in the hole world to love. I hope You will stow this letter safly as a tresher of my faith in You your loyal Son.

He lay listening to the night and charting out the matter of finding his boy in that dog-poor town. Below the canopy the shrieking of possums, the falling and breaking of sticks. It was easy to imagine someone spilling out of the bush for him, yet as he looked about there was only the dark. A night sown with stars. He laid back and watched the moon loll onward into the void. He clutched that letter and kissed it.

Come dawn he stowed his bedding and walked out to pull the snares. In one a potteroo gone cold and wooden. He stuffed it inside his billytin for eating later. Having cleared the wires, he picked a path further west for country he had crossed in the winter, country that he knew in some manner. He descended down the rainforested slope where stringybarks grew tall and full of sun like gargantuan flowers, stopping to study the bush behind him, listening for voices. The low-down dawn light burning his eyes, he crossed a creeklet and mounting the far bank he scared up a host of crayfish that scuttled away to chimneys pitting the soil, and soon the relic rainforest lessened. He left the incline and within a mile the scrub thinned and then, on a sudden, he was standing on a plain of tufted grass that covered the land away to the bluffs. He followed the scrub's edge where there was cover, bent under his load of swag, the billytin in his fingers rattling and him setting a mad pace.

His first sight of the island as a child of fourteen sent out for thieving two overcoats in the winter of 1827 was the sandstone buildings studding the hill above the harbour in Hobart town and when they brought him above decks of the *Woodford* in iron fetters and set him aboard a longboat for the shore he'd thought Hobart a pissing version of his own Blackpool, the inlaying of warehouse masonry much like the stores on Talbot Road, the stark shapes of houses near the same, but then the winter mist parted from the mountain peak above and he knew he was in venerable country, as old as rock, and it wasn't long before he became indentured to the frontiersman John Batman who ran a trade in victualling the army, and here the boy Thomas learned how the island's wilder parts truly belonged to the tribal blacks, a displaced people taking refuge in the hills, and for a government bounty and to secure his land this frontiersman meant to hunt them by whatever means just or unjust, bloody or brave, and he marshalled a party of transportees and black trackers and put into the scrub armed for war and war it was, a bloody war, in which all hands were soiled and Thomas's no less than another's for a killer now he was, an easy killer, and yet while he was diminished by it, made less in God's eyes and his own, he saw in the bullet, the knife, and the club a power that could make a man his own master.

In the early afternoon he climbed a hillock and lay flat to scan the terrain he had crossed. He removed his hat and held it before the sun to shade his eyes. He could see over the back-hills and grasslands he had recently quit and he could see kangaroo mobs and feel their pounding through the earth and see a small flock of rosellas dipping and swinging and making horrible cries. The sun caused his eyes to water, which he wiped on his sleeve and it was then, as he was dabbing, that he saw a flash of white in the far-off scrub. The trees leaned, worked on by a current. He watched and waited, finger halfway to his face. In the bloom of the full sun his eyes teared. Nothing but the wind, the trees ajig, his own track left snake-like through the grass. An uneasy feeling remained lodged in his abdomen as he humped up his gear and left.

On the hard walk down the hill he produced the pocket-book, untied it and thumbed through the banknotes. They were stamped with the Launceston Bank for Savings insignia in fine blue ink and he considered this as he tracked out through a copse of long-ago burnt gums that wore a green fur of regrowth. He counted the notes, retied the cord, and tucked the pocketbook into his coat. Late in the day he forded a knee-deep creek, scrabbled up through ferns on the far side into the land beyond with the horizon light in his eyes, blunt light sheared by cloud, sheared by the whitish trees. Soon he passed that country through and came upon the railway that had been his destination.

He stood gazing left and right along the rails. They split clear through the brush on a bed of blue metal, drawing away to a point in the infinite distance. He dropped his swag and kneeled in the ballast and pressed his hand to the iron. He sat for a moment with it so and then he bent down and rested his cheeks against the bullhead. There was no pulse that he could discern, no movement, and so he stood and looked again along it. The sun was falling into the hills and throwing a thin wafting light over the forest. He resettled his bedroll and made easterly along the clearway beside the line.

I see you over there, the voice said. Don't think I don't.

Toosey had stepped off into the wayside and found a hollow in the feathery infant wattle where he could hide. He'd dropped his swag and was sitting on it to wait for the train. It was a meagre sort of nest beneath parched bush that was flaked with dark smokestack soot but he had a view of the rail line cutting around the bend, tracking up a hill, and that was all he needed. He would see the train before it made the incline, would have time to set himself for the chase.

I said I seen you.

Then you aint seein me right if you still think I give a shit, Toosey said.

On the far side of the track two figures emerged from the gorse. A boy of fourteen or so, and beside him another boy who was younger and grubbier, and if they had anything more than the rags they stood in Toosey could not see it, no bags, bedrolls or blankets. They studied him through the brush. The older one towelled his nose with an overlong shirtsleeve and sniffed.

Has someone given you a touch-up or somethin? he said.

Toosey looked down at the blood on himself. He hadn't noticed it.

Got any grub? the older said.

We are hungry is all, the younger said. We aint hardly had more than a mouthful in days, I swear. A mouthful of bully beef is all we've had.

We aint eaten in days, the older said.

How long till that train? Toosey said.

She'll be along. You'll hear it. Watch for the smoke over the trees.

When?

The boy looked confused. When you hear it, he said.

Toosey smoothed his moustache with the web of his thumb. He could see the boys watching him, gaunt and vulture-eyed. He reached inside his swagroll and found a turnip and lobbed it underhand across the rails into the brush beside them. They disappeared into the gorse. There was a brief commotion as they searched, followed by a longer silence. He sat back on his swag. Something thudded on the litter to his right. They began to call over each other.

I hate them things.

That aint food.

We saw your meat, mister.

Give us some meat.

We aint et today.

You got any bread? Come on, mister.

Among the fronds of bracken Toosey sat listening to the din and testing now and then edge of his knife. He reached and picked up the turnip. He stood. The boys were watching him across the barren of rail and blue metal where nothing grew save thistle, and he drew his arm and flung it hard and collected the smaller one squarely in the forehead. The boy rocked back and toppled into the brush.

Toosey stood grinning. It was a mean shot and he was grinning and thinking it a bit of sport, when the older boy pulled something from the bushes that looked like a mattock or a rake and stood holding it. Toosey's grin fell. He found himself staring into the cavernous eye of a rifle barrel. The boy palmed back the heavy mechanism.

You fucker, you won't laugh no more, will you, he said.

The younger one beside him began to jump with excitement. Shoot the old cuss, Reggie, shoot him in the face. Go on.

I will if he don't give me that meat.

See now, Toosey said, there is no need for this.

Give us what you got there. That meat there and whatever you got. All of it.

Toosey stood perfectly still.

Give it here.

Well come and get it, Toosey said.

The older one made a motion with the gun towards the billytin. His small companion scaled the camber monkey-wise and crossed the rails, dragging a formless shadow over the gravel. The potteroo was stiff and stuck out straight from the can and the boy snatched it by the feet, his eyes never leaving off Toosey. Toosey stood very still, no expression at all on his face, watching the long birding gun that was trimmed on him.

How much you got? the older one said.

Toosey clicked his tongue. He looked away.

I know you got somethin. Turn him over, Georgie.

The younger one put his hands inside Toosey's trouser pockets. Toosey made no move against him. He came away with a long twine-handled knife and a tinderbox and striking iron looped on a length of wire that he dropped on the ground. In the hacking pockets of Toosey's thin tweed coat he found a clutch of snares and tossed them aside. When he dipped again into the hacking pocket he found a letter in an envelope folded and refolded until it had near worn through its creases. The boy studied it. He looked around at his mate.

He is skint.

Keep goin.

I have. There's nothin.

You aint done the insides.

I done em.

You aint.

The boy unbuttoned Toosey's jacket. He reached up for the cavities, found the pocketbook stashed there, and prised it away.

You find somethin, Georgie?

A purse.

Open it then.

He untied the cord. It's bills.

Forget the pocketbook, lads, Toosey said.

Shut your bleedin gob. If we want it, we'll have it.

Not this one. Forget this one.

Seems I'm the man with the piece but.

Toosey lifted his eyes, a dark and glassy brown. How far you think you'll get? he said.

I'll bloody fire on you, see if I don't.

The boy had moved onto the camber and was aiming down at Toosey. He glanced variously at the bush and at Toosey as if he was beset by a whole brace of swagmen more than just this one lonely soul. His finger tapped at the trigger guard in a light staccato.

You won't find us, he said. You aint got a hope. We know these woods don't we, Georgie?

Better than any bugger, Georgie said.

Take the meat, Toosey said. You can have it. But forget the purse.

Come here, Georgie.

I've gone through some hell to have it, Toosey said.

Georgie!

The younger was waving the pocketbook as he crossed the rails. It's bills, he said.

And I will go through more to keep it, Toosey said.

The boy tapped at the steel trigger guard. He stared hard at Toosey.

You don't scare me.

Take that purse and won't neither of you will see another sunrise, Toosey said.

How much is in there? the boy said to his mate.

The younger fingered through the notes. I can't read what they says.

Two hundred pound, Toosey said.

There aint.

Not another sunrise, Toosey said. As I live and breathe.

Show us one, Georgie.

The younger one held up a bill that his mate might read it. Toosey could see the boy's mouth working as he made out letter by letter the denomination. He looked at Toosey.

This says ten.

That's right. There is twenty bills there.

The boy shook the gun at him. Where'd you come on two hundred quids?

A sum like that, Toosey said, by Christ it will send men wild. And believe me when I say I'm the wildest man you shall ever meet.

Try it.

Reggie's your name, is it?

The boy said nothing.

I have a son, Reggie. Not much bigger than you. He'll be on my mind when I find you in the dark. Tonight in the dark. It will sadden me a good deal.

You won't find us.

Sad for your father. Sad I had to hurt a boy who brings to mind me own son.

You won't find us I said.

Shoot him, Reg. Go on. Shoot.

It's just talk, Georgie.

Shoot him. Shoot him.

He won't do it. He's a pissin old windbag is what he is. Don't let him scare you none.

Shoot him. He'll come for us, he'll find us.

Shut your gob a minute and listen. It's talk, George, that's what. Talk. Like it was talk in Westbury, remember? That bugger never come after us and this one here won't find us neither. We know these woods.

Toosey felt it before he heard it. A quivering in the air, a distant violence. He turned and stood gazing out along the gleaming steel with his ear cocked to the sky. The boys heard it too.

She's comin, the younger one said.

Above the canopy to the west seethed a great grey thunderhead marking the passage of the engine as she neared. Hordes of jackdaws and parrots and cockatoos vacated the clearway trees in a single screaming cloud, sent aloft by the steam disturbing the growth by the rails. When her stout black maw drew around out of the scrub and with the blare of her horn it was like the coming of a sea vessel groping through a fog. She slowed on the upward slope and behind the engine came carriages and flatbeds and box-sided trucks and the draw gear snatched loudly along the consist where the slack was taken up. The windows crawling by were packed with travellers of every kind, workmen and women in sun hats and children pressing their noses to the glass. The boy had not removed his eyes from Toosey and had not removed the gun. The carriages rattled behind him in procession.

Georgie, he said over the howl of the train.

The younger one watched the train with stark wonder.

Georgie, make ready for it.

I am. I'm ready.

Mister, you try to chase us and I'll fire a ball through you.

Toosey was staring at the gun.

Fire and be done with it, the boy said.

Toosey ground his jaw. The train shuttled by in a huge commotion.

The boy tucked the butt to his shoulder. All right, Georgie, move.

Now?

Now. Move.

High-sided guano trucks rattled past. The younger one was hardly taller than the running gear he jogged beside but he sprang and caught the wooden siderack to haul himself aboard. The older one backed up. Training the muzzle on Toosey still. At a distance of some yards he turned and slung the rifle and ran.

In the seconds that followed Toosey knelt into the bracken and went about after his letter. He'd humped that sorry-looking thing over the district for weeks and would not lose it now. He stuffed it in his pocket, and his knife with it, and he shouldered his swag and followed the train at a steady lope. Holding his hat, the swag bouncing. Riled like he'd never been. It was the last carriage and he ran between the rails from sleeper to sleeper as the train laboured uphill. Running hard, scowling, he lobbed his swag overhead into a gated tray and caught the hangladder and climbed. The boys had found purchase on the sideboards with the gate wedged under their armpits. The three of them eyed one another across the empty wagon.

There sounded in the dusk's gloom a thundering report and the piece of planking by Toosey's leg splintered. He looked down. A fist-sized hole was punched clean through the board. When he looked up the boys had scrambled over the barrier, the rifle with them, scrambled and toppled into the last of the guano muck, the rifle sliding about, the truck rocking, and they flattened against the boards and covered their heads. A second crack tolled and died along hills and long before it finished Toosey knew what it meant. Every nerve ending in him fizzed at once. He turned and looked downline.

Two figures sprinting full tilt up the straightaway. He could hear their boots crunching in the gravel and could see the pistol being levelled at him. He heaved himself over the barrier as another gunshot sounded and the wood burst beside his ear. He toppled into the guano muck.

Fuckin Jesus, he said.

The boys stared at him, astonished. Who is that?

The gun, lad, the gun.

They fed it out. Toosey set back the hammer and kneeled with it propped at his shoulder. The seekers had made ground on the train, close enough that in the fading daylight he could see how the girl wore a white hood. He wasn't ready for the shock this gave. He'd heard people talk, yet seeing her for himself was another thing. He almost put the gun aside in shame. Let them be, was the thought he had. You've done enough. But another shot smashed the planking by his arm and he felt the wind of the passing lead and he knew for all the world he had no such choice to make. He rose with that firearm and centred the Irishman along the barrel. At this the seekers broke for the sidescrub after shelter and he tracked the Irishman to the left and jerked the trigger. The hammer gave an empty clack. He looked at the pan. It was unprimed.

Where's your powder? he said to the boy.

Aint none.

Do not piss about. Give it here.

The boy shook his head. There's none at all.

What?

It's gone. All of it.

In the bush by the rail line the Irishman continued at a flat run, flushed and heaving as the wash from the smokestack eddied past him. Some yards back his hooded shadow lumbered along and they seemed for a time, the two of them, to be growing smaller. Toosey watched through the holes in the wood. He had begun to believe them gone when the sound of the engine changed. It was losing speed shy of the hill's peak and slowing and the hissing of its pistons grew laboured. Now they gained ground. Toosey wiped his palms on his shirt and then he removed the knife from his jacket. He turned to the boys.

Get up the back, he said.

They talked over each other.

Who is that?

We never done nothin, did we?

What have we done to them?

They're killers.

Get up the back I said. They won't hurt you. Just keep your mouth shut.

Toosey rolled onto his knees and stole a glance over the rim of the barrier and dropped down again. Just get up the back, he said again.

The Irishman was first to make the train. He grabbed the hangladder and heaved himself up. Through the bullet holes Toosey watched it unfold, a run of events as if in a dream, the thick knots of knuckle locking on the rungs, one, a second, and then the corrugated forehead and pinched eyes of Fitheal Flynn as he rose into view. He chose his moment to lean above the barrier swinging the knife. It was directed at Flynn's arm. The blade cut a gash there in the coat and Flynn let go of the ladder, startled, and toppled onto the rails. He crashed and rolled in a spray of gravel. The engine was broaching the hill and the whole train built momentum as the heavier front end descended and hauled with it the long snaking consist. The Irishman clambered to his feet, aimed his gun, and called.

Square off to me like a man. You hear me, Toosey? Like a man.

He fired a useless shot above the truck. The train pulled away ever faster.

A batch of sweat had formed in the ridges of Toosey's brow. He wiped away the damp hair. He looked across at the boys and they stared nervously in return. His small black hat sat in the muck rocking with the motion of the train. He brushed it off, replaced it. The carriage passed further into a wooded cutting and the sun flickered in the overhang of limbs, picking two frightened boys out of the shade at intervals, their eyes like clean spots in the grime, staring through the unsteady light.

Who are you, mister? Some kind of runaway or somethin?

I told you, he said. The freight truck swayed beneath them, the bone-break sound of the wheels. I'm the wildest man you will meet.

The boys drew close to each other, crouching in the guano dust and made pale with it, and they hardly dared take their eyes off this uncommon bushman, for he was not yet done with them. He stood with the sway of the truck, clutching the side gate, and stepped towards them. He put out his hand.

Now, he said. I want the money back.

The older one fumbled from his pants the leather pocket-book and passed it up.

Toosey eased it off him. He stood a moment longer, looking down at them, their arms around each other. He turned and shuffled to the rear and took up a place by the bullet-holed gate. Through the wounds in the wood the country passed by and in time he closed his eyes and appeared to almost doze off, so that when he sat rapidly upright and began to pat himself over it caused the boys some alarm. He slapped at each pocket in turn, felt around inside his jacket, and produced a creased and stained envelope. Once more he leaned back, holding that letter, and like a child with a sugar-rag it somehow soothed him. Lowering his hat across his eyes and leaning back, he locked his hand in his lap and rocked with the ocean-roll of the train.

They descended out of gum forest, Flynn and his daughter, and followed the rails across the flatlands west of Longford. In the late dark the stars hung like points of ice, looking singularly cold and distant. The whole moon steam-white. They walked and Fitheal Flynn sang along a few bars of a taverner's ballad he knew from the old country, tapping his stick to keep time. 'Tis well I do remember that bleak November day,' he sang, 'when bailiff and landlord come to drive us away.' Soon the few faint lights of Longford loomed up out of the plain ahead. They walked ever towards them.

At Longford station they left the tracks and dropped their bedding and other pieces under the raised platform deck. They crouched there beneath it for a time assessing the town across the mud streets, a row of double-height buildings following the curve of the main road, erratic in design and material, a bank with fluted columns of white stone and a plain emporium painted green. Elsewhere, a brick hotel under the sign of a carven coat of arms. Light from the hotel windows spilled onto the street and that was all the light there was for their camp. It would be a long night, one more in a series of many.

They found what small comfort they could under the platform decking sheltered in their blankets, empty bellied. Soon a song started in the hotel that drifted faintly by. Caislin had a wedge of damper that she had wrapped and kept from their last meal and she passed it to Flynn, but he was in no mood to eat. He sat cleaning the bulldog pistol, pushing spent shells with the ejector pin and ramrodding the cylinder with a rag, holding the barrel to the moon and peering through it. She watched him from her slackly hanging eyeholes.

I'm to blame, he said. I had him clean as daylight and I missed.

It wasn't clean, she said.

Near as we will get.

He packed in new rounds from his shirt pocket.

O'Malley should never have given you that, she said.

Let me be worrying about it.

You aint thinkin this through, Pa. What if you had shot him today?

He exhaled. The world would be thanking me, he said.

And if you'd been caught for it?

Flynn snapped the cylinder closed. Aye, well, he said. Would have been a bastard, wouldn't it.

It's the money, she said. That's all we want.

No.

We aint after blood.

Flynn looked up. We're not after money neither.

Caislin fell silent. There was fiddling coming from the hotel that was only dim at this distance, dim and made mournful by the wind.

He could be anywhere, she said.

That made him smile. No, he said. Tis the bills. They're not worth a cuss till he changes them.

Someone might change them for him.

Two hundred pound? Flynn said, his eyebrows drawing together.

Then what?

He does it hisself. Does it at the bank.

Launceston, she said.

Another thing, he's a wife and child there.

Bloody Launceston, she said and her head dropped.

Watch how you speak.

That's twenty mile.

If we be leaving at dawn, we'll make it by night.

I know. Don't make me like it any more though.

Caislin broke apart the bread. She lifted the hem of the hood and passed bits up to her mouth.

Take that off, he said.

No.

You need air. You need light.

He could see the outline of the cotton shifting with her jaw. She chewed and he watched her. Then she removed the hood. Flynn drew a sharp breath. He looked away. Oh my girl, he said.

She folded the hood by bringing in the corner and doubling it through the middle and the cotton was as mottled with stains and was as soft and pliant as a sheet of ancient vellum. She laid it neatly aside on her bedroll for replacing in the morning. She tore the bread and ate more.

Soon Flynn began to cry. It was a quiet sound, constricted, and he wrung his hands and could not look at her as he squeezed his mouth and eyes closed.

My love, he said. Forgive me.

That won't help us, she said.

Forgive me.

Caislin worked the hard wad of bread around with her tongue. That don't matter no more, she said.

I shouldn't have left you there. Left you with the money.

We'll get it back. That will be the end of it.

Flynn wiped his eyes.

Let Toosey get away and where's the use in any of this?

Aye, said Flynn, I know. You're right. Course you're right.

Caislin turned away and stretched out on the canvas still in boots as was her habit. She tugged the blankets around her chin.

Go to sleep, she said.

All right.

But he sat for a long time feeling a familiar ache. She was outlined against the dark, all in black, like a feature of the land. Her breath rising and falling. He grit his teeth until his jaw ached. He squeezed shut his eyes. That one name wandering the blank of his mind. That one thought of pain. After a time he took up the pistol and cracked it and finished loading the cylinder.

The sun, risen from a fire in the hills, had burnt for an hour and below the paltry station platform in their exhaustion they slept. The tin whistle of a guardsman woke them and in the brewing warmth of morning Flynn crawled from their cubbyhole and stood and arched his back, blinking in the hard light. An imposing double-span bridge stretched across the river into town, the stone centre pier set upon an island, and a locomotive was running the whole length of it sending blooms of steam up through the girders. He popped his back and watched the train roll and halt with a horrendous squeal. The guardsman signalled folk to stand clear of the dropaway and blew his whistle and moved along the carriages unlatching the doors of first and second class. Flynn scratched an armpit, sniffed and spat.

Rouse yourself, he said.

But Caislin had stirred already at the approach of the engine and sat gowned again in her hood.

You must be hungry, she said.

I could gnaw off my own arm.

She went about the rolling of the blankets.

The sound of applause caused him to look up. He scratched himself. Pouring out of the carriages were upwards of a hundred formally dressed Rechabites, each wearing across his shoulder a splendid blue and gold sash proclaiming the title of his independent order. Some held aloft ornate banners strung on poles and others carried brass instruments, playing scales to warm their lips, beating senselessly on drums. The crowd applauded and Flynn shook his head. What in the name of fock, he said.

Who are they?

Caislin had dragged out their gear and stood now likewise staring.

Teetotallers, he said. For the love of God, would you look at them.

Elaborately dressed men descended the stairs from the platform into the street. Flynn stood with his hands on his hips just watching them pass. After an interval the two of them humped up their gear and followed. With their week on the back roads they'd slowly acquired the look of derelicts, which by many measures they were. The folk they passed in the road stepped aside at the sight of them. Flynn though kept his head high and looked elsewhere.

The smell of bread brought them to a red-brick bakery sheltered by a painted awning and written with the name Smiths. A bell rang atop the door as it opened and rang again as it shut and they stood in the shop gazing variously at the wicker baskets stacked with loaves and pastries and the sacks of flour piled like corpses. The proprietor emerged tucking a cloth into his apron string and he placed both hands down on the stone counter. Flynn came forward. He pointed at a gallon loaf. He began to speak but the proprietor was looking past him at Caislin.

What are you sposed to be?

Flynn had a handful of coins and he doled them out on the counter. Give me a loaf of that there, he said.

An Irish clown show is it?

Póg mo thóin, Flynn said.

Some mick bloody clown show or somethin, the proprietor

said. He reached for a loaf and placed it before Flynn and took two of the coins. His eyebrows and sidewhiskers were white with flour and his jowls shook when he laughed. The peatbogging clown show, he said and laughed at himself.

They broke bread squatting in the street as the Rechabites stood about conversing in their dozens, shaking hands in a strange fashion with one another, a secret perhaps devised among themselves. They were meant to be a temperance movement, but of late the Rechabites seemed given more and more to the intrigues of politics and the power of a secret. A tent had been erected in the main road where ginger ale was served from a washtub and a woman came past, four mugs in each of her hands passing them out. She came past and she saw Caislin and gave a little start. What the devil, she said and steered away, sloshing ale in the dust.

They had contrived a podium out of apple crates and soon the chief ruler took to it and raised his feathered bicorn and called for quiet. Behind him some fellows held a banner that depicted Jane inviting Jonadab onto his chariot, and stitched across the silk in black lettering was the motto: *Is thine heart right, as my heart is with thy heart.*

Brothers, the chief ruler cried, we are come here today to loudly condemn the making, levying and enforcing of the railway rate.

This was met by wild applause.

Oh Jaysus, Flynn said. It's the rate they're on about.

We should be movin, Caislin said.

Would you look at him up there. I'd like to punch him in the cakehole.

There are three great historic curses, the chief ruler cried. War. Pestilence. Famine. But corruption is the unknown curse. It is corruption that we should fear. Corruption that keeps us in a state of serfdom. Since our inception the Rechabite movement has taught thousands to make their own way to self respect and has created in them a spirit of manliness. We have energised just as many in social and religious matters. We have created among the people the desire for self-government. But the parliament. The parliament, my brothers. That troupe of thieves. That society of cowards. They have abandoned us to the wolves of greed.

Applause and raised hats.

Caislin, her head swivelling inside the cowl, studied the rallied men and women. They're lookin at me, she said.

Who of you has paid the railway rate? the chief said. Who has paid it?

A hand here or there rose.

Who has refused?

Dozens of hands appeared overhead.

I applaud you, the chief ruler cried. Stand firm. The railway rate is nothing less than a crime. The parliament would have us make good the losses of a few speculators. But I tell you this, brothers. We are not answerable for the debts of the Launceston and Western Railway Company. We are not answerable and we will not pay.

Another bout of cheering followed.

But it's easy to rob an orchard when no one keeps it, the chief cried. While our backs were turned, the legislature amended the Railways Act. They voted to confiscate our property, steal our money, and make ruins of our lives. How can they do this, brothers? How can their authority extend even to our property? To our purses? Does it only take an act of parliament to shed us of our rights?

A murmur passed among the crowd of people. Some of them called out.

No, brothers, the chief said. No. It is because they believe us weak. Because they believe the undue exercise of power over the supine and the insipid is their prerogative.

Flynn stuffed into his mouth the last of his bread. Says the man exercising his power over the supine and insipid, he said.

The crowd was mostly families, Sunday-dressed in suits and hats, folk come off the many farms sewed like quilting into the flat land around Longford, come in their carts, come on horseback, come to protest the railway rate that had affected them all, but as Flynn looked across them now, chewing, he saw that barely an eye at all was turned to the chief ruler. The better part had come about to stare at Caislin.

By the blessed fock, he said.

We should go, Caislin said.

Flynn leaned on his staff and stood. What? he called to the crowd. What are you lot of fools looking at?

Many looked away then. Mothers pulled their children close. Fathers crossed their arms. But one young fellow continued to glare. He took a few steps nearer and he had a rag knotted convict-style around his neck that he was adjusting as he spoke. He was a fellow full of his own importance. He loosened his rag and spoke. That leper's got no business amongst decent healthy folk, he said.

Flynn twisted his hands around the staff. Leper?

Get him away. We don't want him here.

What, and you've never seen a hangman before? Flynn said.

He's a hangman like I'm the Queen of Spain.

Caislin pulled his arm. Pa, let's go.

Flynn stood for a time locking eyes with the fellow. The leather of his hands creaked on the hardwood staff. Ever seen a man get dropped? he said.

The fellow nodded his head.

Takes a special breed, I will tell you. Dropping men all day.

He's no more than a boy.

He is what he is, Flynn said.

Tell him to take that bag off. He makes folk nervous.

Well, and it's precisely that he wants you nervous. What's the good of a hangman who calms?

The young fellow rubbed his throat. Perhaps he wanted to

say more, for he drew breath and straightened, but he seemed to think the wiser of it and in the end he turned, stuck his thumbs through his belt, and walked away.

Please, Caislin said, let's go now.

Aye, and we can go, he said as he stared after the fellow. We can go.

He parted the crowd with his staff like a weary shepherd and pushed through and Caislin behind him clutched his knapsack. They passed the crowd in the main street paying no heed to the muttered contempt that came to them. She kept close to her father where the crowd was thicker and he could feel her tugging at the straps of his bag. The street sloped away fringed by buildings down towards the mud and reed flats of the distant river, peopled along its length, and he was peering towards the bridge when the tugging grew more insistent. Wait, she said and tugged. He looked across his shoulder.

Mornin.

The local constable was standing at his side. He was all in black and was as skinny as a pull-through for a rifle. On his cap the crest of the Territorial Police caught the sun and the chin-strap on his lower lip stirred as he spoke. Some concern has been expressed about you two, the constable said.

We're leavin, sir, Caislin said and she pushed Flynn forward.

I'll require you to move along, the constable said.

Yes, sir, she said. We are.

She pushed at Flynn's back, but Flynn would not be moved. He was staring down at the constable. He braced himself on his staff and leaned closer.

Require me what?

You heard what I said.

Aye. Is minic a gheibhean beal oscailt diog dunta.

The constable swayed back. What? he said. What's that you said?

It means is minic a gheibhean beal oscailt diog dunta.

Aint you a barmy little so and so.

Pa, let's move, Caislin said.

She was pushing him when Flynn simply placed one hand on the constable's chest and shoved him aside. The fellow seemed to shrink inside his clothes, made small by such sincere disregard. Away and tug your willy, boy, Flynn said softly.

The constable stepped back. Folk nearby turned to see what had transpired and they were frowning or craning their necks. Flynn leaned calmly on his staff.

See now, the constable said, and he gestured at Caislin, where she stood motionless in shock. I'm requiring you to move along.

Don't look at him, Flynn said.

A brief disquiet crossed the face of the constable.

You want to be looking at me. I'm the cause of your trouble.

The constable switched his eyes onto Flynn.

You see, I belong to the stamp of man as states his principles. My principle is never yield to the Crown.

One or two folk in the crowd had begun to shuffle away. There was talking and pointing, and Caislin seemed turned rigid with it. The constable scanned the crowd and by the time his eyes came back to Flynn he'd drawn his billyclub. This aint County Kerry, he said and he waved that long black finger. Now get yourselves along fore I come up in a temper.

You take me amiss, boy.

I what?

Wave that thing all you like. We're not under your yoke. We don't take instruction from the likes of you.

The constable snorted. That's Fenian talk, he said. I can arrest you as Fenians.

Caislin stirred to life. She grabbed at her father's elbow all of sudden. Leave him be, Pa. Remember what we're about.

Flynn lifted his hand to her for quiet. It's not politics we are talking, he said. We are no part of politics and no part of the law. We are stateless. You understand?

I understand, the constable said. You're anarchists.

I'll make it simple.

The constable watched him closely.

You're a man and I'm a man.

He tapped the stick in his palm. And so what?

So that is all, Flynn said.

I'm a man and you're a man?

Aye.

And what's he? The constable jabbed his stick at Caislin.

He, Flynn said, is the mouth of the lion.

Sounds like politics to me, the constable said.

Flynn's great unruly brows dug together. You would put yourself above me, which I refuse. You're no more and no less than anyone.

The constable lowered his club. His face fell as he considered this. He began to speak but stopped. He cleared his throat. Two pound a month I'm paid, he said after a pause. Two. That don't hold me to much in the way of politics. I take me two and do what I'm told.

There is the root of your troubles, Flynn said. Take pride, man. Be your own master.

They were attracting a rancorous gaze from the crowd of villagers and the lines of sashed and suited Rechabites. Flynn doffed his great hat to them, as a gentleman might. And for all of you, he said, who put yourselves below a waffling fool like that fellow up there. You hang the petty thieves but give the great ones power. Wake up to yourselves. Look around you.

He replaced his hat, set it straight, took his daughter by the hand and led her through the droves of people, the path opening before them as startled folk stepped aside and closed again behind.

Take your leper and go, someone called.

Fenians! called another.

They walked and did not look back.

At the bridge that crossed the weedy river towards Launceston Flynn halted to resettle his load like a mountaineer and drink from his corked bottle. Caislin at his side was still watching to their rear, the huddled set of her shoulders showing her concern. He offered her the bottle. There was a buggy coming over the bridge driven by a stout young fellow smart dressed and as he passed he stared at Flynn and his strange companion, and Flynn in return just touched his hat. The cart rolled on and from the backwards-facing seats sat two children with their mouths agape at the odd ghostly face of Flynn's daughter. Caislin looked away.

The roadside grass sang with summer insects. The fields, boxed with hedges of sweet briar, held flocks of sheep that huddled beneath the riverbank willows or lay like dogs panting with the heat. Flynn had not recorked his bottle but walked with it, slugging from the neck and looking about the country there, the condition of the stock that grazed. Land parcelled up with post and rail fencing and ordered like tiles around the hill's curve. It was all so thoroughly a small misshapen, transported, bastard England that he felt alien in it.

As they walked, his daughter turned to him. You think I should take it off, she said.

Flynn pursed his lips. He swigged from the bottle.

You do, she said. I know.

Flynn said nothing but watched along the river. He drank.

I can't, she said. Not yet.

All right.

But I will. And soon.

Well that would be all right too, he said.

Across the river the Rechabites had struck up a march. The dry metalled road where they paraded seemed to smoke, such was their number.

Well here's how things stand, she said. There's no money for food more than a crown or two. There's Ashley and little Branna we've left with the O'Malleys, without nothin for our landlord, nor for his. And here's you, the man who won't talk to the police.

When we make Launceston I'll talk to some fellows who know some fellows, he said. We'll turn something up. We near had him yesterday in just that manner.

She surveyed the road with her lonely breath hissing in the fibre of the hood. She said nothing further. What more could be said to such a man as himself? What that could douse the blaze of his anger? She knew him better. More than that, she carried that anger too. Handed down from him.

There is a bit of cunning needed, he said. Yes, and rightly there is. Toosey is no sort of fool. Let me tell you something about him, from when I knew him in the Port.

I've heard all your stories, Pa.

Be quiet and listen, he said. There was a fellow in with us by the name of Chauncey Johnson.

I know about Chauncey Johnson. You told me. Toosey smashed him up with rock. I know.

The point being, Flynn said, the point being that we need a bit more sense about us than Gimlet-eyed Chan Johnson ever had.

You Irish aint known for sense, she said.

And what are you? Tas-bloody-manian?

I'm nothing at all. I'm the sole of my kind.

Good girl. That's the way.

The parade began to mount the sandstone highway bridge, the chief ruler at the head signalling with his marching baton and the satin banners of each order floating plumply above the crowd. Flynn looked across at the calamitous sound of the parade and scowled and spat on the road.

Some rat cunning is what's needed on our part, he said. To be sure.

There's nothin clever about killin him, Pa.

Flynn had hiked up his knapsack though and was stepping into the road, the lonely toll of his pots lost among the mounting parade racket. She adjusted her bedroll and followed.

Did you hear me?

Flynn said not a word. He walked on, wearing a look of concern like an etching in stone.

LAUNCESTON

Come the deeps of night Thomas Toosey stole soundlessly out among the rolling stock of freight trucks and carriages into the fringe of reeds at the riverbank. The hills above the river were outlined black before a sheen of stars. He stumbled and cursed through the mud as he made across the banks to the bridge that joined outlying Invermay to the city proper. Before long he was walking through the town of Launceston, casting an eye up and then down the unpeopled streets, his shadow circling as he crossed pools of light below the gas lamps. He passed by the tall gold-stencilled windows of Blundells Glass and China and caught a glimpse of himself dragging over the irregularities in the pane, like his image given back off a lake. With his few sorry effects, his odd round hat. Called from the pits of some wilderness. Not a sight for a weak stomach. He looked away.

He walked up past Prince's Square where in the wind the oak and elm hissed. The houses here were of the failing sort. Rows of untrue fence. Tin rooves scabbed and flaking. He walked to one house that was a narrow conjoined box with a narrow yard in front and stood gazing up at it. There was a light burning behind the curtained window. He removed his hat and smoothed his hair. He lifted the wooden gate and entered, scaled the steps, stood before the door. He knocked twice.

The woman who answered was holding a candle and when the light of it called Thomas Toosey from the dark of her verandah, holding his faded hat and standing at a civil distance, her face fell in ill temper.

Minnie, he said. Good evening.

She stared, her head nodding very slightly.

You look well, he said.

I'd hoped you were dead, Thomas.

He tapped his hat to dislodge the burrs. There were holes spaced around the crown where sun and rain, countless years of it, had eaten the felt. He stuck his finger into one. Wilhelmina—

So did Maria, she said.

He let out his breath. He thought about what to say but there was nothing to say.

Michael will be along, she said. He won't be pleased to see you neither.

I'm not much of a man, he said. I know it.

You're no sort of man at all.

I know it, he said.

You left them penniless, my sister and nephew.

Not penniless, no. I sent them every bit I earned.

Maria died believin in her heart that you despised her.

You're wrong about that. I wrote to her. She knew my feelins.

Minnie brought the door around to close it. Goodbye, Thomas, she said.

He put his hand to the panel. Now hold on, he said through the crack.

Goodbye.

I done the wrong thing.

Remove your hand.

But I come to set it straight.

You left her, Thomas. You can't correct that.

I want me boy, he said.

Minnie inched back the door, one large eye, as white as river quartz, peering around. He isn't here, she said.

Toosey stepped back. He exhaled and looked down at his hat and when he looked up he was frowning. Woman, do not piss me about, he said.

He came here once. He's a troubled boy. Never a minute of peace with him. He wouldn't stay for fear of the police.

Where is he?

I don't know. Such a father, such a son I suppose.

Toosey replaced his hat. He stood quietly staring at her. So help me, that better be the truth, he said.

In the pale light of the flame she looked unwell. Listen, she said, talk to your brother-in-law. You know what he's like. Walking the town all day, gabbing. Chances are he'll know a thing or two about your boy.

Will he be long?

I shouldn't think so.

He looked along the road and looked back at her.

You'll have to wait out there. I won't have you in the house.

Very well.

Minnie stared at him a moment. You never even come to her funeral, she said.

For which I am sorry, he said. Now and forever.

Sorry pays no debts, does it.

No.

He stepped off the verandah. The door crashed closed behind him, the locks turned over. He unslung his swag and dropped it on the ground. Then for a time he sat on it thinking. The truth was this: he had liquored himself up day after day until she, his lonely Maria, could no longer bear it. He'd left her in poverty and she had died. The sun rose and set and that fact never changed. It was a truth to tear him to pieces.

For a long time he thought about going after his boy. He could ask around the pubs. Someone would have seen him. But he lingered nevertheless and late in the evening he saw, shifting among the shadows in the road, one shape deeper and darker than all and when it crossed a band of moon it was, as he knew it would be, a handcart set on a pair of huge wheels, horseless, rolling as if of its own volition. He stood by the gate as it neared. The wheels turned crookedly on the axle, a great worn grindstone set in the centre rigged with pulleys turned as well. Dear Polly I'm goin to leave you, the cart sang, for seven long years love and more. The greaseless hubs shrieked at each revolution. It rolled up before the house and fell silent.

Ho there, Toosey called.

For all his years the knife sharpener had grown gnarled and humpbacked and shaped around his contraption like a trimmed shrub. He raised his eyes off the road and saw the bushman standing, arms folded, by the gate.

Thomas bloody Toosey, he said.

He came forward with his hand out. A tottering prophet, limp with age.

Brother Michael Payne, Toosey said.

They gripped hands across the fence and clapped each other on the arms.

Among the instruments on the cart was a small towel and Brother Payne raised his derby, mopped himself with it, and dried his sparse white hair. He wore a wild set of muttonchops below either ear and these he dried similarly.

You look well.

I'm troubled by a bit of looseness, Payne said. Dare not trust my arse with a fart.

He folded his towel and placed it upon his other implements. Jesus, man, he said. Your hair.

Toosey's mouth tightened. There's three years in it, he said. Three since Maria marched me out. Three since I cut it.

Sounds a Catholic thing to do, Payne said. Punish yourself and think it will be well.

It won't be well. I know that.

No it won't. But you aint come to talk haircuts, have you.

I'm after me boy.

Payne nodded solemnly. Expected you would be.

Toosey reached inside his jacket and removed the crumpled letter he'd carried for weeks. He held it up. William wrote to me, he said.

Yes. I know.

Of all the low acts I've done, Toosey said, and you saw most of em.

I saw a lot.

Leavin them alone is the lowest.

Payne huffed air from his nose. What makes us noble, he said, is a system of compensations. Reward each suffering, recover every debt, repay a sacrifice. You have it in you, Thomas. God don't make us without a notion of rectitude. But the question is, can you act upon what you was bestowed with?

I've come back only for that.

Start by quittin the rum, Payne said.

Toosey spat in the dust. He looked down to where the cud lay and smeared it with the toe of his boot. Says the kettle, he said.

I mean it. Rum is what brought you here.

Three years I've not had a sip. I'm a mended man.

From his pocket Brother Payne pulled a tavern pipe that was carven with harps and shamrocks. He packed it from a pouch and popped a match on the mighty grindstone that was rigged to a flywheel in the bed of his cart. He sucked the flame down to the bowl.

You know where he is? Payne said as he puffed. Your boy?

No, but I reckon you do.

Payne passed him the pipe. Stewart's, he said.

Trent Stewart?

The same.

Toosey put the pipe to his mouth. Lad needs to eat, I suppose.

A lot of the young ones visit. Around noon usually. But that aint the whole of it.

What else?

Well, he said. Listen—

What else?

I'm told he has favourites.

Toosey's look blackened. What's that mean?

He has a room, does Stewart. Out back. Where he shows himself.

I'm not followin.

Payne crooked his forefinger and waved it. Shows himself, he said. To the ones he can trust.

As the import of this slowly settled upon him a series of expressions crossed his face, at first a frown of concern and then, as he understood, his brow began to lift and his mouth to drop. I'll be damned, he said. The filthy beggar.

William knows a villain from a saint. He won't fall into bad ways.

I'll rip his guts out.

Payne wheezed, or perhaps coughed. Don't sound to me like you've mended your ways one bit.

Has someone told the police?

He took the pipe from Toosey. There was a deep and blackened divot upon the crosspiece of the cart where he'd emptied the pipe bowl year after wearisome year, and he did so again now. You would tell them, would you? he said.

My oath.

Then you are a new man.

Toosey took up his swag. He hauled the rope over his head and settled the load. He opened the gate and stepped into the street.

What are you thinkin? Payne said.

That I'm goin round there.

Not tonight you won't. Your boy aint there. Stewart only

gives them a bit of lunch. You want your boy? Wait till he's there before you go kickin up a stink.

Toosey smoothed down his moustaches.

A man like Stewart won't need much in the way of persuasion. Present there on his doorstep. See what he makes of a nine-lived bushman like yourself.

There's another matter too, Toosey said and he turned his eyes away. I need to find William tonight.

You shan't find him tonight, old mate. Not a hope in hell.

Some larrikins wandered past who were taking turns from a bottle, wiping their mouths, weaving drunks, their thumbs through the braces rigging up their pants. Toosey watched them pass and when he looked back there was a bitterness to him that showed in the set of his jaw. It must be tonight, he said. From the breast of his jacket he pulled a banknote.

It was crisp and thick and flecked with blood and Payne looked at it and he looked at Toosey. He snatched it away. Oh, he said. I see it. I see it now.

Tonight, Toosey said. You understand.

You're as thick as bull's walt, Thomas Toosey. And that is a fact.

Toosey made a little grunt.

Oh Jesus, what have you done?

Never mind what I've done. Just help me find him.

Ten years we was in Port Arthur. Workin the land like beasts side by side. You learn about a man after that, don't you?

Those sentiments caused a silence to pass between them. At length Payne said, And the sum?

Toosey looked askance at him.

It's a fair lump, or I'm a prancin fairy.

Two hundred quids.

By Christ, Payne said and tipped back his hat. He stared at Toosey like he was seeing him anew. I thought you was turned away from thievin, he said.

You can't steal from a crook, Toosey said.

Who was it?

Toosey clicked his tongue. A sweat was beading up on his brow and he raised his small round hat and palmed the damp back over his hair. The Dublin man, he said. Fitheal Flynn.

Flynn of the lowbooters?

Flynn of the lowbooters.

Him as pulled his own tooth with farrier's tongs?

The same.

Well, Payne said. I tell you now, without a skerrick of doubt, this Flynn will hunt you unto the end of days for a sum like that. He will dig you up by moonlight and make soup from your bones.

This caused Toosey some unsettlement. He studied Payne across the coarse and heavy grindstone rigged between the wheels of his cart. Doubt it's the money as has him nettled, he said.

Why?

Never mind it now. That's a tale for another time. When I find William we'll leave off the island and that'll be the end of it.

Course, you have another problem too, Payne said. Don't you? He held up the note.

I know, Toosey said.

You need gold.

You're right.

Then forget it tonight. Forget it. Just have yourself at that bank first thing. Change the notes. Fetch the young one. You'll be on a steamer by dark. You'll be off and gone.

Across the town, across the little universe of its lights, Toosey could see the black moonlit flats of Invermay where Trent Stewart kept his place. He put his hands in his pockets. He knew Payne was right but it didn't pay to come out and say it.

Stay with us tonight, Payne said. Have a feed.

Don't think Minnie would appreciate that.

She'll do as she's told.

Like hell. She's as wilful as her sister, he said and the thought of Maria then was like cold water down his back. No, he said. I know a place.

Play it smart, Thomas. Keep your head. Get the boy clear.

Payne doubled the bank note through the middle and passed it to him. Toosey looked at the note for a moment before shaking his head. Keep it, he said. For Minnie and the kids.

It's your burden to carry. I aint about to help you clear your conscience.

Toosey nodded. He took the note. Fair enough, he said.

With that done, he started down Batten Street towards the main road. When he glanced around, Brother Payne was leaning on his handcart watching him, nothing in his eyes but a flagging forbearance, like the world had lost its capacity to surprise. He raised a hand. Toosey touched his hat in return.

Along the footpath his boots fell and the billy rang against his leg. He walked listing places in his head where a man might unroll his bundle, the riverbank, Windmill Hill, the basin, but not one of them was better than an open flat prone to all manner of weather. He crossed streets made grey by the weakish gaslights and when he reached Prince's Square he squatted by the fence pickets and made sure the pocketbook was safe. The remnant heat of day was giving back off the bluestone base. Beyond the pickets, in the fountain square, were flowerbeds in bloom and stands of sapling willow that made a pissing sort of sound as they shifted. He looked along the street either way. Nothing. The windows all dark. The streetlamps hissing. There was one place he knew where he would be sheltered. The bridge by the rail line. He stood. He went on. As he walked his mind worked upon the image of Trent Stewart spitting out his broken teeth.

The bridge was on the far side of town and he was a while making it. He worked his way beneath the wooden span by sliding down a mossy bend and pitching his swag before him. Under the bridge a fire was burning and three men stood before its scant throw of light. They looked up to see Toosey crouch below the supports and stand and straighten his hat. Men, like ghosts of men, tall and sere and attired as if out of a grave for the common dead in ill-fitting jackets and under-clothes stained with sweat. The bridge was known among the town derelicts as a decent place to doss down and they seemed unsurprised to see Toosey. He looked from one to the next, humped up his bundle on a piece of cleared ground, and sat on it. One of them spoke.

Evenin.

And to you, he said.

Holdin any baccy about you?

Toosey looked them over. Wish I was.

How's about any rum?

I got tea and sugar if you got water.

We got water.

Well then, good.

They had a common billy boiling above a pitiful fire of driftwood and weeds and whatever was at hand. Toosey dosed it with tea leaves and the last of his sugar. They watched it steep in silence and when it was done poured a round from it likewise in silence. One of the men was familiar to Toosey and they studied each other through the smoke. Footsteps beat on the wooden bridge above, passed by, and this man was first to speak. He was called Bryce and he was a piece of work. He wore no hat but had a band of cloth tied about his head and like a Chinese gold digger he'd knotted it at his brow. He pointed at Toosey.

I know you.

Toosey looked away downriver.

I know you, he said again. He turned to the other two men. This is the chap give Gimlet-eyed Chauncey Johnson a floggin, he said.

The other men watched Toosey intently.

Old Gimlet-eyed, one of them said. He was thin from hardly eating so that when he fetched himself another drink from the billy his collarbone hollowed out and the slack skin of his neck pulled taut. That were twenty years ago, he said.

Bryce waved his mug at Toosey. Tied his hand with a rag and a piece of brick, he said. That made a job of it.

They all watched him. Toosey threw his dregs on the fire in a cloud of steam. For a time nothing more was spoken. They each watched the coals throb in the debris of driftwood, mosquitoes coming and going along their bare hands, enormous mosquitoes the size of moths, and all the while Toosey sitting as if deep in study and never removing his eyes from Bryce. Toosey soon cleared his throat and spoke.

I weren't the one.

You what?

Was the Irish fellow. Irish-Flynn. Was him as hit your mate, not me.

Bryce grinned. He was mostly toothless and his gums and the stubs of his teeth shone luridly in the fireglow. That's a lie, he said.

Toosey watched him though the heat haze. Was Flynn who give him the name too, as you well know. Given him on account of the gimlet he stole and was flogged for.

That's some pretty nonsense, Bryce said. He was called Gimlet owin to the oddness of his eyes. And it was you who give him the name, not Flynn. You. That's why he come for you.

The fire popped and sparked.

I never touched the man, Toosey said.

Bryce stood up sharply. Then I'm a liar, am I?

Toosey also rose.

I won't be slandered, Bryce said.

And I aint slandered you. So sit down.

Tell them I aint a liar.

Toosey clicked his tongue. History is the art by which we live our lives, he said. You have your history and I have mine.

History, Bryce said and gave a shaky smile. We can talk about that all right. Let's talk about it. Why don't you tell us why you was in Port Arthur? Eh?

This caused Toosey to stiffen. Shut your mouth about that, he said.

The lowest act of all.

She was a murderous lying bitch, Toosey said. She done it, not me.

That's your story? She done it? What a man you are.

Toosey held his eyes a while. The sound of horse-clops somewhere in the still, the murmur of the river. Bryce chewed the whiskers on his lower lip and did not look away. At length Toosey stepped into the dark beyond the firelight, and unbuttoned himself and took a piss. He stared over the river at rows of ships moored or made fast to the dock, the hulks of black along the bank. Around the fire the delinquents watched him. Something was spoken among them. He buttoned himself and went to unroll his bedding. He started to shuck off his boots but then thought better of it. He lay back on the canvas, hauled his blanket up, felt for the pocketbook and removed it from his jacket. The other men spoke in quiet tones and shifted about. He stuffed the pocketbook into his pants where it was safer.

A cart crossed onto the bridge. As it passed the commotion filled the hollow underneath and grit fell through the bridge boards, fell on his cheeks, on the water, disturbing the surface of the river with rings upon rings. Toosey lowered his hat over his eyes and waited. He heard the men mutter between themselves and he heard the fire hiss as it was fed. He listened for boot-steps heading his way through the weeds but there was only the whisper of the fire, the squealing billytin. Bryce, in a low voice, called to him through the smoke.

Toosey, he said. You got any more tea, cobber?

By daylight he was abroad among the early-risen citizenry. He had turned his shirt inside out and braided back his long grey mop, tying it off with cord, but he nevertheless made for a ratty sight lugging his roll of sailor's canvas. In the first glare of morning he walked up Tamar Street where a fish-barrow trader pushed his load and called his trumpeter and cod and where the factory hands lingered in threes and fours to smoke. They all watched Toosey pass for the angle of his hat, set low and to the side, was something sinister. At the corner he turned for the centre of town along Cimitiere Street. Here, the tall row houses crowded up the road and cast elongated shadows while opposite the upper-storey glass was of a thick gold, like a plate, full of the horizon sun. Soon he was passing shopfronts embla-zoned with names in neat type, Jones and Son, Robert's Drygoods, Chung Gon, and he knew himself close to his des-tination.

In the inner streets of Launceston he stood below the tele-graph lines gazing up and down the carriageway. There were canned-goods emporiums and coffee palaces. Coaches idled by under loads of netted luggage. Toosey walked on until he found the place he wanted. It sat on the corner curiously out of unison with the frugal local style. Horizontal bands were sculpted into the masonry, and fluting into the parapets and columns. The monumental decoration seemed to tell of the spirit of wealth taken hold in the colony. He resettled his swag and crossed among the carts plying the street towards the Launceston Bank.

It was not yet seven. Toosey perched upon the stone steps

waiting and eyeing the folk in the street and after a time he pulled the envelope from his pocket. The paper stained brown, seasoned with the ash of campfires. He opened the flap and lifted the letter. The pencil had begun to fade. He watched an ice wagon come along, tilting to and fro with the weight and the horse making a racket on the hard-packed road. He watched the merchantmen at their shops unbolt and open glass-panelled doors for a day of trade. Folk crossing in high collars, scarves, women with little bonnets on. The slow advancing of all things, the slow decay of the letter. They kept their eyes away from Toosey, as he well knew they would.

The doors swung on nine and he was first inside. The ornate ceiling was hung with a clutch of glass gaslights that gave a tolerable warm glow above the rank of tellers. Toosey approached the first stall smoothing down his moustaches and studying the stretch of white cornice as he shrugged off his swag and dropped it at his feet. His billytin clanged. The other patrons looked around at him. He delved inside his trousers for the pocketbook he had borne these last weeks, opened it, smiled, and pulled out the banknotes. As if he had some business being there.

Makes for a sight, don't it? This whole place.

I suppose it does, the teller said.

Would give a man a convulsion, Toosey said as he looked about.

Behind the barrier glass the teller drummed his fingers on the desk pad. His hair was parted in the middle and pomaded down so it appeared to be made of tar.

Well? What will it be?

Toosey held up the notes and counted them onto the counter. He pushed them forward.

I want these done up in gold.

The teller looked down at the notes. They were stained with blood, the prints of fingers, in a vivid biblical red. He fanned them out. Each more filthy than the previous. Wrinkled up and tacked together where the stains had dried. Relics of a frontier where men swore their debts in flesh. He looked at the notes and he looked at Toosey.

Say again?

Gold. Need them changed for gold.

What is your name?

Atkinson.

Have an account here, do you, Mr. Atkinson?

No, I don't.

The teller looked him over. How did you come by this money?

Come by it? I earned it. Worked like a bastard for it.

The teller tapped the pile of notes together and then counted them onto his desk pad. He gave Toosey a long and steady glare.

Wait here, he said.

He went among the desks in back of house until he came beside another gent in a drab frock coat and bow tie. As the teller spoke into his ear this dour gent turned to squint at Toosey through his glasses. Toosey removed his hat, palmed back his hair, and placed the hat upturned on the counter. He smiled at the gent. Some small discussion was had and shortly the teller returned with the fouled banknotes. He tapped the stack a few times on its edge as he considered Toosey across the counter.

Why don't you open an account? Collect the interest?

No. I want gold.

You understand that two hundred pound in gold is much more than a man ought safely to carry.

Toosey looked away. He muttered to himself, some profanity. He looked back. I aint bothered by a bit of work, he said.

I don't mean that. I mean what if you're robbed?

They've tried that already. But here I am.

The teller drummed his fingers. All right, he said. All right. If you mean to insist on it.

I insist, Toosey said, and replaced his hat.

It was agreed as a figure of a hundred and eighty-four lately minted Melbourne gold sovereigns. The teller counted the pieces into a cotton sack that he handed across to Toosey and Toosey knotted the cloth and rolled it into his swag. When he heaved it to his shoulder the coins rang inside the canvas like a string of muffled bells.

He was turning to leave when the teller leaned close to the barrier glass and said, Must have been a decent bit of work you did.

Toosey's face blackened. What?

That's a lot of money for a labourer.

Toosey took a long breath. He looked around. He settled his swag and stepped away from the counter. Several men were queued at booths and they watched Toosey coming past but looked promptly away when he caught their eyes. He was about ready to break someone's nose.

Outside the sun lay like a pour of hot pig-iron, giving off a sharpish heat while the air yet felt cool. He cut along St. John Street attended by the sound of coins to where blocks of light and dark lay cast between the rows of stores and the street was full of people. As he walked here among the many boutiques and dried-goods emporiums, his demeanour changed. He held his eyes forward, locked shut his jaw, tugged his hat. He soon built to an awful temper. He had in mind a picture of Trent Stewart holding his bloodied mouth. He walked the town streets, his thoughts at work, his forehead furrowed, but he could not go after Stewart yet. There was something needed doing. Before they could reckon things out, he had to leave the gold somewhere.

Along a short way was an overhead sign showing a silver painted sphere and bearing the title Star of the North Hotel etched into the inch-thick wood. He stood below this sign glancing between it and the hotel, a weatherboard block resting on a base of freestone dressed with cement, ornamented by iron balustrading running under the window boxes. The effect was to garb what was otherwise a mongrel sort of place with some pretence of hospitality. He was mulling over the prospect of going back to that goat-faced teller to make a deposit and glancing up and down the street, scratching his balls through his threadbare pants. He tucked his bundle under one arm and climbed the stairs.

At the reception desk the automatic smile of the clerk fell as Toosey crossed the lobby with a billytin making a hollow toll, grim in his bloodied clothes and his bruising. The clerk lifted his hands in protest.

Sir, he said and his voice was strained, we have a dress policy.

Toosey looked around at the frieze-patterned wallpaper that was faded and torn. The wainscotting scarred with the marks of dragged trunks.

I must ask you to leave.

He removed his hat and slapped it. Bits of grass seed fell in a light rain to the floor. He placed the hat on the counter. The clerk cleared his thoat.

You have a strongbox in here, I suppose, Toosey said.

Sir, I—

Toosey dropped his bundle, making a whump that filled the grand cavern of the lobby.

Sir, I'll call for the constable if you do not remove yourself.

Toosey began to fish through his swag for the coins.

Sir?

I aint walkin to another hotel and I aint goin back to the bank, he said. He sat a new sovereign on the desk. Just need the use of your strongbox a while, he said.

I'm sorry, sir. No.

Eh?

It's for guests only.

Toosey gazed hard into his face. Then give me a room.

The clerk levelled the guestbook on the counter and adjusted the pencils beside it so that each was spaced apart, set straight, finding some kind of peace in this ritual. When he was done he looked up at Toosey with a weak smile. Sir, he said and he cleared his throat. Sir, I think you have the wrong impression of the Star of the North. We are a well-reputed hotel, thus the requirement that you be neatly attired in order to take a room.

Toosey snorted. His jaw below the tufts of his whiskers worked back and forth. He looked about the lobby. This arsehole town, was all he said. He reached into his swag and produced another of the coins. It flashed like a struck match in the light of the window.

Two? the clerk said.

Two. For you to overlook your policy.

There was a small silver bell upon the counter that the desk clerk lifted and shook. We best ask Mr. Chung, he said.

Good, Toosey said. Call him out.

All was quiet. The clerk watched the door in the panelling behind him. He rang the bell again.

Maybe he'll find me a bleedin room.

The clerk was ringing the bell furiously.

After a moment the panelling swung back and a tall and slender man with slick dark hair appeared. He closed the door and stood and crossed his hands at his waist. He was plainly oriental. His eyes flicked to every part of Toosey. His face remained calm but his nostrils flared slightly at what he saw. He smiled and bowed. Ah, he said. Welcome to Star.

Toosey looked at the clerk and he looked at the oriental. He frowned. Is this a wind-up? he said.

No, sir.

I am not the sort of man you wind up.

This is the owner. This is Mr. Chung.

The oriental was so tall he looked down on Toosey.

Toosey slowly replaced his hat. He levelled it, set it right. To hell with you, he said. Scruffing his swag, he turned and started towards the doors.

Oh, Chung said. Oh you a mean bastard, huh?

Toosey looked around. That's right. One as prefers his own kind.

What your name?

He stopped. He crossed his arms.

Your name?

Johnson.

Let me tell you, Mr. Johnsons. I am mean bastard too. Oh yes. You like that?

Toosey was laughing openly.

We mean bastard. We see each other.

You see me, do you?

The oriental eyed Toosey's battered hat and canvas roll, and his smile began to broaden. I am from Guangzhou. We say stand straight and do not fear crooked shadow. I stand straight, Mr. Johnsons. Do you?

Straight as a rod.

Chung smiled and bowed, as if his point was thusly made.

I'm offering two gold vickies, Toosey said. Two. For the right to lodge somethin in your strongbox.

Oh lot of money.

I can as easy take it elsewhere.

No, Mr. Johnsons. No no. We help you.

Will you now.

You want my strongbox. You have valuable thing. Yes?

Toosey reached inside his bundle, fished around, and pulled the money sack. Chung's narrow eyes grew round.

Ah, he said.

Two is fair. Two for the use of your strongbox. That's the simplest two vickies you'll ever receive.

Chung was staring at the sack. How much? he said.

A hundred and eighty five.

Oh.

I'll be back for it. Might be anytime, might be midnight when I come. Might be tomorrow. But when I come, you be ready to give it to me. Right?

This very safe hotel. We keep money safe.

There is no need to concern yourself, the clerk said. Mr. Chung is here day and night.

Oh yes. We take care of money.

Toosey inclined his head slightly. Whenever I come. No question.

Yes, sir.

Oh yes.

I want a receipt for it. The whole amount.

When he dropped the money sack on the counter the sound of all the coins seemed to call them to attention. The clerk stiffened. Toosey stood drumming his fingers as the clerk scribbled out a note and handed it over. He filled in the guest register and pushed it across to Toosey and Toosey wrote Chauncey Johnson in ill-formed letters and signed it the same. He laid his sovereigns in the crease of the book and pushed it back. Chung, standing dead still, could be heard to breathe. He spread his gloved hands.

Welcome to Star Hotel, he said.

He approached the bushman around the desk and smiled. Without warning he picked up Toosey's old bundle. Toosey caught it by the rope.

Unhand that.

I take you to room, Chung said.

Room be blowed. I only want the safe.

No no. I take you room. Good room.

He had the bundle under his arm and was motioning for Toosey to follow. A huge flared staircase filled the centre of the lobby and Chung mounted the first step and began to climb.

Give us that here, Toosey said. He crossed the lobby and ascended after Chung.

Nice room. This way.

The landing was lit with dim oil lamps placed in sconces and Chung led him to the end of the hall and, looking back, smiling at Toosey, he pointed to a tall pine door that was inlaid elaborately with blackwood to make an eight-pointed compass or star. There was a delay as Chung slipped on his glasses and fed a key into the lock. He glanced up at Toosey.

Just a moment, he said.

The key knocked in the latchworks. Inside was an enormous posted bed buttressed either side by stout-looking bureaus, the timber marble dark and waxed to a high shine, and over the floor a square of Asian carpet. Chung dropped the swag and moved off to draw the curtains while Toosey walked a turn around the room, picking up ornaments and replacing them. He opened the door to the bathroom and peered inside to where a great claw-footed tub was stationed above a spread of cream tiles grouted in black. He frowned and backed out and glancing around his attention was taken with the sideboard upon which stood, like something a child would drink, a row of tiny whiskeys and rums. Chung was crossing the room to leave, but Toosey clicked his fingers.

See here, he said and clicked.

Yes?

There's someone else. A boy. I might bring him here later.

You need company, eh?

What?

I know nice girl, Chung said. White girl.

Toosey just stared at him.

Chung was smiling, his eyes jovially narrow. You like I send company?

No, said Toosey and waved him off.

Very clean girl. Very nice fanny.

No.

The oriental nodded and bowed. Toosey was picking through the miniscule bottles of whiskey, bottles of gin, when he saw Chung still lingering by the door, still grinning.

I know nice boy. White boy, yellow boy.

Away with you.

Chung backed out of the door, bowing, displaying the part in his hair. Toosey reached out and smacked the door closed.

The window onto the street was glazed with an oily grime. He stood, watching the folk drift below like phantasms, rippling and stretching in the streaked glass. Watching for someone, he realised, as he leaned on the frame. He polished a clean spot in the glass to better see. He wouldn't breathe easy this time. That mad Irish mongrel would come, there wasn't a doubt in the world.

Find the boy. Get off the island. He sat on the bed and ground at his eye with the heel of his palm. It was two weeks since the letter, and who knew how long before it. The lad, alone all that time, street-living, a gentle-hearted little thing hardly ready for it. Toosey walked again to the window and looked out, pondering what pitiful few choices remained to him. But all he could think about was his boy and the deviant Trent Stewart with his wattle-grub cock hanging through his fly.

He left the room and went downstairs.

Outside, the heat had brewed into a thicker sort of thing that dried the throat. He crossed through streets where barefooted children called out wax matches at a penny a box, mopping himself on his sleeve as he went. At the crossing with Tamar Street he stopped and looked over the row of cheap-john shops and corn stores towards the river, slick and brown like the outfall of a sewer, and beyond that to the low-rooved homes of Invermay. He felt again for the knife inside his coat, resettled it, and set out.

By noon the Rechabite parade was swarming over the farming town of Perth. The chief ruler, wearing his bicorn like a rooster strutting, called a halt and marshalled his followers into ranks, arranging soprano and baritone apart. Satisfied, he led them into a hymn that carried on the hot baked wind. The citizenry of the town lined the main thoroughfare. They were a beggarly lot that wore straw hats and sad linen smocks. They stood in silence watching the marchers sing. The women each with a herd of children. The menfolk, glaring, sunburnt from labouring in fields and gardens. There were three separate public houses along the main road and noon drinkers emerged blinking and naked-headed into the sun only to be set upon by recruiters waving paper questionnaires for a place in the order.

Fitheal Flynn and his daughter observed all this from a distance.

I ought to have shot a few of them, he said.

Caislin quietly stared. What a lovely song, she said.

Tis the sound of inducement.

They were quiet a while and then she said, Wouldn't it be wonderful to join a choir?

Ah, and you will, my love. You will.

Flynn shuffled off along the road for Launceston and left Caislin gazing at the odd festivities, standing alone, and soon, lifting her voice, she began to sing along. Flynn was climbing the long hill ahead and her song played above the farmland

and the road, catching at the strings of his heart. He looked back at that singular figure, covered, dressed as a man, and a great despair rose in his chest. What had he made of such a precious soul? What sort of beast?

The highway was in heavy use. It had been corduroyed in places with split logs and outside of Breadalbane they passed a team of fourteen paired steers hauling a eucalypt slab of such a weight that it cracked the thinner of these boles. The bullocky called good afternoon to them with a waving hat, a gesture that Flynn returned. All day they passed travellers coming along, a woman bent under a load of kindling, leaves in the morass of her silver hair, itinerant men walking the road for work, boys in bare feet, boys as thin as beggars. By late afternoon they were crossing the Kerry Lodge bridge on a steep river gully. Caislin ran her hand over the parapet walls where indentured men had placed a coping of broken stone, men like her own father. Clear water trickling, the sound of the river. Her hand following the wall. The winding highway led through the valley wheat tracts and the market gardens of Youngtown and they passed fields and lone farmhouses and they passed the tall white houses of the well-to-do. Elsewhere clutches of huts nestled like hogs asleep in a mud wallow. The paddocks feathered with button grass.

Do you remember the toffee Ma cooked up?

Through the eyeholes two dark wet jewels staring at him. Flynn looked away to the wooded slopes of the valley. She loved to see you eat, he said.

It got stuck till I couldn't chew.

That's how she liked it, he said. Thick like.

I could never eat it.

And she would laugh. Watching your fingers in your teeth.

They walked half a mile in silence. Some of them toffees I tossed in the grass, you know, she said after a while.

Oh did you?

They made my jaw hurt. I hated them.

Flynn put his age-speckled hand on her arm. Never mind.

Do you think she'd be mad?

No.

I shouldn't have done it.

Well, and by God, girl she is gazing down from up there in fits of laughter. Not one ounce of love did she hold back from you. Not for any reason. Forget something as silly as that.

A scrap collector came leading his belled and tasselled horse by the bridle. He stared at the hooded girl. Standing in the centre of the road, leaning on his staff, Flynn watched him go by.

It's ones like him you ought to watch out for, he said.

Should I pray to her? Caislin said.

Over what?

Tell her where I put them toffees.

He took her by the hand then and led her along, a sombre lump in his throat. He could not answer.

What they needed was shelter. Off the road in the backways, among the painted board cottages, there remained homes earlier generations had abandoned, huts of wattlestick caulked with clay, rude barns fabricated from logs. They picked along the outer parts of a hill where the road was dry, scanning the hovels dormant in the fields for one they could use. Many appeared to have collapsed in disrepair but smoke ran from the chimneys nonetheless. Occupied by what downcast creatures, who could say.

Did they make you build things? she said. She was trailing along behind her father some yards, one hand tucked under the rolled blanket roped on her shoulder.

Who, my love?

The soldiers. The wardens.

At first Flynn said nothing. He gazed across the hills as if in thought. I built a blessed lot of road, he said at length. It was hungry work and we were always hungry.

What was you in the Port for?

You know why.

Hittin some bugger.

Aye.

Did you hurt him?

A long silence. The tapping of Flynn's staff on the road. Not as much as I should have liked, he said.

They walked another quarter mile before Caislin said quietly, What was he in there for?

Who? he said, but he already knew full well.

That man, she said. Toosey.

Flynn stopped. He looked back at her. Girl, don't be wasting thoughts on him.

Is he a killer?

They hang killers.

Then what? she said.

Then it doesn't matter, does it?

So tell me then. If it don't matter.

Aye, he said and pointed his stick at her, that's your mother's canniness you have.

I want to know what sort of man he is, she said.

What sort of man? he said with a snort.

That's right. If we are to do him a mischief, I want to know.

Well, you aren't as canny as I thought if you need to ask that, he said and he turned and continued on. And it's him that did us the mischief, he said.

I imagine he robbed some squatter. Or bushranged out west.

Flynn kept walking. It's not a fit subject for a girl.

She hurried after him. I'm not a girl.

Yes, you are.

No, I'm a woman.

She said it very plainly. He looked up at the sky, gripping his staff, his soul wringing inside him. Ellen, would you listen to her, he said.

Did he steal a horse?

Bejaysus, how would I know?

What do you know then?

All I can tell you, he said, is what I was told by that spiteful lot of men that was generally at Port Arthur.

Behind the cloth her black eyes narrowed. I don't want lies, she said.

That rogue is flush with lies and fock all else.

Flynn walked a while without saying more. Gazing over the hills, over the pallid fields of wheat. When he turned to her his face had soured. There was a girl, is what I was told, he said. I don't know, a servant girl, ex-government. Like as not a girl without much in the way of sense. Point being, Toosey had her with child and this was all a long time ago, to be sure, but it was told to me as such.

How long?

Twenty years at least.

It sounds like what Jilly Connell done.

Aye, and it might have been. Only Jilly Connell done what was right by his girl. He married her. Toosey has no notion of rightness at all.

So what? He was gaoled for that?

That's not the whole of it, no. When the little bastard was born this girl had a fit of the nerves. There was some conspiracy between the pair of them. God knows what. But the wee'un was killed.

How?

Put a cord about its throat. Tied it off. They done the deed and buried it by the river, which wasn't clever. It was turned up by and by. Wrapped in a piece of towel and some brown winsey, I was told. Wearing a little apron.

Caislin walked with her hands in her pockets and her eyes down. She kicked a stone. Might it not have been bad luck? she said.

Twas bad luck. They should've hung him.

I mean, might the girl have blamed Toosey for her own neglect? Or might the wee'un have just died?

Flynn snorted. More fiddler than dancing man, is our Toosey.

Caislin took another swing at the stone. Why should anyone want to kill an infant? Their own infant?

You can ask the man hisself when we find him.

A few yards further up Flynn found what he was after. Within a field of thistles stood a dark and smokeless shack dropping bits of its palings and sprouting weeds along its roof thatch. The door hung slightly ajar and inside all was still. Flynn lifted his staff and pointed to it. Caislin looked at the shack and looked away without a word. Thus it was agreed upon.

They stepped over the low drywall and picked through the scotch thistle for the front door, Caislin watching the road over her shoulder. The door was a few handcut planks suspended off a hinge of rope and Flynn pushed it back with his stick. Sun shafts pierced the dark where the roof stood open to the sky. He looked around the room. There were blankets and other bedding strewn over the stone floor and on one wall a table stacked with empty tins and candle stubs in jars. They moved into the room and pulled the door closed.

It was a long and peaceful hour they wasted removing their boots and socks to let their feet dry and eating the last crust of Longford bread. Caislin was seated against the wall on a pile of mouldy blankets and nodding her head now and then in sleep. Flynn watched her from the corner of his eye as he wrapped his blisters in shreds of sheeting. He whistled.

Oi, he said, don't you be drifting off now.

Let me bloody sleep.

We can't stop here. And watch your mouth.

Let me sleep a minute. Please.

Like hell.

He threw a wadded length of sheet at her.

Please, she said. She was clasping her knees and bracing her head upon them. The sun through the ceiling cast light over her frail white feet but left the rest of her in darkness. Flynn said no more on the matter. In time there rose a rhythmic breathing from the shadows where she slept, long and even and calm.

So when later he heard talking, at first he thought the girl was muttering in her dreams. He peered up from his work of mending the satchel straps with knotted rag. The sound seemed to waft through the breach in the roof and he bent his ear to it. Voices, coarse and loud. He stood to look out of the window hole and he saw, lifting their boots over the drywall and approaching, a band of young men, a good few of them. He had time to shake Caislin awake and seize up his staff before the door bundled open.

The first of the gangers stepped inside the hut. He had a strangely stiff gait and his shadow wormed like a dying man in the oblong of light cast on the floor. When he turned and saw Fitheal Flynn the ganger had time to cease smiling and knit his brows together before Flynn shoved him to the ground by his shirt collars. A general cry went up from the group outside the hut. The other gangers had mounted the verandah and were crowding about the door but when they saw Caislin, a fable horror, hooded, holding coolly by her side the bulldog gun she'd drawn from Flynn's belt, they stopped dead and stared.

Get along now, she said.

But they could only stare.

She lifted the pistol and cocked it. Get along I said.

The sound of the turning cylinder sent them breaking for the low drywall, vaulting it for their lives. Caislin stepped outside, the gun still up. She watched them flee down the road holding that pistol on them all the while.

You're in me snug, said the young fellow laid out on the floor. He was struggling to his feet.

Flynn came to this ganger and with his staff cracked him a settling blow across his head. The youth tried to cover himself and Flynn jammed one boot flat between the fellow's shoulders and pressed him out. He propped on his knee as he studied the sorry sight pinned below.

A wonderful piece of luck, he said to the lad.

This is my place.

What is your name there, my son?

You can kiss my arse breeches down, you can.

Flynn struck him again. Your name?

The fellow clamped his arms around his shaven head. Jane Eleanor Hall, he said cringing.

Flynn's feathery eyebrows lifted. Playing games will get you hit, he said.

I aint playin. I'm a girl.

Well, Flynn said, you're the ugliest girl I ever saw.

Go and be buggered.

Jaysus, and where's your hair?

Go to hell.

Best you smarten up, Miss Jane Eleanor Hall. For you have yourself in a nice little quandary.

It's comin, she said. Tell Rabbit I will have it soon.

She was pressed down hard on the floorstones and even bending her neck about she could not see Flynn. I don't have it yet, she said trying to twist out from under his boot. The devil knows how, but I will have it. I swear I will.

From her place on the floor she could, however, see Caislin. She stopped her struggle and stared. What's wrong with him? Is he sick?

In the column of sun the cotton cowl was brilliantly white, the folds below the nose twitching with each breath, the fathomless pits of the eyes. The ganger rubbed her bruised head. You aint Rabbit's boys, she said.

No, lass. We are not.

Hall bent her neck around. The lack of hair made her eyes look big. A pair of showy bastards is what you—

Flynn drove down the butt of his staff. She cried out.

Listen to me, lass, lest you come to end your days on this here floor. Shut your mouth and I'll remove my boot off you. Can you do that?

Hall nodded slightly under his stick.

All right?

All right, she said.

Flynn moved back and stood before the door. He gripped his staff and watched as the girl drew first to her knees, rocking back into a crouch with one leg cocked out stiffly, the tears in the grime of her face leaving clean streaks. Her eyes jumped back and forth between them. At length Flynn addressed her.

Your place, is it?

The ganger nodded.

Then I apologise. I believed it empty.

Silence. The ganger seemed to be waiting for her fate to unfold. When nothing happened, when they merely stared at her, she climbed to her feet in a series of practised hops, cocking her lame leg out to the side and backing away to the wall. She seemed wholly keen to disappear into the darkest corners of the hut.

Flynn removed his droopy hat and fanned himself with it. She's hotter than Satan's arse, he said.

Why's he lookin at me like that? Hall said. She was watching Caislin, watching her hold the bulldog gun.

And a nice wee snug it is too.

Is he sick? Why's he starin at me?

Save for the great bloody hole in the roof.

Tell him to take that bag off, Hall said.

Flynn snorted. He won't make hisself known to the likes of you.

The ganger pressed back against the wall, blooms of mould blistering the spoiled paint.

But I will tell you his name, said Flynn, for tis a name well known. A name even you will know.

Never seen him before, she said. How could I know his name?

But you do.

Jane Hall backed away further.

This here man is Jack Ketch, he said.

A look of concern crossed her face. It aint, she said. Ketch is a story.

Who says stories aren't real?

You're shammin me.

Tis Ketch all right, said Flynn.

Hall edged another pace towards the corner.

I should think a fine young city arab such as you, Flynn said, would come to hear of the man Ketch.

They call all the hangmen Ketch, she said.

They do. Aye, they do.

Tell him to take off that hood.

There was a long pause as Flynn pulled his stick close and settled his weight upon it. He looked her head to toe. Could you find a man in town, Miss Jane Eleanor Hall? A man who didn't want to be found, say. A man called Thomas Toosey but who uses different names. Last week it was Atkinson. Jaysus only knows what it is this week. Could you do that? Would you know how?

I never heard of no Toosey before, said the ganger. So hows about you leave me be.

Here Flynn paused to hang his hat off the weighted bulb of his staff. I will confess that Toosey has his reasons to avoid me, he said. We have an account to settle with him, you understand.

Hall looked from one to the other.

Having known Toosey many a year, having spent a portion of my life in confinement with him, you can trust me when I say that he is fairly due to the gallows.

Jane Hall seemed not to hear. Her eyes cut about the room.

Are you listening, Miss Hall?

Yes sir, she said.

God forbid you come to harm merely cause you didn't listen.

Please sir. I'm listenin.

You should understand I provide this counsel for your benefit.

I'm listenin. I am.

Shall I continue?

Yes sir.

Flynn reached up and smoothed his sparse hair across the width of his forehead. I run cows on a tenancy in Quamby, said Flynn. Run them for beef. Was a good year for beef, did you know that?

No.

Oh, and it was. We made us a profit, my three daughters and I. Sold eighty head up Deloraine way and took our banknotes home for safekeeping. Never trust a bank, Miss Hall. What are they, after all? Feeding off honest men like march flies.

Yes, sir.

Flynn wrung the neck of his staff, the leather of his hands creaking. But somehow this man Thomas Toosey got word of it, he said. And in he come. He waited till I was away, watched the house I reckon. When he come my daughter was alone.

Talk to the traps, said Hall, if he's stolen from you.

Lass, tis Ketch and I shall settle him.

For stealin a few quids? she said.

Money is not the matter.

Kill a fellow for stealin, she said. Why in hell would you do that?

If it was the stealin, said Flynn, we should have our money and let him be, by God. But the blood that beats in him is old blood, tried in war. It was the blacks he fought as a boy. Indentured to a frontiersman in the east. Now it's whichever poor soul he happens upon. He is a powerful fiend, is Toosey, and murder follows him about. Just two days past we saw a man who'd fought Toosey fist and claw. Oh, and he fought. And for it he was killed.

Police round here are nasty bastards, Hall said. He won't get far. They'll hunt him out for you.

You aren't one of these who bow down in fear of the law, are you, Miss Hall? A moderate woman? Crawling in fear of words on paper?

She looked at him. Eh?

The lessons of Paris are learned, the lessons of Ballingarry. Are they not?

She propped hard in the corner of the hut, staring back at him. You're a mad pair of bastards, she said.

The madness is to meekly submit, he said. Meekly lie down and accept servitude. Withdraw your consent, Miss Hall, and they cannot control you. That is the lesson of Ballingarry. Civilisation is a lie. The grand lie. Told by masters to servants. He smiled, exposing his brace of crook teeth. I see a fortuity in meeting you, he said. A girl who knows the town, knows how to hide herself, knows how to ask around.

Jane Hall curled back her lip. You want a cripple to go hunt a killer? she said.

Not hunt. Lay eyes on him, that is all.

Lay eyes on him, he says. I think you have me mistook for another. I aint cut out for this.

You're cut fine for my purposes.

And what if I find him? Hall said. What then? I'm bloody lame.

Mostly in these cases, he said, the horse thinks one thing and the rider another. I expect you shan't even look for him. You'll hole up snug somewhere and wait for us to pass through. Would you do something like that, lass?

Jane Hall cocked her head to one side. She kept quiet.

Of course you would, Flynn said, such is your nature. So let me propose an offer, to be sure of your loyalty. I'd be willing to pay for word of Toosey. Let's call it a pound for a sighting. Two for his whereabouts.

She looked at him and her eyes glistened.

Hearing me, are you? he said.

She licked her upper lip. Ten, she said.

Flynn lifted a single woollen eyebrow.

Ten pound.

His hands on his stick creaked and twisted.

I find him. I show you where he is. You give me ten.

Flynn shook his head. No.

It's my neck I'm riskin, aint it?

Flynn gave a slow shake of the head. Take a look at Ketch there, he said.

Eh?

Are you lookin?

She nodded.

Get yourself a good long eyeful, don't be shy about it.

Yes, sir.

A man remade in the image of a beast, Flynn said. A man given over to blood as the mouth of the lion is given over to blood. Is he not?

Hall blinked rapidly. She straightened up.

Make war with him at your peril, Flynn said.

To show their sincerity Caislin tucked the gun into the loose band of her trousers. She pushed back her sleeves and there were foul blistered scars along her forearms, bound about in part by stained bandaging. Hall looked into the black pits centremost of the hood and was rendered silent by what she saw.

So you'll have your ten, lass, he said. But you would not be wanting to upset Mr. Ketch here.

No, sir. Thank you, sir.

You would not want to disappear, say.

No. I wouldn't do that.

I should think not.

If I can show you where the mongrel is, she said. If I can take you to the place. That is worth ten.

Aye, you'll have ten.

Flynn dipped into his pocket and produced a knotted leather purse and shook some coins into his palm. I am entirely sincere about this, he said.

He put out his hand for the young ganger and it hung there, solitary in its intent, until Hall shambled forward out of the dark corner, plucked the coins from it, and pocketed them.

Entirely sincere, he said again.

What's he look like? she said. Your man Toosey or Atkinson?

You will mark him by his hair which he keeps long and braided like the Indians of America. He's near sixty and perfectly grey, wearing always a billycock.

Give us a day or two, she said. I'll need a day or two.

You have everything to gain, Miss Hall.

He stepped clear of the door and he held out his arm as if to guide the young ganger through it. She hobbled slowly forward. On the threshold she stopped and looked them over, one then the other. He spat in his hand and put it out to her. They shook.

How will I find you? she said.

No one forgets a hangman, lass, do they now?

No, she said.

So ask around, he said. We won't be far away.

She looked at them both and shook her head. She hopped into the afternoon heat, her halt leg scything through the this-tle and tussock grass, and mounted the drywall into the road. It was quiet thereabouts and she moved alone over the rutted mud and through the fringe of land with only the rhythmic scrape of her leg disturbing the silence. When she was out of sight down the way Flynn said, We need to be leaving.

Why?

If she finds Toosey, she might come the queer with him. Perhaps propose to sell him our whereabouts and therefore enlarge her own profit in this game.

Caislin dropped her head. That was our last few shillins, she said.

Spent well too, if it turns up Toosey.

Unless she comes the queer with him.

Then it's a mess of a business, right enough. But it's a mess anyway, so there you have it.

And here's us with nothin to eat. Not a bite.

Flynn held up his hand and tapped on the gold band he wore. It was so scuffed and dull that it looked almost part of him. Time has come to sell this, he said.

No, don't do that.

Listen to me now. I'll put the ring into pawn. That is all.

No.

We'll soon fetch it back.

It's the last thing of hers you have, Caislin said. It's all you have to remember her.

Remember? My treasure. I look at you and I can never forget your mother. I don't need a ring.

Yet he moved off to retrieve his knapsack, his stick, and for a time he could not look at her. For in truth he was not sure who she was, this girl in outsized pants rolled at the ankles, outsized coat and shirt, cowled in a stained cotton flour sack. He had made of her something she was not. He shouldered up his bag and stepped outside. Forgive me, Ellen, he said to the sky.

They convened beneath the lessening sun. A road led away up the sloping hills into sparsely placed blue gum and sassafras saplings, above a carpet of infant bracken, and they were wary,

Flynn and his daughter, as they stepped over the low stone wall slouched under loads of bedding to put forth upon the road. They looked for a moment towards the distant town spires hooped in smoke and the river traders at anchor before turning away and making for the open woods. A half mile of distance had them among thin trees. Flynn tapped his staff as his daughter followed behind like some mythic animal made tame.

Launceston's the other way, she said.

I know.

They walked on further.

Where are we going? she said.

Just up the way.

Caislin looked around. The track was a pair of cart troughs lined with stands of black wattle and gum left for shade by squatters.

Why? she said.

Flynn kept walking.

She lowered her eyes and followed on.

Later a mounted cattleman cleared them off the path as he came through at a gallop and he whooped and cracked his riding crop on the animal, crouching in the saddle as the horse thundered beneath him. They stood by and watched him pass. Through their legs they felt the ground tremble. The horseman made a wind that stirred the bark rags and raised the birds. He left a track through the scrub where he'd ridden, and the seekers stepped back onto the road, themselves silent, treading among his divots. Further on Flynn paused near a pair of huge fallen trees. He turned to survey the thin woodland and he put aside his staff and climbed the trunk. It was a long time dead and collapsing in rot. He jumped off the far edge. Caislin in the wayside, waiting, saw him stick his head above the trunk.

This will do us, he said.

For what?

For the night.

She dumped her bedroll and sat on it.

They soon had an arrangement out of sight of the road with a ring of fire rocks that held the billytin. Not that they carried any tea to brew, nor anything by way of food. It was only the habit of weeks on the road that did it.

I'll be for walking into Launceston, he said and he began gathering his coat around himself and neatening his sagging hat.

What about me?

He stood up. No, he said.

Am I to stay?

Aye.

Alone?

Flynn stood looking down at her. He put his hands on his hips. Remove that thing and I'll take you, he said.

She lowered her head. The mottling shade cast through the canopy crept over the cotton.

Taint prudent to be having a hangman in the town, he said. Folk will talk. If Toosey is around he'll soon hear.

Caislin sat in quiet.

You don't need it. Throw it away.

He adjusted his listing hat. When he looked at her again his eyes were soft, his lower lip heavy. Throw it away, he said.

I can't.

The girl I remember, Flynn said, my daughter, she was a brave one. This girl before me, well. Who would say as much about her? Tucked away in her costume, hiding away.

He started tearing then, without sound, his lower lip aquiver and the lines around his eyes deepening. You are the pulse of my heart, he said after a time.

I know.

But I want my daughter back.

I know.

Where's my daughter?

In the trees the breeze made an ocean sound. Flynn dragged a hand across his cheeks to dry them and he reached to the small of his back and lifted the pistol from his belt. Take this, he said.

She looked away.

Don't be talking to anyone now, he said.

I won't.

And keep hidden.

Just leave the gun and go.

He passed her the stubby gun gingerly. She dropped it on the dirt and sat studying it over her knees, hunched, the ears of the cotton sack wilting in the damp and the heat.

If some bastard comes near you—

He'll get shot, she said.

Aye, well, and will you do that?

I'd rather not have to.

No.

Course, she said and looked up, you know what happened last time you left me alone.

Flynn nodded. I know.

But you'll do it again anyway.

He turned his eyes along the road. My beautiful girl—

Don't say that.

Take it off. Come with me.

No. I told you. Not yet.

He exhaled. He stepped onto the road. Then I'll be here by dark, he said.

He tramped out along the track that led to town, leaning on his staff. When he looked back at the campsite his daughter was staring at him. She'd removed the hood and her naked face floated sadly in the scrub. The sight of it stopped him. She did not wave or do otherwise than stare with the gravity that had lately become her chiefest part. He touched his hat to her and walked on. A cold stone hanging in his chest.

Invermay. Here lived the dregs drained from the town, funnelled into one hole. For no one of any influence would inhabit a quarter as cursed with mosquitoes and as openly pitted with rat nests as was this part of town. A flat swamp edged by a marshland of tall reeds and deep mud. Toosey, his billycock lowslung upon his head, made his way in the early afternoon through the shabby and ramshackle homes in the back alleys where garlands of washing as if for some festival festooned the verandahs. The mud in the street had dried to hard shale that cracked as he walked it and the silt beneath rose through his bootprints. He went, his eyes shifting warily about, with his fists stuffed inside his pockets.

Further on he passed children conferring on a vacant plot of land. It was serving duty as a tip, overrun with castoff bedding, bits of blown paper, coiled wire. One of them was screaming. He halted in the street and called to them and the children scattered. The screaming continued, the cold and horrendous sound of murder, and he saw the small fire they had burning and saw the cat they had somehow made fast to a fence slat. He crossed through the debris to the fire and stood looking down. The cat had its hindquarters burning in the coals and was shrieking and thrashing. It was bound about with wire so that its eyes and bloated stomach bulged. He turned a circle, looked around for the children. They were nowhere he could see. He spat. In the end he brought his foot down upon the cat's head, and again until the woeful noise stopped. He wiped his boot on a grass tuft. He moved on.

By and by he came to the premises of Trent Stewart. It was a grim house of unpainted boards and he stood without the cast-iron gate gazing up at the second-floor windows. The eye-holes of a skull. He lifted back the gate and mounted the verandah. Without removing his hat he raised the knocker on the door and let it fall.

It was opened by an old hollow-cheeked matron. She peeked around the jamb, studying the grim-looking man on the step, the holed jacket he wore, blood on the shirt beneath. She must have been seventy at least and had a look about her like she'd been licking vinegar.

Only children in here, she said. We don't take men.

I aint come about a feed.

She squinted at him.

You have a boy sometimes, he said. Goin by the name of Toosey. Master William Toosey.

I told you no men allowed.

I'm only askin to see him.

Who are you?

I'm his father.

The matron turned and called over her shoulder. Mr. Stewart! There's a fellow out here.

The whump of boots tolled somewhere inside the house and soon a big round-bellied gent rolled up behind her in the hallway. He peered over his half-spectacles.

Yes? What is it, Mrs. Crowthers? he said.

This chap wants to come in.

I should like to see my son, Toosey said.

Sorry, we don't allow men on the premises.

Told him as much, the matron said.

We allow girls and boys and girls and boys only, Stewart said.

Listen, I don't care what you allow and I don't want to come in. Just let me boy out here on the step and there won't be no trouble.

Stewart pushed back his glasses. This really is improper, he said.

Improper can go and fuck itself.

Mrs. Crowthers made a small strangled gasp.

Well, Stewart said. Well now. There is no call for profanity.

Let him out front here like I told you then.

The children are eating. You will have to make arrangements to meet your son elsewhere. Outside of lunch hours, of course. I am sorry.

You could get real sorry yet, sunshine.

With hardly a movement Toosey had drawn his twine-handled camp knife and was holding it by his side. The blade was lean and tapered and the corrosion on its steel stood darkly in the light. Stewart saw it and seemed suddenly to understand the quality of the fellow on his doorstep. His cheek gave a twitch.

Look here, he said, but Toosey placed his free hand on his chest and shoved him backwards. He pushed through the doorway into the narrow hall. A rack hung with coats toppled as he crashed past and he paused upon the patterned hallway runner surveying the rooms that ran off the corridor, his mouth hardened into a line.

Stewart took his chance to flee. He ran onto the verandah and descended into the street in a series of awkward falters. The matron tailed him, stumbling. From the gloom Toosey watched them go. He shook his head and spat. He opened the first door in the hall. A sitting room occupied by leather armchairs, a commode stacked with rows of books. Next came a kitchen, in the shadows an iron stove, the pots on top steaming poisonously and making a rattle. There was a window across the kitchen and he could see in the rear yard a wooden outbuilding beyond a mire of stagnant water and refuse and strings of washed clothes. He passed through and pushed the loose latchless door at the back. Voices of children were coming from within the paling building that looked like a chicken house. He stepped into the yard towards it.

When he entered they looked up as one from their plates. A dozen or more of them, arranged along a narrow table. In the centre of the table a pot of soup, a board with a loaf of soda bread. Some of the children put down their spoons, some stood and backed away. A boy near to him spoke.

There's no men allowed in here.

Where is William? he said.

Here.

A boy at the rear of the place, younger than the rest, stood and pushed the crate he was sitting on. He was in a tweed coat patched with hessian and his hair hung dull and dusty. Toosey studied him across the room.

I'm William.

Toosey clicked his tongue. You aint him, he said.

That's the only William here, mister.

Well it aint him.

He looked around the table. If Stewart had chosen these children with some rule in mind it was of a range Toosey could not discern, for they were a mix of the young and the half grown, orphans off the street or runaways or thieves, dressed in adults' clothes so that they seemed to have been magically shrunken, one boy wearing a woman's bonnet, another girl exhibiting a scar like war paint lengthwise down her forehead and over an eye that was consequently white and unfixing. Toosey had seen a scar such as that before, on a man hit with a red-hot stoker. It was at this girl that Toosey found himself staring. She addressed him.

You got a cheek comin in here, she said.

There's not much time, Toosey said. He has gone for the constable I reckon.

Then best you leave, mate, the girl said.

William Toosey is his name, the boy I'm after. He lived out by the park. Cimitiere Street. His ma has died of late. He's on his own.

I know him, said one of the boys and he was sitting holding a spoon of soup before him. Will Toosey, he said. I know him.

You know where he is?

The boy put down his spoon. He stared up at Toosey with a pair of frank green eyes. He was red haired and his face was all over freckled, even to his lips. In the town, he said.

No he's not, the boy beside him said. I saw him near Thrower's.

When? Toosey said.

This mornin.

He won't be there now, the redhead said. They will have given out the bread already.

What do you want him for anyhow? the scarred girl said.

I'm his father.

You look like a bummer.

Toosey looked down at himself. I've had a time of it gettin here.

Why aint he with you? If he's your son.

He will be, by and by.

The girl narrowed her good eye. My pa come huntin about for me, she said. Come in here like you are. Where's that Molly? Where's that Molly? I'll bloody murder her.

A little round of laughter went up among the children.

Well, he's never found me yet, the girl said.

The children nodded.

Toosey pulled the letter from his pocket and unfolded the paper and held it up. He's asked me to help, he said. See. I want to help.

He'll be out by the Coach and Horses, the redhead said.

Or buggerin around at Rabbit's.

Toosey studied the row of grubby faces at the table. You should be with your families. All of youse. Not here with this Stewart. He's a fiend.

Stewart feeds us, the scarred girl said. My pa don't feed me. Stewart's a decent sort and you're an old tramp.

Some of the children nodded. Toosey's face grew dark.

Go on, mate, the scarred girl said. Get out of it.

He reached into his jacket. Which of you can find William?

The children watched him.

Bluey, he said and he pointed at the redhead. You can find him.

The kid sat with his mouth open, breathing through his nose.

There's a gold vickie here if you can show me where he is, Toosey said and he produced the coin from his pocket.

The redhead boy jumped off his crate and rushed forward, but now all the children jumped and rushed at Toosey. He gripped the redhead under the arms as the children bunched around him. He carried the boy out into the sun.

I can find him, the children were each one saying, I can find him. Give me the coin. Give me the coin.

Toosey walked through the mud in the yard hauling the kid. He did not look back at the rest. They called to him and tugged at his jacket, following in a pack, but he did not look. For he would move fast or face arrest. He reached the low stairs to the house and pushed the redheaded boy forward and the boy started to climb and then stopped. At the head of the steps, standing in the kitchen, was Trent Stewart. He had a cricket bat and when he lifted it the round damp stains of his armpits showed.

Children, he said, children, do not follow this man.

Toosey thumbed back his hat brim and stared up at the fellow wavering in the doorway. They met eyes across a few measured breaths. Toosey was first to speak.

So help me I will knock out your teeth.

He began to climb the steps, dragging the boy behind him. Stewart backed away and raised the bat above his head. On the blade was a series of red troughs from the ball. He clenched his fingers around the leather grip like he meant to swing it but when Toosey reached the top of the steps Stewart started reversing among the racks of hanging spoons and cookpans, tracking prints in the scattered baking flour. Toosey never removed his eyes from him. He worked Stewart backward with that baleful glare. He walked through the kitchen into the hall-way dragging the redhead along with him.

Stewart called to him. You won't get far. The police are near.

Hearing this, Toosey paused. He stood in the hallway scratching at his whiskers and staring out the open front door to where the startled matron was waiting in the street. Others had congregated with her, men and women and children. He scratched his whiskers and then he turned and stood framed in the kitchen entrance. Stewart raised the bat again.

That boy of mine comes back, I want you to tell him I'm in Launceston.

Stewart swung tentatively to keep him away.

Tell him I'm at the Star of the North.

The police is who I'll tell, Stewart said and waved the bat.

Toosey stared. You're seein me as genial as I get. If I have to come back you'll find me different.

With that said he walked off down the hallway holding the boy by the hand. A few folk had congregated outside. He came down through the front gate, adjusting his hat, his eyes straight ahead. As he walked out among the gathering, walked out leading the boy along, they parted around him and formed up again as he passed. No one spoke. From windows white faces watched him come along the laneway. He led the red-haired boy out of that place in silence.

WILLIAM TOOSEY

In the early afternoon two slim boys, lank as saplings, came up through the buckled hovels of Invermay. They were animated, talking incessantly as they walked, and only looked up now and then to see where they were before bending together once more in chat. One of these boys was William Toosey. With the sun and dirt he was almost dark and his mass of hay-coloured hair was grubby enough to stand on end. At Holbrook Street they left the footpath, crossed the street and went on. The boy beside William was barefoot and he walked with his lean arms hanging straight down and his feet slapping the hard earth.

What did it look like? William Toosey said.

Like anyone's looks, the boy who was called Oran Brown said.

Just pulled it out, did he?

Right out.

Didn't he say nothin?

Oran moved stiffly. His feet were bruised and it slowed him. He said what do you think about this, but I didn't think anything about it and I told him so.

William Toosey bent down and picked up a stone and threw it. What would anyone think of a fat fool who shows himself? he said. They'd think him mad.

It looked like a thumb, Oran said.

You know what I would've done?

What?

Cut the blinkin thing off.

How?

With me knife.

You aint got a knife.

I got a knife.

William Toosey reached into the pocket of his trousers. They were deep pockets and he had to sway to reach the bottom as he fished about. After a moment he brought up a small brown object, which he held out. Oran tried to touch it but William snatched away his hand. He unfolded the blade and laid it on his palm, grinning, and let Oran see it. The blade was short and wide and stamped with a cutler's mark at the thumbrest. It was set in a handle of stained and varnished pine burl.

Fetched it out of Johnson's, he said as he admired it. Johnson never even saw me.

Oran wanted to touch the knife so much that he was hopping. He kept pawing at William's arm. Give us a go, he said.

No.

I only want to hold it.

William lifted his hand a little and let Oran take an eyeful. Gleams like pale fire rippled in the steel. Oran clutched at his arm.

What a beauty, he said.

It aint sharp yet, but I'll sharpen it.

William carefully folded away the knife. The action was still tight and always gave him a start when it snapped shut. He slipped it into his pants.

Don't go back there with Stewart no more, he said. Don't go when he calls you.

He give me half a crown.

Bugger that. Bugger goin back there with him.

Do you reckon?

Course I reckon. ·

They walked on.

They crossed the street then, throwing reedy shadows on the road, the two of them, past tenements of tired board before drawing up in front of Trent Stewart's place. It was fenced with dark-coloured palings and the boys stood by, clutching the posts, gazing up at the house. A woman in a neighbouring yard watched them across the washing she was pegging up. She had a child tied in a sheet on her back, another clasping at her skirts, and another crawling in the uncut grass. Oran scratched his lousy hair. He was nervous and it made him scratch all the more.

What did I tell you? William said.

I'm hungry, said Oran.

What did I tell you?

Said don't go back with him.

Well don't.

Come on, I'm hungry.

I aint muckin about. Don't go there with him. He is mad and it aint safe.

It was Oran who'd brought him first to Stewart's, showed him in, and got him fed in the workroom. Without that soup they were long nights lying in the dark. He'd gone to find Oran after seeing his Aunt Minnie and Uncle Michael and their horde of children. His aunt had cried and cried for the news of her dead sister, struck with a terrible grief. He knew his father would soon come to find him, knew it like he knew the tide would rise, and when he told this to his aunt she grew outraged. He's killed her, you know that, she said. Killed her through sheer neglect. William would not stand to hear his father slandered and told her so. Then get yourself out of here, she said, for I will slander that man with my last breath. At the time a few days living on the tramp around town seemed an easy deal. He had friends who knew no other life. Friends like Oran Brown and Lally Darby and the Henry brothers. Orphans. Kids without a soul in the world save one another.

He knew street life from chumming with them so he left his aunt's house without a fear. His father would soon bowl into town. But it had been weeks now. Weeks of hunger and hiding. Watching for police. He and Oran slept wherever it was dry, ate wherever there were scraps, and stole wherever there was opportunity.

Be sure and do what I said.

Oran nodded.

Run if he calls you.

He was still nodding. He had not washed in weeks and he smelled of turned milk. The smock he wore was falling off his shoulders from where it had torn on a nail. William hung off the fence assessing the pitiful sight of him.

There were things he wanted to tell Oran. Important things, he thought. Words his mother had said. The way she would tuck in his shirt, or comb his hair from a cup of water. He didn't know how to explain these things but he wished he could. It seemed important that Oran should know too, that while their days were a deep and lasting hardship, beating sun and bitter night, bruised and bloodied feet, that it would not always be so. They might huddle in the dark and weep with hunger, one beside the other, whisper in fear like fugitives, but there were times and places in his heart that warded off the pain. Likewise did Oran need the old and the ever-remembered to comfort him.

He pulled the knife from his pocket. Here, he said.

Oran looked at the folded blade. He took it.

Keep it to hand.

He was cupping the knife. He just looked at it for a time, and in time tucked it into his smock.

All right, he said.

Where you can reach it.

I can reach it.

If he calls you, leave straight away. All right?

All right.

If he touches you, cut him.

Yes, Will. I'll do it.

William lifted the gate latch and let the boy through and they climbed the steps together and knocked on the door. There was no answer so William made a fist and pounded harder.

It was Stewart himself who opened it. He squinted at the boys through his spectacles and when he saw it was William Toosey he seemed to puff up, blinking rapidly, and he stepped onto the landing and caught a grip of William's shirtfront.

You, he said as he hauled William to the gate. You can keep out of my house.

What?

Keep out.

He shoved the boy into the road. William stumbled and fell. He did not understand. He lay staring up at Stewart. Then he stood and moved towards the gate. Stewart yanked it shut and pointed at him across the pickets.

If you come here again I shall give you in charge of the first policeman I meet.

Oran was crouching on the verandah wearing a bewildered sort of a gaze.

What have I done? William said.

And tell your father the same.

A spark started inside of his chest. It flared until he felt hot all over. What? he said. Who?

Stewart was thundering up the steps. He put out his arms to shepherd Oran before him through the door. William clung to the fence and called, leaning over, his voice cracking in his throat.

Was my father here?

That was enough to make Stewart turn. He turned and posed on his verandah, arms cocked on his hips, jacket tails kicking where he pushed back the flaps.

Your father is a brute.

Was he here?

A brute and a madman.

Was he here?

I have a gun in the house. Tell him that.

I don't know where he is, Mr. Stewart. I aint seen him in years.

Stewart descended onto the first step and pointed his finger. I shall not hesitate to shoot. I will put him out of this world. Tell him that.

I don't know where he is.

Stewart dropped his hand. A shameless, disgusting brute, he said. Poor fathers make poor sons, William. Steer away from that fellow.

He has come to help. He has, I know it.

Stewart moved off for the door. He stopped, one hand cupping the knob, his head bowed, and looked back at William with a lift of his eyes. He's at the Star of the North, he said.

Thank you, Mr. Stewart. I mean that. Thank you.

Stewart shook his head sadly. He twisted the handle and disappeared in the hallway darkness.

The sun in the unmarked sky blazed. William could hear his heart at work. He was sweating and his blood was working and he stepped away from the fence into the road where deep shadows crept outward from the homes like spills of ink. The Star of the North, he whispered as he trotted towards the end of the road where the river in its banks of mud, its weed and whip-thin willow, washed past. His father was here. His father was looking for him. He began to run.

S tanding in the squared shade of houses. Dry, hungry, hot. Toosey's heart had somewhere begun missing beats and he mopped himself and waited for it to settle. A desperate heat was descending over the city. It rippled above the black slate rooves like fumes. He would find his son and they would sit and eat, as they had in other, better times. They would eat and talk about Maria and he would try to put across why, when she was the only candle in a terrible dark, he had left her alone. But that time had not yet come. Here and now he needed to find William. He turned to the small red-haired child by his side.

Look at you, he said to the boy. Sired out of a fox, by the colour of you.

The child stared up at him, for all the world meaning to look angry and seeming instead like the sun was too bright.

What's your name?

Robert, said the redhead.

Bobby.

It's Robert.

Right, Bobby. Where's this boy of mine?

The boy pointed along the street.

You sure now?

Down there. I saw him.

They walked Brisbane Street to where the boy had pointed. The road ran through a gorge of stone merchant buildings, two sheer walls, tall and ordered, and some stores fronted with awnings, some with signs. Geometric shade lay on the dirt. The sun in the slots like mortar. Along the road he could see a number of horse carts and a great rising dust. They walked on and as they neared he saw a number of folk milling, a hundred or more. Something was happening. He slowed his pace.

You saw him down there? he said.

The boy nodded.

When?

Today.

Toosey exhaled. He tipped back his hat. Even from here, he could see teams of city children wandering the skirts of the crowd. Bobby came to stand beside him.

How is he? Toosey said. I mean, is he well?

Bobby looked up. He shrugged.

Thin as a crown piece, that child, he said. Ever since he come into the world. I hope he's eating somethin. Boy needs to eat.

The crowd seemed tame enough but he squinted up his eyes and watched a while anyway.

What does he . . . I mean, what does he do mostly? Does he have friends?

I'm his friend, Bobby said.

Do you go fishin? What does he like doin?

Bobby just looked at him.

You fish, don't you? Children always fish.

The child dropped his head. He fiddled with the thin rag of sleeve bunching at his wrist.

Fish, Toosey said. I should teach him how. Soon as I can.

Will you show me too?

You?

Bobby nodded.

Don't you have a father for that?

He walked on and the child followed. The crowd had amassed in the road before Bell's Mart. They milled before the door to the purchase room or lined the footpath under shelter in their hundreds. Toosey stood in the street and he was not sure what it meant, this gathering. Most folk looked to have come straight off the land or out of factory work, but a few were dressed as if for Sunday service in top hats and coats. A hawker with a wicker basket walked the crowd calling out rye bread, sausage, salted herring, while another chap was selling nobblers out of a keg of brandy hanging from his neck. On the bed of a cart an angry-looking bald man stood to speak and a round of cheers immediately rose from the crowd. He took his place and there was an uneasy air about him as he raised his hand for quiet. He carried a newspaper rolled for an impromptu gavel and the noise died off as he clapped it in his palm.

We will not pay the rate, he cried. We will not pay it. We will not feed the salaciousness, malice, brutality and moral abandon of this parliament. We will not pay the debts of the wealthy. We will not bow down, will not retreat.

The crowd cheered and hooted.

We will not pay, he cried. Why? Because we know. We know that whenever they send city bailiffs to claim our property and the parliament allows it, whenever a family loses their home and the parliament allows it, whenever private citizens are robbed to pay the debts of a few shareholders and the parliament allows it, we are reduced, cut away to almost nothing, cut by a brotherhood of butchers thinly disguised as a system of governing.

A great cheer followed.

We know that after all these crimes have been enacted, he cried, all these lies furthered, all these trespassers given leave to steal, all these men beaten and whipped for defending their families, all these patriots humiliated, at the end of all the sordid greed and the arrogance, a vast wound will have been opened and day after day our island will bleed out its heart-blood. All of it done in the name of the Launceston and Western Railway Company. All of it done to fund the disaster that that railway has become.

The crowd hooted.

But it was not the campaigner crying from the cart that had Toosey's fullest attention. It was the children wandering the edge of the crowd that he watched most intently, pauper children, scrawny and barefoot, rugged in scraps of shirts or jackets, tendering little cups into which would be sometimes tossed a penny or a shop token. Toosey stuck his hands in his pockets. He didn't like a busy town. With the noise and uncertainty. He liked a grass plain. A lonely road. He wiped his mouth. But there was little else for it. He could easier fish out his soul with a boathook than he could leave his boy behind.

You saw him here? he said.

Bobby was standing close beside his leg. The crowd seemed also to disturb him.

Kid, he said.

The boy looked up.

I said you saw him here? Today?

He nodded.

Right. That will do you then.

The boy dropped his head.

Get yourself home.

He rooted out from his pocket the sovereign and pushed the coin into the boy's grotty palm. Take it, he said. Have yourself a feed somewheres. Get a new shirt.

The boy hardly moved. He would not look at Toosey. The scraps of his shirt gathered at his armpits. When will you take me fishin? the boy said.

Toosey hooked his thumb through a belt loop. Don't worry about that, he said and he stood regarding the boy, the pitiful state of him. Listen, he said, take care and don't lose the coin. That's a lot of money.

But the boy wasn't listening. He crouched in the centre of the street and began to scratch at the dirt with his new sovereign. The balls of his knees, so bulbous through the holes in his pants, looked the only sturdy part of him. Toosey smoothed his moustaches. He thought to walk away and might have at other times of his life but what he did instead was finger another coin from his coat and then he crouched, knuckles to the dust, knee bent, and placed it in the child's hand.

Go home, he said. Someone will steal them off you.

There's good fishin by the wharf, the boy said. I seen them catch eels there.

Toosey straightened up. He gazed down the road. Eels, he said. They're not good for nothin anyways.

The child crossed his arms over his knees and buried his face in the crook of his elbow. Toosey adjusted his hat and looked about and when he looked back at the boy he couldn't think of another word to say. He moved away beneath the awning cover of Brownhill's butchery.

In time the child stood, coins in hand, of which he seemed unconcerned. He went away in a daze wiping his nose. A few yards along he caught his feet on a cart trough and fell. Toosey took a step towards him. The boy stood and walked on. Grit on the legs of his pants. His nose running. Toosey exhaled. He'd been holding his breath and thought himself suddenly daft. He straightened up and walked the other way.

The great unruly crowd had started funnelling through the purchase-room doors and he stepped to where he could see it all. Through the narrow doors they shoved. Some fell. There came ever more of them from along the streets until they numbered rising several hundred. Dust rose curling away on the brief riverwards wind. Men like long dull shadows inside it. But there were more here than purchasers. A small mob had begun to build that was off to one side of Bell's, a corps of armed men and fellows with clubs and blades, one with a breech loader and one with a coiled bullwhip, looking around themselves, assessing the play. They gathered at a cart not sharing a word but merely staring at the purchase room with intent.

Toosey was uneasy about all of this. It looked concerning. He reached into his jacket and felt for the knife. He watched the men in the carts. They sat quite still, staring. He saw one lift a rifle and lay it down and he saw one kick a box of cartridges and that was enough. Whatever it was, whatever was happening here, the larrikins and the idle boys had drawn to it. He stood by, grinding his jaw. It would be a proper rumpus in the absence of the police. It was a turn of events for which he could not have accounted.

Let them burn, wouldn't you say?

Toosey looked around. A man had come to stand beside him. He could see where the man had a big dip of tobacco in his cheek and he thought he might have seen the man before, in prison, or on a forested back road. What? he said.

I said let them burn.

The whole arsehole place can burn for what I care, Toosey said.

The man rolled his chew to the other cheek. There's a chest a drawers in there as belongs to me cousin, he said. I swear. I will burn the place fore I let a man bid on it.

Toosey frowned at him. What's this auction for exactly?

My cousin, he said and he spat. My cousin is a proper weakling. About any man at all could push him clean out of the way. They come through his door, the sheriff and them others. Just come straight through it. First thing they laid eyes on was this chest.

What, they're selling property taken by the sheriff?

Not while I'm here. I'll burn the place before I let a man bid.

Jesus, Toosey said. I aint missed this town one bit.

The purchase room filled with all it could hold and the rest, those left outside, the elderly, the laggard, clustered up around the wide stencilled windows of Bell's. Soon the street stood vacant but for the few carts, the few men perched in the beds, and here and there a wandering child. Toosey studied the faces of each. One a little girl in a loose summer dress. She held her cup to a loutish type leaning on an awning pole, her other hand above her eyes for the sun. The lout tossed her something. Then away she went to the next fellow she saw, displaying the blackened soles of her feet. Was that how his boy had survived these weeks? Begging?

A high-sided cart pulled by a black mare in blinkers rolled down the Charles Street hill with the squeal of its axle horrible like a crow. The people in the street gave way before it and some of them were waving their hats and the surly teamster on the bench lifted his hat to them in return. It pulled up before Bell's and Toosey saw now that a troupe of men were squatting in the bed. They were six, all dressed in black, and they had on black gloves, tall hats wreathed in black crepe, and wore stern expressions to a man. They dismounted one by one and stood looking about.

Now you will see it, the fellow beside Toosey said.

A murmur went through the crowd lining the windows. Some stepped away and others removed their hats as if out of respect for these dour men and everywhere people in the street began looking back at the six undertakers. Toosey stood with his arms crossed, watching. Everything about it made his hair stand up.

The six in black dragged something heavy off the cart and laid it in the dust and they stooped down, and when they stood they had mounted lengthwise along their shoulders a grey clapboard coffin. At the windows folk abandoned their places wholesale. The crowd drew back entirely from the doors and the undertakers lumbered up to the wide entranceway with their load and dropped it. Foremost of them was a huge bull-necked fellow, thick-jawed, his shoulders distending the seams of his coat. He pushed back the coffin lid and retrieved from within it a tall forester's axe. The women screamed. One fainted dead away onto the road. The undertakers shouldered up the coffin and ducked through the doors inside the purchase-room darkness.

The fellow beside Toosey swigged from a flask of spirits. Let these six do their work, the fellow said and he motioned for Toosey to take a drink. Toosey shook his head.

Damn the rate, the fellow cried. Damn the railways.

Toosey watched the room for what would follow. Long instants of silence. In the crowd, folk craning their necks the better to see. Toosey narrowed his eyes but nothing in the sunless dark inside had shape or substance. Then came a roar. The devil-like pitch and intensity startled him. That was followed an instant later by an even more tremendous howl inside the purchase room as the place fell into general panic. People rushed for the doors, clambering over benches, over chairs, and women screamed and men pulled them by the arm and some fell and were trampled and some fought over the backs of folk gone down or climbed from pew to pew and the crowd rolled outward from the doors like the bursting forth of water, the undertakers among them kicking and lashing out, while in the street some of the armed men began to give fire overhead, the small sharp reports of revolvers and with them the heavier thud of rifles. The windows of Bell's shattered as folk began to spill from there onto the road, gripping their hats, running, looking back at the scenes inside the purchase room and shouting, and all along the street echoed the endless crying of horses, the breaking of glass, screaming.

For a while Toosey just stood watching. He could not quite believe it. The crowd drew away past the stores and hotels and a core of a hundred or more men led down the street in a march with glass breaking everywhere as larrikins started to loot. But even as he stood with his arms folded and his uneasy feelings turning to outright alarm, he saw the town's vagrant children in twos or threes. He saw the girl with her cup. Children bewildered, running to one another, huddling up. The whole scene awash in gunsmoke. Toosey tugged down his hat.

Here you are, he said to himself. The ex-drunk. The thief. What have you to show?

A fresh round of gunfire made him flinch.

Whatever was left of his wicked life, and he knew it might not be much, whatever was left was owed plainly and honestly to his child.

He started forward into the smoke.

THE RIOT

J ane Eleanor Hall crouched by a gas lamp on the crest of the Charles Street hill and surveyed the town below through her fingers. A numberless crowd covered the streets like a carpet, pitted in part with the holes of bonfires. Men loped through the smoke and dust, men blacked up with charcoal to hide themselves, wielding hoes and clubs and axes, hooting and whooping. The depth of noise made the whole air tremble. Above the rooves smoke scudded in a band of utter black. She held her face and could hardly breathe. Her gut knotted up. The town had lost its mind.

It took her a while to understand. The railways. The levy. She exhaled and rubbed her head. All week there had been warnings that if the auction went ahead then blood would follow. But this was more. This was rebellion. Gangs in masks moved store to store smashing the plates of glass that lined the street in a weave of silver. They dragged furnishings into the road to feed the fires. She looked across a town obscured by smoke billows. The people of this place were not suckers. They would not bear the debts of another. Now the railways' shareholders and the men of Kennerley's parliament would truly learn it.

She crouched there a long time. She had set about finding the man Thomas Toosey, the finding of him, the getting back of the money. Now her gut was knotting and her breath stalling in her chest. She rubbed the stubble on her head. At length she stood. She might have returned to the hut. Maybe even to

Rabbit's place. She might have stayed away from the trouble. Stayed safe. Instead she began to descend the hill. This was not the hour for fearful ways. She needed to act.

Her father had often led her along this road for her leg, for the bettering of it he always said, and he would take her hand crossing the roughest holes and then have her walk alone so that she would give the leg the strength it needed, and him talking, always talking, calling her the bravest girl about and darling Janey in his rough whiskey voice and pointing over the river to the new station building dressed in its flags and bunting and promising her a trip to Longford or beyond in first class, for he was a railways man, a navvy, working a pick and barrow and laying out the ballast, and that was how he came to be retrieving a charge from its blast-hole while it was still wired and his death was instantaneous, the foreman had told them, instantaneous, as if that excused it, but that was no word she knew, a girl of fifteen hardly lettered, and her mother flew to claw out this fool's vocals when he said there would be no money forthcoming for the funeral, no widow's pension, by order of the Board of Directors and owing to her father's status as a temporary hire, and in the end it was only Rabbit the tapman who'd help, only Rabbit with the five pound they needed to see him rightly buried and he gave it so freely, did Rabbit, that her mother never thought to question the debt, the interest that doubled it, and their now-alarming lack of income, and short of paying it off Rabbit had other ideas for her mother that would put her on her back at a shilling a fuck, and little Janey too, he said, who was plenty old enough for cock, and so here she was now limping her way towards the sundering town in the aid of murder, made the tool of men once more, for all that she'd sworn otherwise.

Drawing closer to the strife the source of it became apparent. There were five taprooms along that emptied men into the street with mugs, bottles, pitchers, waving them aloft, calling boorish toasts variously to the premier, to the king, to the railways, and then lastly to the railways' lawyer Mr. Douglas. One of the drunks put up a call that was taken on by every man.

Up to Douglas's! Up to Douglas's!

She limped on with that howl in her ears. Ahead, the crowd in their numbers was flinging rocks through the windows of some flash-looking place and uprooting the paling fence and tearing out the garden. She walked the slope of the street with her eyes down. Men in packs of three and four broke doors and dragged chairs through the tended flowerbeds of the wealthy, laughing like crazed men, laughing and swearing. When she rounded into George Street the crowd there had a banner: Don't Pay The Rate. They were chanting the same slogan over and over. Beating kerosene tins. Hollering. From a gas lamp they'd hung a half-finished guy, a sad figure wadded with hay and with a tiny head of carven wood lolling weirdly in the rope. He wore a top hat of black felt, a silk vest. On his face a painted scowl that told of his hatred for the common man.

As she stood there watching the guy turning in his noose Bunyip jogged up beside her and crouched. He was breathing heavily and sweating. He hung his long thin arms over his knees and dropped his head, heaving air in and out, dropping beads of sweat on the dirt. She felt better to see him but she put her back to him anyway. Bunyip had a purse from somewhere, which he emptied into his palm. A few shop tokens, tanners, a shilling coin. He tossed the purse in the street.

A shillin, he said. In an hour out there. And look at em all.

Naff off, she said.

Oh lovely that is.

She turned to him suddenly. If my leg wasn't so bung I'd bloody kick you senseless.

Who was they anyway? he said.

What a friend. Leavin me like that.

They might have shot us, Janey.

I ought to truss you up, she said without looking around. Truss you like that scarecrow there.

Who was they?

They was after someone. Some fellow called Toosey.

What a queer bloody thing to wear. A hangman's hood. He looked a proper loony.

She let him sit in silence a while, letting him stew. Then she said, This fellow. The one they want. They'll pay ten pound for him.

Ten? What's he done?

Stole some money off them. A lot of money by the sounds of it.

Ten, Bunyip said.

He sorted through the bits in his palm. He picked out the coins and pocketed them. There remained a few shop tokens, which he pressed into Hall's hand. That's for you, he said. He had hold of her wrist lightly at first but it tightened as he pulled her closer. There's somethin else better than ten pound you might offer me, he said. He held her waist and breathed into her neck.

If you say it's me titties I will cuff you one.

They do get me enthused, he breathed.

Long hair, she said and pushed him off. Perfectly grey. Wearin a natty little billycock. If we can find him—

You could pay off Rabbit.

Yeah. The whole lot.

Christ, he said and looked around sharply. Christ, long hair. Like in a braid?

Braided, yeah.

I seen the cove. Oh bloody hell. I seen him, Janey. Just lately. Bunyip took off.

Oi, she said.

They followed the agitators parading in the centre of the road. Among the hundreds of men and women and the woollen drifts of smoke it was a job to see anything. On Brisbane Street every place was closed. The tearoom had sheets of roofing tin pitched before its bay window as a primitive barrier, great tall sheets rusted and stuck through with nail holes, and covering the door were battens affixed directly onto the frame. She looked around at the miscellaneous destruction as she followed Bunyip. The dire work being done on properties nearby. Teams of boys stoning shopfront glass. Two men in waist aprons chasing them off with sticks. Hall turned her head, taking stock of it all.

Where's the police? she said.

But Bunyip wasn't listening. Everyone saw him, he said. Your man the Indian. He was talkin to the city kids. Askin about somethin.

He pushed past a circle of gents and lightly patted the pockets of one chap but took nothing. They went along by the Launceston Bank and turned up the hill.

Talkin about what?

How should I know?

You sure it was him?

Grey hair worn long. Black hat. It was him.

She scanned the street. Smoke drifting through the scenes of bedlam. Bunyip led her further to where the crowd thinned outside the merchant quarter. They stopped before a huge flat-fronted brick-and-render cottage fringed neatly with shrubs of rose and lavender and saplings of willow. There were others at the door of this place, trying it. Some of them kicked at the panels. Before long the wood splintered up and the frame gave way and they filed inside. Bunyip scratched his chin as he watched the men, scratched the onset of beard.

Where's the bleedin police in all this?

Oh you only just noticed, she said. Sharp one you are.

Bunyip watched the men. One chap toted out a load of pewterware bundled in a sheet and behind him came another with an oil-painted English landscape, broad and heavily framed, and on his head a stack of top hats. She knew what he was thinking and she didn't like it.

That ten pound will see Rabbit off my back, she said.

Won't be an easier profit than a bit of carried-off silver.

You can't take it through the streets in daylight. That's mad.

These buggers are doin it.

It's ten pound for trackin him home. Findin where he's holed up. That's as easy a ten as I know of.

Ought to be your ma payin it back. Not you. It's her as spent it.

She slapped him on the shoulder. Oi, she said. He was my father. Blame the railways if you want to blame someone.

Bunyip kicked a stone along the road.

Rabbit won't give you a fair price, she said. Not a hope. He'll pay whatever he likes and what can we do about it? Stamp our feet? We won't get no ten pound off him.

Hold on there, he said and looked past her. Hold on. Here comes the johnnies.

A line of municipal police had deployed at the corner. They were uniformed in black and wore black leather ankle jacks and white sashes slanting crosswise to their belts. A crowd had gathered in counterpose to them, and called, Don't pay the rate! Don't pay the rate! The municipals formed up and stood facing the crowd. Each man with a long wooden stave held out, each with his eyes jumping. Their sergeant, marked so by his sabre, stepped forward. He called on the rioters to cease their vandalism and disperse or be hauled before a magistrate on charges. The rioters jeered. The sergeant pressed his gloved hands to his hips and waited for the catcalls to die away but the din grew only louder.

What are they playing at? Hall said.

From the skirts of the crowd a rough sort of woman was yelling through her hands, Give em some, boys! Give em some! Her call fired something in the mob. Others of that body took it up. One man broke, and a next, and a next, and soon the group in its entirety was pouring down the slope.

The constables raised their staves. In those moments their nerve was tested to its utmost. A rolling influx of rioters smashed around them. A blow felled the sergeant and knocked loose his peaked cap and spattered his blood across the road and the sight of it sent some constables into retreat. They ran doubled over, lashing out with their sticks, while fence slats and stones and bottles rained down on them. Only when they had made some distance up Brisbane Street at a sprint where the savings banks and estate agents kept house did their attackers break off.

This is some hard game, she said.

Aint it though.

Such was the wash of noise that she could feel in her chest the shouting and the crying out. The blood-soaked sergeant rose and like a drunkard staggered about the street and fell and rose again. He was followed by a troupe of children calling cries of dog shit or weakling. They threw stones. They spat.

Come on, Bunyip said.

He walked the slope keeping his eyes ahead and Hall went after him. They headed down by the town park where folk now sat in their dozens drinking. There were fewer people in this part of town, less noise, so when Bunyip reached out and punched her in the arm she started in fright.

What did I tell you? he said.

Bugger off.

He punched her again.

Ow, she said.

Look.

Away by the gates of the park three men stood in a loose sort of circle and in the centre, sprawled on the ground, was a boy. The boy was in fact Oran Brown, who was regarded by most as a fair hand at fistfighting, but he was bloody about the mouth and painted with the dust in which he'd lain. The men standing around paid Oran no mind though as he flailed and tried to rise. Their attention was directed wholly upon one another. Bunyip said something then but Hall didn't hear him. Her ears had filled with the sound of her heart like a fresh salt wind and she began to backtrack and wheel away.

That's the one, he said.

From the side of her eye she watched the group, two louts in straw boat hats, the third man, a mean looker, kit in a thin coat and with a small billycock set artfully low over his brow. This last man had a long ash-coloured braid slung across his shoulder and it was this feature, his hair as the Irishman had described it, that gave him up as the miscreant Thomas Toosey.

Bunyip was staring at the men.

Don't look at them, she said.

Your easy quids.

Get your eyes down.

They carried on past the park gates. From there they could see Toosey standing dead centre of the roadway, feet spread, his jaw working side to side. The men in straw hats seemed set on softening him up for they stepped past Oran Brown making their hands into fists. But this fellow, this Toosey, had drawn a chipped and rusty knife. He held it to one side and with a tip of his head motioned for the men to keep coming. They looked at one another and they looked at Toosey. They stopped. Toosey flexed his fingers on the twine handle. When he then started towards them in a languid stride they began to backtrack. They turned tail and ran.

Oran Brown lumbered to his feet. He looked like he might run with the men but he did not. Toosey came to him and he tucked away the knife and bent to one knee. He addressed a series of questions to the boy, each of which was met with a small quick nod or a shake of the head.

What's he sayin?

I can't hear.

Don't stare. Move that way a bit.

Oran Brown tugged something from his shabby pants. Something modest enough to cup in his palm. He held it up. Toosey's expression changed. He turned to study the park, the stands of elm and oak. He turned to study the road. He seemed to be pondering where next to go.

What's he after?

How should I know?

He looked about the street. With each turn of his head his braid snaked. You could see his qualities in the state of his dress. The wire-taut tendons of the neck. He surveyed the street once more and when he lowered his eyes and started into town she dug her elbow into Bunyip's ribs.

Right, she said. Move.

Bunyip grabbed her by the elbow and pulled.

Oi.

Tell me that aint her.

We need to follow him.

Janey, he said and he was shaking her arm. Look. I reckon it's her.

Eh?

There lying sprawled on a plot of lawn by the caretaker's home the lone figure of a woman. She was face down, the black shroud of her hair spread about. From out of her skirts stuck two long white legs shod with little boots and the long white drawers of her underwear plain to see. Like a castaway washed ashore from a shipwreck. Baked dry in the belting sun.

For pity's sake, Hall said.

It's her. Aint it?

They crossed the smoke-blown street to where she lay. Hall knelt in the grass and shook her by the shoulder.

Ma.

In one hand she still held a bottle. Hall knocked it away.

Ma, she said again.

Her mother lifted her head, looking about as if seeing the place for the first time. Her eyes wandered as she studied her daughter.

Janey, love.

What you doin down there?

Her head fell again. She closed her eyes. Let me lay a while, she said.

Like buggery. Look at you.

They had themselves one arm each. With a grunt they lifted her clear to her feet and held her there while she found her balance. Hair was plastered to the sides of her face where she'd lost all the pins for it. Dress was crusted with mud. She dried her mouth on her arm. Janey, she said. Love. I've found you.

You're in a proper state.

Her mother said, What have you got for me?

She began to lead her mother away.

What have you got?

Forget that, Hall said. We're goin home.

Who's this? She was looking at Bunyip.

John Berry, marm, he said.

You know him, Hall said. He comes around. Now move. We're goin.

Her mother snatched her arm away and stood swaying before Bunyip, straightening her matted hair, pushing it from her face. Henry's boy, she said.

That's me, marm. I'm him as give you them caramels, remember?

She tried to fix her unfocused eyes upon him.

Hall took her mother by the arm. That's enough, she said.

They kept house in Invermay and Hall meant to see her there, but it was a miserable state she was in, as unsteady as an infant, and they had nearly to carry her. They weaved through groups of men, who were leering at her mother and making lewd finger gestures. There was nothing else for it. She had to see her home. The men would be on her like tomcats. They walked and her mother tottered between them.

Along the road as it rolled away to the bridge the stores were shuttered and the rows of warehouses at the riverfront stood silent. The unrigged river ships hauled on their ropes with the outgoing tide. The chimney spire of the gasworks rose colossal on the plum-skin sky. It was to these things Jane Hall looked, for to look elsewhere, to look at the packs of men that operated or the black breath of fires raking the dusk, was to be made sick with fear.

What've you got for your dear ma?

Nothin, she said.

Be honest.

A half-crown is all I got, just a half, Hall said and she reached into her pocket and pulled the coin. Her mother held out a damp palm.

Buggerin hell, she said and gave over the coin.

What a good girl. Always somethin for me. A right good girl.

A good girl wouldn't give it to you.

Hall led her by the elbow. Down through smoke and broken glass and mobs of men and women. Her mother was heavier than ever as her shoes dragged and her head slumped. At Tamar Street where the low wooden bridge spanned the river she lifted her head and said, A good girl, my Janey.

Hall huffed and looked away.

They crossed the bridge with the boards shifting wherever they stepped and the nails squeaking, and crossed into the narrow alleys of homes in Invermay. They kept a place here, she and her mother, a house of unpainted scantling with paneless windows papered over. Her mother was dead asleep by the time they carried her to it. They carried her to the door and lay her down and the long bovine snores issuing from inside her chest seemed to rattle her every part. They fished out her key and flung back the door.

Get her legs, Bunyip said.

Right.

They swung her inside and laid her among the scraps of stained and thinly worn rug covering the hallway floor.

That'll do, Hall said.

Bunyip crouched beside her mother, smoothing back the curtain of her hair. She is a picture, he said.

Yeah and what good has it ever done her?

He stood up. I would marry her and keep her well. My oath I would.

Hall punched him hard in the arm. Shut your trap, she said.

What? I would.

You're a child, John Berry. What's she want with you, for cryin out loud?

Sixteen aint a child.

You're as thick as manure you are.

Kiss this, he said and showed her his finger.

Along the wide carriageway crowds of people milled. They gathered on the corners at public bars, packs of larrikins, swindlers on the roam, and here and there little groups of the respectable shaking their heads at the shameless upheaval. They walked, Hall and Bunyip, as far as the Royal Oak and there they stopped. In the street there numbered near a thousand, a great vengeful mass ranging in the laneways and roads like secret cults abroad for the end of days and some had torches burning for light in the slow falling evening and many handed around quarts of indian rum or other things as they spoke in one enormous noise. Hall and Bunyip stood so close their shoulders touched. They walked the edge of the crowd with their eyes flicking everywhere.

It had a murderous feeling. The glow of the fires. The dark and, above, the grey pebble moon. Hall stood for a long while watching. People filled the sloping street like a thicket. They were singing and drinking. They raised an effigy on a broom handle. A battle standard for an army of paupers. A ragged army risen up to eat the hearts of the rich. Perhaps she should have joined them, for the sake of her father dead these months at the fault of the railways, for the sake of her mother driven crazed with grief after it. But she had not the shamelessness. She knew the owners of these stores, these hotels and taprooms. What relief was there in spreading misery? Beside her Bunyip frowned at it all.

You ever see that many people? she said.

Don't go breakin your head about it, he said. We'll keep smart.

The mob advanced to the junction at Wellington Street and turned towards the river and Hall and Bunyip followed.

I don't feel well, she said.

They won't hurt us none. Just stay close.

A murmur passed through the larrikin crowd and soon they moved in their numbers and settled on the road beneath a line of sister buildings of plain colonial style that walled the street and the last of these was caged by wrought-iron spikes and boarded over in the windows. It was the police house and the rioters hove up before it in a squall of smoke and song. They brought the effigy to ground and put torches to his clothes and like a treasonist of old he was quartered and his wooden head mounted atop the ironwork and doused with whiskey and set alight. Larrikins began to scale the pickets. Refuse was thrown. Flaming bottles.

They will tear down that place, Bunyip said.

Hall swept her eyes across the fringe of crowd in the firelit dark. Aint that Oran Brown there?

He narrowed his eyes. Where?

Down there.

They began to call together. Brownie! Brownie!

Oran Brown was standing away from the body of people with his head hung low and his arms dangling and when he heard that cry he looked around himself with some alarm. He saw them waving. He came trotting over. Even in the darkness Hall could see that he was blacked about the cheeks and had blood on his shirt and neck.

What the hell, she said.

Oran licked his fat lip. Yeah, he said.

Who was it?

Some fancied-up Melbourners.

You look a fright.

Feel all right though. Went to Rabbit's just now for a nip. It worked wonderful.

What did you take from them?

Oran shrugged. Nothin. I had me fingers on a few coins is all. That's the shame of it.

And Toosey? she said.

Who?

Him. With the long hair.

Oran looked at her and looked at Bunyip. Why's everyone want to know about that old bushman for?

He helped you, Hall said.

This caused Oran to blink a few times, as if caught out. Well he came up, he said. Here's me gettin a hearty bastin from the Melbourners. He came and says leave him be, boys.

Why?

Oran blinked. They was goin to kill me, I suppose.

Only it seems a drastic thing, don't it? Seeing off them two chaps for a pissin little city kid like you.

He lowered his head.

Out with it, she said. Did he want somethin? Did he ask you somethin?

Oran looked over at Bunyip. You're right about her, he said.

Aint I just.

Hall crossed her arms. She turned and stared out across the crowd.

They was goin to kill me, he said.

I saw him talkin to you. Didn't he say nothin?

How come if you saw them Melbourners you never helped me?

He has you there, Bunyip said.

She watched at the crowd rattling the police-house gates. The two boys waiting for her answer. Me ma was in the horrors, she said at length. We was carryin her. Tell him, Johnny.

Drunker than a sailor, he said, and still lovely as ever

Like you've never been the worse for liquor, Johnny Berry.

Here Oran pulled from his pocket a folded jack-knife, the handle of varnished burl, and snapped the blade into place. He did ask one thing, he said. Wanted to know if I knew his son.

What son?

He's out for his son, Oran said. Lookin for him.

In her innermost deeps a knot began to form. What? she said.

Oran held up the knife. Will Toosey, he said. Will give me this knife when I showed him Stewart's rooms. He's been dossing on the street since his ma died. Fairly a beauty, aint she.

Hall dropped her head and pinched the bridge of her nose. It unfolded for her in a neat series now. Toosey had a son, a vagrant boy like Oran. A boy with no mother. She squeezed her eyes closed. Toosey talked to the city children because he was after his son. Someone worth more to him than his own life it seemed. And she meant to put herself between this bushman and his boy. There crossed upon the plain rag of her mind in black and heavy letters the upshot of it all: this was a mighty cartload of trouble.

Lifted it with little Nobby, he said and wiped the blade.

She kept her eyes shut. Paying down Rabbit's debt was the name of it, but to see a man, a father, swing for her debt was a hard-hearted thing.

Did you tell him? she said and looked up. Bout his son. Bout you knowin him.

I told him.

And what?

What?

Didn't he say nothin?

Ask him yourself, Oran said. He's right there.

She looked around sharply. Eh?

The only light was the light of fire in the road, a bonfire lit from fence pales. She studied all that darkness. The rioters clustered before the police house and in the freer road behind was a lone shifting figure barely more than a shape. His gait as he turned and started away was an upright stride like a fellow unafraid of a fight, shoulders squared inside his coat. He seemed to be seeking someone, for his head swivelled as he stalked about and Hall knew for a cold fact who he was after.

Bleedin fuck, she said.

Toosey began to track out through the ranks of people and into the wide road, straight of back and looking around. The townsfolk fell about like tomfools. They danced. They tossed bottles and stones. Toosey among them, a guarded man, sober of bearing and wary of where he was. It made him all the more menacing. This was not some twit from the backblocks; it was a man who knew how to carry himself. Just like her own father had. There came the clout of an even darker thought then that caused Hall to close her eyes. It could be that Toosey was no murderer at all. She was playing the foxhound to this Irishman, unwise to his motives and unwise to even the smallest facts of the matter. How could she be sure? What was her proof? This Irish meant him harm and there was no doubting it. But did he even deserve it?

By the time she opened her eyes she had settled on a different course. You're right, she said to Bunyip. You're right, and I'm a nelly. Better a bare foot than no foot at all. There's neater ways to get a quid than this.

Bunyip was frowning at her.

What? she said.

Where's Oran off to?

Eh?

She turned around. Oran Brown was strolling away, thumbs hooked in the band of his pants.

Oi! she said. Brownie!

He kept walking.

Where's he goin? she said.

Bunyip wiped his nose. How should I know?

Toosey was lingering at the thin edge of the police-house crowd and they watched Oran Brown alter course and start towards him.

What's his game? she said.

Christ, you don't think he would—

Oh the little prick.

She bolted after the boy with her crook left leg swinging outward and her plain stubbled dome bobbing in that queer gallop. In a few yards she caught a grip of his collar. Whoah there, she said. Where you goin?

He pushed her away. Somethin I have to tell him.

The bushman?

Yeah.

She scruffed hold of his hair and hauled his head down.

Ow, bloody hell, he said.

She looked into his face. Reckon I won't do nothin, is that what?

Oran pried at her fingers.

Is that what?

No.

Then where you goin?

He helped me. I ought to help him back.

By gabbin on your mates, she said and twisted his hair.

Ow, Jesus, he said. It's not you. There's another fellow as well.

What fellow?

A queer old Irishman.

Hall let him go so suddenly that he stumbled to his hands and knees. You know about him too? she said.

Spoke to him not an hour ago, Oran said. He's come for your bushman.

She looked across to where Toosey drifted in the firelit dark. His attention was directed towards the stragglers lurching about in liquor and singing tavern chants, clinging to one another, strangers and lovers alike. No, it was the children. Some slept in the road or on the doorstones of townhouses, the derelicts, whole squadrons of them, slinking about to rifle through the pockets of the unconscious for pennies and tokens. It was to these children that Toosey had directed his attention. So when at that moment there came looming from out of the otherworld of the crowd a tattered fellow holding above his head a long and heavy staff, Jane Hall was the only soul to see it. Sharp tendrils of fear unfurled in her midriff. She raised her hand to call, to warn him. But there was no time and there would be no warning. The Irishman was upon him.

The first blow caught Toosey across the shoulder and sent him sprawling. Tied to the staff was a cloth bundle and meat and pastry came bursting out in wads that skittered across the road and rained down. Fitheal Flynn swung that stick overhead. He struck Toosey and buckled him flat. A circle widened around the pair as folk pushed back in fear and Toosey stared up at the Irishman as if he could not quite conceive of what he saw. He scuttled rearward from the club that came fizzing past again.

Give em room, someone was saying, let em have at it.

Hall limped closer. In those moments Toosey had reached into his coat and produced his blade. A long dull thing the colour of rot. He held it in his fist as if it was nothing, staring at Flynn. He rolled to his knees on the dirt and like a dog grinned up at him. Flynn gestured with the point of his staff.

Get up, he said.

Toosey rocked onto his heels.

Get up.

It's a rum old business this, Toosey said.

Flynn was dark of eye and darker still of intent. He pulled the remnant cloth off his stick. Make ready for it, he said.

Proper little scrapper you are, Toosey said and he stood. Proper little battler.

Proper as a judge.

They locked eyes across a few yards of road.

They will kill each other, someone said.

Hall began to scan the ground, seeking out a rock or a bottle or a stick to pelt at the Irishman and drive him off. Toosey, however, would not be drawn into a brawl. He broke off and pushed out through the ring of men. Flynn shouldered his staff. He went after him. Hall watched first one then the second vanish into the black beyond the ring of firelight and she kicked the dirt with her stiff leg and said, Of all the bleedin—

Then she followed them into the night.

Rabbit's Taproom

In the early evening Fitheal Flynn left his daughter quartered in a roadside camp, feeling heavy-souled for it, thick of head, and with evening falling he crossed down out of the scrub towards the southerly part of the city. He moved through the rows of low-rooved hovels at Kings Meadows and further down through fields of maize and cabbage and potato that studded the black paddocks, framed by wild hills beyond, and as he passed people in the road he stopped and begged pardon and asked after a place to eat. The sun had descended past the hills and these folk looked at him in the dimness, shook their heads, and could only apologise. He walked further into town.

At dark, Flynn saw a man leading a mare fully eighteen hands in height by the underhalter and he paused to make an enquiry of him. The fellow presented a strange lopsided leer, beckoned him closer, and in a voice like the rattling of corn husks directed him to a taproom known to serve late hours. Flynn thanked him. He headed for the place as told.

It was a wooden shack, this place that might have been convict built. At one end a chimney gave forth a gruelly smoke out between the cracks in the stonework. A sign hung that showed a black rabbit perched on its rear. He stepped onto the sagging verandah, wiped the dust off a window, and peered through. A terrific carousal was going on inside. There were men and women shrieking through a drunken song without melody. He stepped back, looked up and down the street, and for a moment scratched his armpit and considered walking away. But there was his daughter hungry and alone and he removed his hat with more thoughts of her and entered.

Say now, Flynn said to the publican and he dropped his upturned hat on the bar. Say, you wouldn't be having some food someplace?

At the dimmest end of the counter, beyond the throw of light from the only oil lamp, the publican stood in conference with a long-coated fellow. Neither man looked at Flynn. They talked in hushed tones that were hidden from him for the singers at the tables had not ceased in their merriment since he entered. The fellow in the coat passed across the counter a hessian sack that was half full of something heavy and the publican stashed it below the counter in a cautious move. Flynn made a fist and knocked on the countertop.

Say, you wouldn't be having a scrap of grub, would you?

Now the publican looked up. He was a huge man, wide through, his gut resting on the clearing bench behind the bar. Among the unwashed mugs was a bottle of Grumbleene, which he picked up and unscrewed.

Speak up, Paddy, he said and took a draught.

I've come after some grub.

The publican lowered the bottle. His eyes were wet. His face inside the folds of his corpulent neck was tiny. Yet for a big man he was quick. Something caught his eye across the room and he fetched up a wooden mug and pegged it viciously in that direction. Oi, he called. Think I aint seen you there.

A child, a girl, was fossicking below a table after flakes of tobacco. The cup struck her in the side and caused her to flinch.

You want the whip again, do you? he called.

The girl ran. She made for the door, tugged it, and vanished outside.

So, the publican said and turned back to Flynn. It's grub you're after then.

Flynn crossed his arms. He looked at the publican and looked at the door.

Well, speak up.

Aye, Flynn said. Aye. But I've only a few bits.

Strange times indeed when the Irish walk in with nothin in their pockets, the publican said grinning.

Listen, my friend, if you're after having some food to sell be a good fellow about it and let me see it. Or else you can go and fock yourself. I shall be royally entertained by either.

The publican laughed. He laughed and he reached down beneath the counter and brought up a tied cheesecloth and dropped it there. He loosened the knot. Within it was a lardy pork pie. Mould had coloured the upper crust and the filling was jellied and rank-looking. Flynn frowned at it.

One shilling, the publican said. And you won't find better tonight, owing to the troubles.

Can you not do no lower than a shilling?

The publican sighed and his face fell like a thespian's.

This is the last few bits I have, Flynn said and pulled out a handful of coins, and you are welcome to them. Only, can you not give us something else as well? We are on the road, my daughter and I. We haven't eaten today.

There were kegs arranged along the rear bench, the contents of each being marked on the scantling behind, and the publican pointed at one among the row that had whiskey scrawled in chalk above it. I'll pour you a finger of that there, he said. Let you numb yourself for the buggerin I'm about to give you. Eh? How's that sound? I can't be no fairer than that for the Irish.

Flynn propped his elbows on the bar. He ran his hands over his thin hair. Be making it generous then, he said.

The publican walked away to the whiskey keg, his great bulk rattling the glasses in the crate, setting the oil lamp on the counter jiggling. He loosened the tap and let fill a threaded jar one-third full.

As he did this, Flynn leaned back from the counter and took up his hat and turned to survey the room. In the farthest corner a pair of men huddled over a hand of All Fours, the irregular light of the oil lamp leaving them in twilight. Pipe smoke suspended in geological strata dimmed the room to a yellow glow. He stood surveying it and replaced his hat. At the tables sat some coarsely bearded seamen and two whores in shawls of crocheted wool, rouged around the eyes and cheeks. They drank from wooden mugs, filled pipes from a common bowl of weed. A squalid man at the rear held cocked before him a tankard, his whiskers spumed with porter.

The publican placed the jar by Flynn's elbow. Flynn drank. He sat down the jar. His eyes watering, the publican began to speak but then stopped. The door had clattered against the wall and they all turned to see outlined darkly on the doorsill the shadow of a boy. The boy came into the light, a young and lank and sickly-looking thing. Blood dripped from his nose, which he smeared across his face as he stumbled forward. He was barefoot and dressed in a torn smock. Across the tables eyes raised and settled on him, seamen, revellers, whores, wary of whatever trouble this was. He slumped at a bench and dropped his head.

Fetch the lad a stiffener, someone said.

Flynn set his hat upon the freckled dome of his head. He stepped past the bleeding lad, his mind at work on how he might make his way in the falling dark outside and find the bush road where his daughter was waiting. He had one hand on the door bolt when he saw where he'd left the pie, the only food he had, upon the counter. He slapped his thigh. He crossed past the lad who by now had attracted a crowd and fronted up at the counter and hitched the pie cloth upon the knob of his staff to carry.

There was every sort of question being put to this lad about the nature of the violence unfolding in the city and the gangs going at it, the actions of the municipal police, the ruin being waged. They dragged up chairs and took seats about the boy, leaning close to hear what he had to tell. The boy was bony and frail but there remained a harder edge to his gaze that was not fogged by the pain he was in. Beads of blood formed and dripped off the point of his nose as he gave some answers. The gamblers, the seamen and whores, they all listened intently, as if in the listening they might show their hatred of the railway rate.

We ought to be out there fightin, one said.

You aint a fighter, John.

No, I'm a fucker, he said and they laughed.

Better if these dogs paying the rate are run out of town, the publican said. Better by a long shot. Run out or hung up and I shouldn't care which.

He came around from the bar and stood, hands folded on the great mound of his belly. And what in the name of Heaven have they done to your face, Oran Brown? Caught fiddlin something, was you?

The lad threw back a decent part of his drink and sat the glass before him, twisting it in his fingers and shaking his head, looking a sorry specimen. It was couple of Melbourners is who, he said. One reckoned he felt me hand tuggin at his pocket. What a joke. I never went near his pocket.

No, the publican said. Oh no. Course you never.

Here the lad looked up and held his glass out. Pour us another, Rabbit, he said. I'm in a deal of pain.

They ought to have killed you, the publican said and he hiked up his trousers and turned away. I bleedin well would've.

They tried it and I took a fearful basting, the lad said. I believed I was done for. Then up come this third fellow. I thought he was some island chieftain or a Chinese digger or somethin cause he wore a braid of hair down his back like nothin I ever seen. He calls on the Melbourners to leave and they just up and ran.

The lad paused to mop his blood. He was reaching for a rag among the detritus of clay pipes and bottles on the table when a heavy calloused hand pressed down upon his arm. He looked up at the face of Fitheal Flynn who was leaning in to him, blue eyes like insets of sea ice, the ruts of his brow grown hard.

You saw him?

Oran looked nervously at the others. Saw who?

A man with long hair.

I just said that, didn't I?

His hat?

Eh?

The hat, lad. How was it worn?

Small I think. And black.

Flynn leaned back, stepped away from the table. Where?

Oran wiped his nose. Along by the town park.

The taproom was quiet as everyone present watched the Irishman push back his creased, shapeless hat. Flynn looked around the room at the many men and women mustered in the smokey dark and he gripped his staff and sighed. Without another word he stalked into the pallid dark of evening.

THE LANEWAY

D own through the valley streets. Bare unpaved paths. Homes of split peeling weatherboard. On the evening sky the smoke was mantled like sunset cloud with the glow of fires and as Flynn drew towards the centre of town there came drifts of it curling through the rows of townhouses and alleyways. In the distance the low thrum of mayhem. He walked further and shortly rounded into a wide thoroughfare and there spread before him was a crowd wandering in the dark, men and boys with slats and chains and rocks. He slowed as the racket of voices grew. They spilled from side lanes, streams of them, and some were staggering in liquor and others, wounded and red with blood, seemed to have left off from a war. Flynn watched them go by. They wore kerchiefs tied across their faces or were blacked up with charcoal. Men discharged from the lies of gentility. He studied it all with great satisfaction. He smiled.

He walked the roads around town tracking the outflow of rioters back towards the source and before long that trace led him to arrive at the police house. Here a scene of pandemonium was unfolding. Men in their thousands, wild men, their sound like flocked crows, had laid siege to the barricades and were pelting the police with whatever came to hand. They scaled the police-house palisade in numbers. They threw burning chairs, burning stakes. The fence shook under the weight pushing on it. For a while Flynn simply stood and watched. It was a sight, good God it was. Toosey would be in there, he knew it. But he stood and stared and for a while he felt it might be the birthings of something bigger, a cousin to the sublime enterprise in France and the beacon-fire it had become for burdened peoples everywhere. He smiled with great satisfaction.

A boy in Dublin he'd been once, starved thin as a stick and shivering in his duds, and he'd seen his father die in the front room of their tenement reduced to a grey frail fellow laid out by a fever and his mother stayed a full day beside their father after death, moaning, twisting her hair, and Fitheal and his older brothers waited as well but could not feel what she felt and felt only hunger and in the days and years to come he'd follow her to the foreshore of Dublin Bay to pick cockles in the morning to sell at the market for a night's lodgings, his mother like a husk, hollow-souled, and he was an older boy by then, meaner, and he struck a fellow that grabbed his mother's buttocks and knocked his jaw out of socket and that was the close of his youth, that instant, for he was taken and tried, a child still, at the quarter sessions with his mother screaming go bhfuil sé ina leanbh from the gallery and he was sent within a month to the arsehole end of the earth in the rat-swarmed hold of a British hulk beside a hundred just as young and that was so long ago that the green home of Ireland was fading in his mind like he'd left his thoughts exposed to the sun, his dear broken mother just an impression, his brothers the merest ghosts, faceless all and long lost to him, and he stood here in the street having passed the times of his life well nigh through and there was nothing of it that did not soon fade, nothing that lasted, save the thought of his mother in that bleached past of ancient crying go bhfuil sé ina leanbh, as he wanted now to cry for his own girls.

Near the gates the mob surged and gave a roar that Flynn felt at the corners of his chest. He surveyed the crowd. Bonfires rose in the cutting wind and gave light that called men from the blackness and they were a mob of louts made up alike from respectability and the lower orders, revelling in the names and feats of rebellion. He wrung the neck of his staff and looked up at the hills from which he'd lately descended to where the faint lights of the shanties stood. His eldest girl up there, and elsewhere, far beyond, his youngest two. He gripped his staff. He walked forward.

The crowd pressed in at the gates of the police house. He walked into the thick and was jostled side to side and in the ceaseless motion of that great body he pushed himself forward, shepherding men aside with his staff. A drunk lay trampled on the road holding up his hand for help but Flynn stepped over him and continued. Where the crowd grew dense around the palisade he lowered his shoulder and bullocked through, his head turning and his eyes sweeping about for sign of that man he'd sought across the districts of the north. The man he would not be kept from.

He was some time at the task. He cut through the herd from hem to hem. He walked the tattered outer edge. It was as likely that Toosey had seen him first and fled. He walked on anyway, circling about and cutting back through. He saw the same faces every time. A woman with her dress torn away and her undergarments displayed. A group of well-mannered gents watching as if for sport from a distance. He was at this work an hour or more. The fence of the police house still stood and the crowd had begun to lessen. He crossed out of the crowd and found himself on clear road the far side of it, overlooked by tall and sombre town buildings, the piled coals of bonfires. He stood a moment and straightened his hat and when he turned to walk on he saw there by the wrought-iron palisade something hallucinatory, like the terminal moment of a dream. It was a fellow standing apart, standing and looking across the throngs, down his back a long braid of hair.

Flynn dropped his head and sighed. A terrible feeling rose

in his throat with the sound of the crowd and he wanted to turn away but he would not. He sighed and when he lifted his eyes they'd grown hard and he lowered his staff and pushed through the people with it. The pie in its cotton cloth swayed. Now had come the culminating instant and he would not shrink from what was right and needed. He widened his grip and strode forward raising the stick wildly overhead and clubbed the madman Toosey across the neck in a foul blow.

Toosey fell. Flynn swung his stick hard. He struck Toosey over the back and flattened him on the dirt. Segments of pie spun. The stick kicked in his hand. The world narrowed around the pair of them. The cave of their feud. He lifted again and Toosey like the bar brawler he was scurried back as the bulb bounced by his legs.

Get up, Flynn said.

Toosey rocked onto his heels.

Get up.

It's a rum old business this, Toosey said.

Flynn pulled away the strip of cloth. Make ready for it, he said.

Toosey stood. He had drawn a knife and was letting it hang in his fingers. Proper little scrapper you are, he said. Proper little battler.

Proper as a judge, Flynn said.

They will kill each other, someone said.

A second passed where they locked eyes, two veterans of combat, their stars aligned in deadly heat. The men around them had begun to push back the circle. They were calling and yelling but Flynn saw only that creature placed by God's hand before him.

Toosey was wavering though. He clicked his tongue and dropped his head. He broke away and bashed out through the crowd, knocking folk aside with his elbows, and Flynn hiked up his stick and followed.

Among the press of bodies he could see the hat Toosey wore. He picked through the stragglers at the edge of the crowd, looking either way along the street, in the lighted upper windows of pubs and shops and stable houses the shapes of people in seclusion, below in the deep dark gloom men at war, and he turned his head, searching, and when Toosey came looming out of the night like some ancient miscreation with his long, sharply worn blade he had no time to defend himself.

The knife caught in Flynn's jacket. He hissed, for the point had stuck in his ribs. Toosey gripped his throat, his knife arm pushing, and there passed an interval of struggle where they tested strength. They strained. Grunted like bulls. Then Flynn planted his feet, leaned, and gave an almighty shove that sent Toosey staggering across the road.

He touched his chest. A leak of blood in his shirt. He wiped his hand and clutched his primitive club and he cried out to Toosey, Well now I'm focking angry, is what I am.

It seemed to cause some upset in Toosey and he stumbled and bolted, and Flynn went after him in a lumbering gallop. There were men everywhere in the street and Toosey sidestepped as he fled, barrelling by them into a narrow back lane fitted between the stone and brick buildings.

Flynn slowed then stopped. The lane was dim its whole length but spoiled in parts by shears of moon that angled in over the rooves. Among the shadows stood the man Toosey. He was holding the knife at his side. He spoke.

Let this lie, old mate. There is no good will come of it.

She never hurt you, said Flynn.

No she never.

You miserable bastard, I will stove your head in.

Listen to me, Flynn. I never meant—

There is a vileness in your heart that I mean to quell.

Listen now, fore one of us is killed. My son is without a

mother. I required the money, you must understand that. I required it for him.

In the darkness Flynn was deathly still, a figure of black. He switched grips on his staff and pressed the point of it to the ground.

Maria is dead?

She is.

There was silence. Then Flynn said, She was a good girl.

The best of them all.

Tis not the money though.

Toosey spat to the side. No, he said. I expect it aint.

Sure, and I would rather it wasn't this way. I'd rather Maria had lived.

That makes the both of us.

Flynn stood quite still, taking his measure. But it is this way, he said.

I shan't go easy, you know. Not even for a chum.

Nor I.

Toosey raised the knife, flexed his fingers on the twine, then lowered it again. You think I'm villainous? Is that what?

Flynn stared quietly back at him. Hell is full of good wants and good wishes. Full up to the guts. You will add to it as well.

It was an accident, that is the truth.

Judging you is not my concern, Thomas Toosey. Stoving your skull is what I'm about.

You righteous Irish prick.

Aye, and make ready now.

Toosey began to circle, bearing his weapon up, strings of hair in his eyes. The blade appeared in a beam of moon and then vanished, like a light doused in the dark. Toosey crabbed around, circled right and cut back left and Flynn turned with him. But the Dubliner had reach on his side and he used it. He swung a blow at Toosey that bounced off his leading forearm. They broke off and circled each other, weapons up. Toosey raised his voice.

That's weighted with lead.

Flynn swung hard overhead at him. Toosey raised his arm to take it. The bulb struck full weight and Toosey cried out. He skipped backwards.

It is.

Fuckin Jesus.

Toosey was cradling his arm and doubling over. Flynn swung the staff again before him in a double-handed pass that sounded through the air and the effort caused him to hiss and scowl at Toosey. The return swing caught Toosey across the knee and upended him. He fell to his back. Flynn seized the advantage and strode forward. He lifted the stick and pummelled the bulb into Toosey's chest and drove the wind from his lungs in a loud expulsion. Before the next blow fell Toosey rolled. He found his feet but his head was hanging low and the knife was only loosely perched in his hand. He stumbled backwards out of range.

Flynn moved with him. He swung high, the staff whistling in the quiet, and brought it down like an axe across Toosey's lifted arm. The thud it made was woeful. Toosey yelped, yet he did not retreat. For in that action Flynn had exposed his belly and Toosey leaned and buried the blade clean to the handle.

A second passed where Flynn was standing over him in numb silence, a long subsiding wheeze releasing from his lips. He looked down at Toosey with a grimace, the staff going slack in his grip, slipping down by Toosey's ear. Flynn stepped slightly and shuddered.

The blade ripped sideward with a vicious flair. Flynn rocked back. A knot of cut blue bowel hung through the slit in his shirt and he looked at it like he didn't know what it was. He slumped to the ground, grasping for his staff for what good it might do him. He toppled.

Toosey cradled his arm at his waist. A huge welt had formed and he could not close a fist. He braced it against himself. At length he reached down and picked up his knife and wiped it clean on his pants and placed it in his teeth. He turned to look at the Irishman.

The ground greased with blood, pooling blackly in the dark. The Irishman was tenderly returning the cords of intestine into his wound and his hands were bloody and shaking. For a time Toosey just stood gazing at him splayed out there in his mess, fumbling with his internals. He walked over to Flynn and knelt with him.

Flynn tried to sit up. He held the ragged gash, his eyes on Toosey. Toosey sat forward over him and took the knife from his mouth and with a single forceful motion he punched the steel into the heart's hollow. Blood ran around the weapon, ran hotly through his fingers. Flynn clawed for Toosey's neck. Toosey raised the knife and brought it down again. Then he stood and moved away. Flynn's eyes tracked him as he paced. He watched the Irishman in return.

Don't you linger, you bastard, he said.

He walked up and down watching the mouth of the lane, the men out there in the smoke. Flynn wheezing softly in the dark. He paced and he waited for Flynn to die. Flynn lifted his hand and let it fall. Soon he sagged inside his clothes and lay still.

Toosey slipped his jacket tenderly over his bad arm. He dried his hands on the lapels and he crouched by his old friend. A pair of pearl-hard eyes alight in the moon, his mouth agog. Flynn looked like a child seeing suddenly the shape of a constellation. If there was more of a world beyond that laneway it was to him peripheral in those brief beats of the heart. All he knew was that man, those eyes. He shook out the jacket and laid it over the Irishman.

A lump was growing on his forearm. He tested the contusion with his thumb and the pain was fearful. He braced it to his chest and found some small relief. It was broken, but it didn't matter now. He needed to get away from here and that was all he could think about. He stood and began along the lane and after a few steps he stopped and turned back. There was something else. Squatting again beside the dead man he reached into the jacket and retrieved William's letter and he kissed the greasy paper and placed it in his shirt pocket. He walked to the street. Into a world wholly new. And he was pale as a figure of carven bone.

The Star of the North Hotel

He cut along the road where the cave-mouths of shops stood, the plate glass smashed and spread about in a frost of shards. There were men here looting clothes, shanks of meat, camp lanterns, some calling to each other and one man making off with a rifle yoked behind his neck. Toosey watched them pass from the dark of a lane. Keeping to the shadows, he crossed to a stable and bent and washed his good hand in a water trough, brought up his boots and rinsed the blood there as well. He buried his face and took a drink. Across the way the druggist was on fire. He dried his face on his sleeve. Smoke tumbled upward from the window frames and ran along the portico. There was an odd greenish tinge to the blaze. A man was attending to it with a bucket, tossing water through the windows. The fire, however, grew only fiercer. At his last toss he dropped the bucket, put his hands on his head, and knelt in the street. He began to cry and call to God. Toosey dried his hands on his pants and moved on.

He would have a few hours before the municipal police found Flynn with a knife in his heart. Then he'd be holding a spread of cards he could not play.

On reaching the Star of the North Hotel he hung off a distance watching the place. There was moon enough to see by and what he saw made him swear. A group of men, one with an axe, were at the door of the place. The shining head winked on the backswing then the thud as it buried sounded along the street in a rumble. Glass and splintered wood littered the path where they'd destroyed the windows each side of the door. Toosey stepped into the street, cradling his arm, sweat falling off the point of his chin. The axe struck and the door buckled. When the figures moved out of shadow he saw how they weren't more than boys, thinly bearded and built slim through the shoulders. The axe had left a great fissure in the panelling of the oakwood and they peered inside now and whooped and cheered. Toosey came forward.

Ho there, he called.

The five of them formed up on the top step.

Ho yourself, old bloke, the first one said. He was young and wore his felt horseman's hat angled after the fashion of the louts around town. He hooked his thumbs through his braces.

Toosey pulled his arm close. That's my hotel you're breakin.

She's the night for it, aint she lads? the one with the axe said.

They gave a uniform laugh and turned to study the place. It made for a miserable sight, dark and half sacked.

Get away from there, Toosey said.

The five looked among themselves.

What's that he said?

Told us to bugger off.

Did he?

Believe you'll find he did.

The foremost man spoke. What did you say?

Aint nothing in there worth takin, Toosey said. Get along and leave it be.

See? What did I tell you?

Old man must be full, one said.

Looks like a bush tramp.

They peered at him through the moony dark.

What's he think he'll do?

Never mind him. Just have at the door.

They stepped clear while the axeman levelled the head

before the locks then hiked up the blade behind his ear and struck the centre panel. The wood made a bone-crack sound. He jerked loose the axe and lifted it. Toosey spat on the dirt. He was half wild with the pain in his arm. He wanted to chase them away but he was at a loss. One-armed and weaponless. Thoroughly outnumbered. This would not be simple.

He was looking around the street for help when his eye was called to movement inside the hotel window. It was fortuitous timing, for as he looked up the Chinese proprietor showed his head over the registry desk, his white gloves two bright points in the gloom, fumbling with a small palm gun. Toosey frowned. The door kicked under the blows of the axe. He looked to the men but the men had not seen the proprietor perched behind the desk now cocking the pistol. He began to back away.

With the last blow the door collapsed suddenly inwards. The louts rushed forward, all of them calling and whooping, holding their hats, and they stood gazing around at the cheap chandelier and the wide curving staircase in the middle of the lobby and it was dark enough that they did not see the proprietor lean and fire from a recess beneath the desk. The muzzle flash showed them posed like wickerwork mannequins in the dark. All the men cried out. His next fire lit them faltering and colliding at the head of the steps, wearing a common look of dread. Toosey had shifted well back from the scene when they burst forth, taking the steps at a sprint, bolting up the road.

The proprietor darted through the inner dark of the lobby. He took position and fired through the window. The men skidded and changed course, lurching for the deeper shadows before the row of shops. Toosey backed away.

Run you mongrels, he called after them.

At that sound the proprietor turned and fired wildly at Toosey.

Stop that, Toosey called. I aint the one you want. Stop firing.

Another round fizzed by.

Chung! Put that thing down.

You break my door, the Chinaman called. You break my window.

I never done nothin.

Break my door, you get bullet.

The hotel interior lit for an instant as he fired. The round kicked up dust on the street.

I mean bastard too, he called. We two mean bastard.

My gold is in there, Toosey cried. Why would I break your bleedin door?

You get bullet you come my hotel.

I don't want to come in. I'll stay where I am. Just toss the gold out. That's all.

Get away my hotel.

Toosey thought about what to say next. He needed the oriental to see sense. But poor luck that night knew no halt. From a side road two territorial police emerged, brought no doubt by the sound of gunfire. They were mounted on a pair of bay mares fitted with black saddlebags and tack and the riders had on tall custodial helmets and long trench coats that covered the stirrups. When they saw the pack of louts running through the intersection they glanced at each other and kicked their horses into life. Within a few yards they'd ridden down the five and, drawing batons as long as swords, the officers beat them from the saddle and raised cries from the men at each blow.

Toosey watched for a chance to run. Horses reared and men fell, screaming horribly, and one of the constables was caught by the leg and hauled halfway from the saddle but holding on to the cantle he turned his mount and spurred her up the street. Toosey broke for the mouth of a back lane along by the hotel.

In the street the wailing of horses. Elsewhere the distant chant of the riots. He crossed into the lane in a burglar huddle and trudged in the blackness past a broken cart jacked up on bricks to where a pestilent bog of washwater lay, and beyond, rounding into a bend, following the rear wall of a theatre, he found a back entrance here below a broken gaslight. He looked around. High up, a line of women's stays strung on a line between the walls. The doorstone of the theatre stained with mud. Everywhere piles of refuse. He wedged himself down in the door and braced his arm to himself and ground his teeth for the pain.

In the dark he lay listening. Were they looking for him? It wouldn't be long. A dozen people had seen him at it with Flynn. He tried to think but the hurt in his arm was immense. He needed to leave and he knew it. He needed to get out of town. What o'clock was it? He looked at the stars. Dawn was hours away. And somewhere in the guts of it was his boy, the only sort of good his life had ever known. Hold that thought as close as you would hold him, for it is all you will get now, fool.

The Lane by the Hotel

It was gunshots that woke the boy from a shallow sleep. He sat up. A pack of men broke past the mouth of the lane where he lay hidden, all holding their hats, three, four. Then a fifth. Looking back. Wearing grins of terror. Some foul-sounding voice cried, Run you mongrels! as they passed and more shots popped and the street was briefly lit as if by lightning. The boy sank back below the springcart where he'd taken shelter, a wheelless wreck set upon stacks of bricks. He hid there and listened to bootsteps fading on the road. For hours he'd been waiting for his father to come along, tucked away in the deep and cobwebbed dark. He crawled further into the blackness.

This was the second mob turned away tonight. The first had come at dusk. They'd started on the hotel's broad double-door, kicking at it, likely after money and grog, but the fellow inside had begun to give fire out of the windows. Those fellows, like the ones just now, had rightly fled. He huddled in the shadows under the cart and held his breath.

His trouble wasn't finished though. In the street rose a new sound, of horses bellowing and men screaming. He crawled out to where he could better see. Two mounted police, as black as snakes in their leathers and long coats, were riding down the larrikins and giving them blows about the head, wide swinging blows that sent blood, and the larrikins fell and cried out and the horses reared, pawed the air, their eyes grown immense. The whole scene like something rendered on a canvas. He edged back into the gloom under the cart. He hugged his knees to his chest.

He was listening to the drama in the street, trying to keep perfectly quiet, when a shambling form cast in silhouette came along the lane. It was holding its guts and bending low. It entered the dark like it belonged there. Feeling its way down the wall. He watched, flushing with dread. He backed towards the unlit alley behind the hotel and made ready to bolt but stopped. The shape was coming past. He looked up. It had on a round hat. It moaned. He saw then how it wasn't the guts but an arm that it was cradling. It seemed in pain from the sound it gave. The outline of the hat against the light of the street was round and squat and there was no denying it. He crouched in the deep moonless dark below the cart and let the creature pass.

George Fisher, Agent

In those long years alone after Batman's militia disbanded, the boy Thomas Toosey, now a ticket-of-leavesman free to sell his labour, wandered the roads of the conquered north and worked at whatever the season needed and these were hungry years when for a bowl of stew he would hoe turnips dawn to dusk and sleep in the rags he lugged on his back, warm with the rum the farmers gave, always rum, and as an older man he met on the road to Launceston a girl who served as a cook to a publican and they took a slipshod house together, this girl Mattie and he, for she was certainly pretty with her milk-white hair and they worked and were happy and the child that came in summer was the sweetest thing he'd witnessed, white hair like his ma, pink skinned, and he would hold his finger for the child to suckle and kiss it and sing its name like a song but Mattie grew eccentric in the month from its birth and took the child away, locking the bedroom door, crying and crying, and she would say the child was born of someone else and was not his and Thomas knew it to be so in his heart but did not care as he was the one who nursed and fed and bathed it, no other man, no other father, and when he returned home one cool May evening to find their meagre rooms empty, he felt the loss like a sickness, a slow onset followed by a long enfeeblement, in which he drank and drank and hoped to die and it was a while before the constable came, a week or more, to arrest him for infanticide on the sworn statements of Miss Matilda Welch and her employer Mr.

Henry Scales and he was taken and gaoled and bound over for trial by the coroner owing to the belt found tied about the infant's neck when it was washed from a shallow grave by rain, a belt belonging to Toosey, and the judge agreed that Mattie had left the child behind with Toosey who Mattie swore in court was the father and that Toosey, in a fury, a jealous temper, had strangled his boy and buried him by the river and for this crime and given his past offences the judge sentenced Thomas John Toosey of Cameron Street Launceston to ten years in the Port Arthur penitentiary.

Toosey woke in a frantic state, clutching his arm. A mass of greyish smoke stained the sky above the alley, the sun somewhere unseen. It was hot and dry and his mouth was gummed shut. It must have been late morning. He palmed back his hat and straightened his legs and he was leaning forward to stand when he saw a young lad staring at him. Toosey took his time to look again. He rubbed his eyes and feigned indifference. His doltish heart beat hard, half believing it was his boy. He dared not look. He took a breath, lifted his head.

The lad crouching against the wall of the lane was not William. He was as red eyed as a sawmiller and grubby enough in the face to pass as black. He wore his shirt untucked, his boots unlaced. He stared at Toosey like he'd asked a question and would hear it answered. Toosey wiped the crust from his mouth as he considered the lad. Likely a thief, come to turn him over. On a better day he would have wrung the little bugger's neck. The rattling of carts over the road's furrows carried on the air. In the end he just stood and smoothed his shirt with his good hand and started off along the lane.

In the street before the hotel a horse and cart waited idly in the road. It was loaded with the debris of wood and glass and the huge Clydesdale harnessed to it shied as he passed by, tossing its head, jerking the cart about. There were some Chinese boys sweeping glass on to a shovel and they leaned on their brooms and studied Toosey. He was haggard and mad with pain. The boys shifted out of his way.

I know, he said. But it's the galled horse that will kick the worst.

They could only stare.

He mounted the steps and entered the hotel through the ruined double-doors. The clerk stationed there at the lobby desk lifted his head. On seeing Toosey he dropped the ledger book and he started to call for Mr. Chung. At the same time he produced from below the counter a small over-and-under derringer finished in nickel plate with a two-part extractor that would put a wound in you like a shovel hole. He directed the gun at Toosey and his hand shook so much that the works could be heard rattling in the casing. Toosey stopped.

You better ship that thing, he said.

Do not come any closer.

Get it off me or be called upon to use it.

Chung, suited and gloved as ever with his black hair slicked back, stepped from his office in the panelling at the rear. He saw Toosey and his face clouded.

Get out, he said. Get out.

I want me gold, you yellow mongrel.

But Chung took the pistol from the clerk and raised it and levered back the hammer. I shoot you, you dog fucker. You pig fucker. Get out.

Don't come that caper with me. We had an agreement.

Agreement? Chung said and then followed it with few phrases of Chinese. You break agreement, Chung said. You take everything. You take my money.

Like hell I did, Toosey said and came a pace closer.

Chung fired a round into the floor that splintered up the boards. The clap in that high wooden hall was immense. Toosey froze. He raised a palm. Steady on, he said.

I shoot you. Right there. Shoot you like dog you like to fuck.

Toosey stood with his good hand upraised.

Shoot you in balls. Chung directed the muzzle downward at Toosey's crotch. You want I shoot balls? How you fuck dog then, huh? How you fuck pig?

Toosey switched his eyes from the proprietor to the clerk to the handgun and back as he gauged his dilemma, hounded by a pansy and a foreigner armed with hardly more than a toy. What exactly have I done wrong here? he said.

Mr. Chung was robbed last night, the clerk said and he appeared the most nervous of them all. They took everything in the strongbox. Our banknotes. Coins. The whole lot.

Your friend, Chung said. Your friend take it.

What? Toosey said. What friend? Who?

They break my door. Break my window. Your friend. They use axe. They take my money. They take everything. Here Chung bent down and pointed at something behind the desk. You see? he said.

Toosey leaned to get a look. There was a strongbox standing open at floor level that held some sheets of paper tied with ribbon and envelopes. Nothing else. His eyes when they cut back to Chung had a wild quality to them. No, he said. No no no. They was sons of bitches. Not my friends, not at all.

Chung looked confused. He still had the derringer trained on Toosey. He cupped the butt now with both hands.

I tried to stop them, Toosey said. I tried to help. Why would I steal me own money?

Oh you lie. You lie.

Damn me, I'm not lyin. They was at your door with an axe. I wasn't about to let them in here so as they could take what they like. Take my gold.

A moment passed where the three of them stood staring, each unsure, each taut with anger. Toosey lowered his hand. Was it the same fellows? he said. Are you certain of it? Cause I saw a couple of territorials properly clean them up.

I see, Chung said. I see with my eyes.

And they come in here and opened the safe?

They make me open safe.

Why didn't you shoot?

I shoot bullet, I miss. No more bullet in gun.

Toosey was breathing hard through his nose. His eyes cut from one to the other. You cockless bellycrawlers, he said. Couldn't keep a horde of children from robbing us blind. Sweet Christ.

I wasn't here, the clerk said. I went home at six.

Toosey ignored him. The brim of his hat had cast his whole face in shadow. You ought to bend a knee and thank God I'm impaired, he said.

Chung glared and that was his answer.

A round railway clock on the wall ticked in the quiet. Toosey took a deep breath and let it go. So listen to me, he said. Are you sure it was them? Cause if it was them, I'll soon find out. This town's too small to hide in.

I get the police, Chung called. Bring them. We see about money.

No. No police.

Get police. They find money.

No. Not yet. We don't need em. I'll find the bastards. Just answer the question. Was it the same men?

Same men, Chung said. Same. I see them.

No need for the law to stick his nose in then, Toosey said. I'll have our money back. Just give me time before you have the law involved. Just a bit of time.

Chung said not a word, his narrow eyes dark and unreadable. The fall of light through the window lit him grimly pale. At length he lowered the gun.

With a last long glare at them Toosey turned and left. Outside on the footpath the Chinese boys emptied buckets of glass into the horse cart. He stopped in the sun and stood and let the heat steam the damp from him. A hot wind was coming up the river. It heaved over the rooves of the city where like stalks of barley the chimney smoke bent before it, a desert wind from out of the red heart of the mainland lifting the dust off the road into little devils and setting the weathercocks all acreak.

He looked along the road and looked back at the lane where he'd slept. The wind stirred his hat. He closed his eyes. His arm pounded in time with his heart with a pain that shut his thoughts to all else. He felt ill. The heat in the air and the heat in his arm seemed part of the same devilment. He swallowed with great effort and considered sitting in the street but he knew he would not get up again. He kept his eyes closed a moment longer. He could not summon the courage to face what he had to face. A life in which he'd traded away his last hope at peace.

He breathed in and breathed out. He opened his eyes and began to walk. Among the folk in the street were men full of drink and holding one another in comradeship, men asleep in doorways like sick and needy vagrants. Toosey walked towards the part of the road where he'd seen the territorials warring with the louts who stole his money. He thought he might find there some sign, some intimation of who they were or where they'd gone. He walked holding his arm to himself, cold sweat streaking down his backbone.

He'd come along the street a dozen doors, past shops, past tea rooms, before he looked up and saw standing beside the road, in the maturing daylight, the boy from the lane. He was tall, thin, angular. He just as brazenly stared at Toosey as he had in the laneway. But in this light he was somehow changed. Toosey tugged down his hat. He headed towards this lad and the lad fingered the ends of his shirt like he was nervous about it. As Toosey walked he began to see things that unnerved him too. The lad had a brace of moppy hair but lightly coloured, like grain. His face beneath the grime was softly shaped and familiar. He came towards the lad and stopped some yards short.

The lad fingered his shirt. I've found you, he said.

Toosey nodded his head. He looked away. He blinked and blinked and his eyes ran anyway.

The lad continued to stare.

I'd say you have, said Toosey.

For a moment he dared not look at the boy. His boy.

I remembered you, William said.

After a while Toosey turned back. His eyes wet and narrow. He said, You've grown.

The lad looked down at himself. He let go of the hem of his shirt and pocketed his hands.

Toosey nodded some more. He was pressing his mouth tightly shut. He could hardly see. I would not have picked you, he said.

Ma is dead. I sent a letter.

Here, Toosey said and he fumbled for the innards of his coat. He pulled out the letter. I still have it.

Wasn't sure it was the right thing. Sendin you a letter.

You needn't be afraid. I've quit the drink.

William seemed unmoved by this. He wiped his nose on his sleeve.

My boy, he said. A rotten man would not come. I have come.

Yes. You have.

Look at you. All grown by now.

More or less.

I pictured you as you was. Little, with short hair. Three years has altered you no end.

A faint expression passed over William's features, brief as a spark. Regret or remorse or something else. Then it was gone and he hardened over again.

How did you find me? Toosey said.

Stewart told me where.

Stewart. I was going to knock in his teeth.

William was studying the blackened arm Toosey carried. Could you even do it with that?

I would school him, Toosey said and lifted it tenderly. Arm or no arm.

I thought they had shot you. Them last night.

Who?

The ones outside the hotel.

Beneath his moustache Toosey's mouth pulled sidewards. I went round the whole town yesterday after you. Then here you are, right where I was sleepin all night. What a lottery.

The Chinaman said you would soon be back. Said you had money in the safe. So I waited.

Oh my boy. Come here. Come here.

William came. Toosey hugged him one-armed around the shoulder and held him close. They were moments full of nothing else but the feel of his boy breathing and the feel of his blood slamming like something at the cell bars of his rib cage. It was done, he was found, and they would not be split. He held the child tight and it was close and it was wonderful.

She went quick, his boy said. I had the doctor there. But she went.

We'll miss her.

I tried. I brought the doctor.

She was called away. When we are called, we go. No one can help it. Certainly not no doctor.

No.

We shan't be apart now. Not never.

No.

I'll keep you near. I promise that.

The boy was holding him tight now. His arm hurt and he did not care.

I promise.

I promise too.

Listen though, Toosey said and he leaned away. We have a task. We must get moving.

He began along the street and the boy followed.

Today. You and me. We are leavin on the first boat.

Good, the boy said. I've had enough of this arsehole place.

Toosey smiled at him. Aint we a fine pair, he said.

George Fisher kept office at the river end of the city among the breweries and rows of warehouses, the granaries mounted with great flywheel elevators for the lifting of sacks and barrels. It was a ground-floor office, red brick, sashed windows dressed with curtains of stale yellow, the glass in the door stencilled in gold with George Fisher Agent TSN Company. Toosey clutched his arm to himself and stood gazing up and down the empty street. Mid-morning. There should have been people everywhere. Instead there were level towers of black rising from the fires in town. Everywhere the signs of damage. He stepped to the door and beat on it.

There was silence. Then came a call: There's no money in here.

The voice was hard-sounding. Toosey shifted about. Are you Fisher? he said.

More silence. There were bootsteps and the curtain was pulled back. A bald man in the window frowned out. He was elaborately whiskered save his chin being shaved naked. He looked around the street. I suppose you think I'm going to let you in, he said through the glass. Just throw back my door.

Don't bother me how we do it.

There's not a penny in here, you know.

Toosey pulled a sovereign and showed it. Passage is what I want, not your damned money.

Fisher's expression moved. He leaned into the glass.

Next passage out, Toosey said, wherever it bloody goes.

Why should I believe you?

A long silence. Toosey sighed. He bent down and slid the sovereign under the door. Take that as goodwill, he said.

He heard the bolt being knocked back and the door cracked open an inch or two. Toosey cleared the sweat from his forehead. William pushed back the door for his father and held it while he stepped inside.

Fisher was sitting at a blackwood desk behind stacks of manifests and bills of goods and receipts for duties paid and notices of duties owing. He was made small by these various piles, small and old. He rocked forward in his chair and removed his pince nez and tapped his chin with it.

Have a seat then, he said.

He squinted as William shut the door and they crossed and took a seat.

Nasty business, he said. That last night.

Don't reckon it's done yet neither, Toosey said.

Fisher nodded once, like he was winking. Nor do I.

There was a pencil in his shirt pocket, which he produced. He began to scratch something on a pad. You want passage then?

If you would.

For the pair of you?

That's right.

Fisher dragged a pocket watch from his vest and snapped it open and read it. The *Derwent* steams out for Melbourne this evening at four, he said, provided that her crew present fit and healthy. That leaves you not very long at all.

Sooner the better, Toosey said.

Fisher brought a ledger book off a pile of such books and such papers. He thumbed through it. He sat his eyeglasses on his nose and leaned down to the book nearsightedly. He licked the tip of his pencil and began to write. Very good, he said. Now. Tell me your names.

Smith.

Fisher looked up. His eyes were oversized through refraction. Mr. and Master Smith?

Mr. John Smith and son.

Fisher filled out the ledger. When next he spoke he did not look up. John Smith?

That's it.

I get a lot of John Smiths.

Toosey snorted.

If you're an old government man, Mr. Smith, I need to see your papers.

Toosey sat his hat in his lap. He was still for a moment. He dug into his pocket, pulled out a fistful of coins, and picked through them in his palm. He sat on Fisher's desk a pile of six gold sovereigns and pushed it forward.

There's me papers, he said.

Fisher took off his glasses. The coins among the books and inkpots on the desk had the look of something arcane. He studied the coins and he studied Toosey. He laid his glasses on the ledger and leaned forward. I need to see your pardon, he said. A full pardon. Signed and official. I can't let you leave the island without it.

Six vickies says you look the other way.

But Fisher was growing angry. It's always a bellyache with you government hands, he said. Think you can buy your way through? Think the rules don't apply? Well, I am sorry, Mr. Smith. They do.

He stood from his chair and moved around into the office as if to show Toosey the door but Toosey had spread his legs and was sitting back cradling his arm.

What's this? he said.

You had better leave.

Toosey gave a grim sort of smile.

My next move is to fetch a constable. See if it isn't.

They told me you was a hard man, Fisher. Told me well.

Mr. Smith, if you kindly please. Fisher opened the door and gestured outside. William stood and started for the door but his father caught him by the arm.

Let me make it seven then, Toosey said. The seventh being payable upon my touchin the deck of the *Derwent*.

Twelve.

Eh?

I want twelve, Fisher said and he shut the door and stared hard at Toosey.

No.

Then you need to find yourself another passage.

This here is all I have. The whole of it.

And it doesn't cover me for the risk I'm taking.

Toosey watched him for a while. A real bloody hard man, he said. He stood and replaced his hat and came forward with his hand out. Twelve it is, he said. Keep them six, plus the one I slipped under the door. Five more payable as of when I reach the deck.

Payable at the wharf, said Fisher. To me. In person. Or else you don't sail.

Toosey's hand hung unshaken between them. At the wharf then, he said. He lifted his hand a little and Fisher took it.

The agent wore a scowl as he shook Toosey's hand and he turned away, perched once more at his desk and picked through his piles, making notes. Toosey was leaving when he spoke again.

I don't have to tell you that our arrangement is a confidential matter, he said and he raised his huge owl's eyes. Do I?

But Toosey did not look back. Just get me on that boat, he said and herded William out the door.

He stood in the road with his arm giving him hell. Sweating and suffering. The boy was staring at his arm and looked concerned. Toosey hauled it closer. A queer feeling was growing in his chest. It might have been the pain or it might have been the heat, but he took a few staggering steps and halted, and stood swaying. Miss that steamer and they'd be left in town without tuppence to their name, and soon to be sought by police. He gritted his teeth for the satanic fire in his arm. He squeezed shut his eyes.

You don't look well.

Just let me have a moment.

Want some water?

No.

I can find you some.

He had to sort it out. The whole plot had come unlaced in his fingers until he was left with only the rankest of choices. Have the sovereigns by four or place his neck squarely in the noose. It was a choice but no choice at all. When he opened his eyes it was to a different world. He took a long breath and let it out. He drew his hat low over his forehead. He set off.

Where we goin?

To see your uncle.

He won't lend you no money, you know. Ma asked him plenty of times.

He'll lend it to me or I shall burn his house down.

William followed at a small remove. He took a hop-step now and then to keep pace with his father. What about the money you left with the oriental? he said.

Gone. Stole by them cocklickers last night.

Them ones chased by the territorials?

The same.

They walked southward into the town's heart. Small groups drifted in the streets and the smoke and they kept clear of them, watched them pass, before venturing forward. A chestnut mare came cantering riderless along. It was panicked and wore a lather on its flanks like soapsuds. It circled and cantered back. It had on neither saddle nor headstall nor bridle but was as naked as a brumby. They stepped to let it by. It left dust where it had been and soon the dust settled and the way was empty. They walked on and when they crossed into Brisbane Street they were presented with a pandemonic scene.

Before the taproom on the corner close to fifty men lurched about, sodden in liquor. The publican had taken to giving away pots of grog that his establishment might escape the general destruction levelled upon other venues. It was a sight to behold. Toosey and his boy lingered outside watching drunks clamber across the counter for the taps and kegs, more animals than men, flailing about in the spilled beer, rough-looking rogues with beards and broad hats and behind the bench serving girls working like the infernal damned at the task of refilling cups. They stepped over a man lying in the road, fouled with vomit. Stepped over broken bottles, broken chairs. There were men swaying in the shade, near at the level of catatonia. On a bench seat Toosey found a pint mug dosed with whiskey, which he picked up, swirled, and held under his nose.

Who's that? William said.

He was gazing down Brisbane Street towards the town. Toosey followed his eyeline to where a boy stood dead centre of the road staring at them. They saw that the boy was stiff in one leg when he turned away slightly. His head was shaved to a stubble. If he had anything to say for himself he did not venture it but merely stood in the street making a quiet study of Toosey across his shoulder. Wind lifted grit off the road in a wave and when it settled the lad was watching him still, hands in the pockets of his loose pants like some work-shy drudge.

Don't think I aint seen you, Toosey called.

The lad looked away.

Eh? I'm talking to you. Be ready for a fight if you mean to bail me up.

The lad shuffled away to a wall and leaned on it, crossed his arms, crossed his feet.

Sweat melted into Toosey's eyes, which he blinked away and, with a lengthy sideways glare, he commenced upon the street. Behind them, trawling up the eddies with his odd leg, came the stranger. Best we move along, he said to his boy.

He was watching you before, William said. When you was in the hotel.

Was he just.

Do you know him?

Not from Adam.

They passed crook-looking weatherboard stores next to tall freestone lawyers' houses with their brass plates and at the corner Toosey paused to allow himself a view to the rear. Rows of buildings. A merciless sun. Inebriates of all stages wandering in the bitter light. He clicked his tongue as he stood surveying the street each way. The lame boy was gone again as fleetly as he'd appeared.

That don't make me feel well, he said.

I saw him once, William said. He was a caller at Stewart's.

I've not more than a shillin anyhow. If it's robbery he wants.

They walked on a while among merchant buildings and meagre homes and folk drifted by, liquored men, boys, coming from the troubles.

Callers, Toosey said at length. Is that what Stewart said you was.

Mostly.

What else did he say?

William picked a scab on his elbow. Said we was lost and fallen children in need. Said he alone of all the city would see to our hunger. But that part wasn't true. Plenty of folk fed us. Them at Thrower's Hotel would. That fat bugger Rabbit would too if we took him something.

He could not look at the boy. Did he lay a hand on you? he said.

No.

Cause if he laid a hand on you I'm payin him a visit right now.

No. He never.

Toosey shook his head. He spat. I swear, he said. What a fiend.

It's Oran Brown is the one. Stewart always picks him out. Takes him to a room in the house. I give him a knife yesterday and told him to cut off Stewart's worm next time.

Where'd you get a knife?

Stole it. Out of Johnson's.

So you stole a knife, give it to a kid, and told him to cut Stewart's cock off with it?

That's about the guts of it.

You're a pint of whiskey, you are. Jesus.

William looked down at the road. He perhaps didn't quite know what to make of his father. He picked his elbow as they walked and kept quiet.

Think he would do it? This Oran?

Like as not.

I'm of half a mind to let him alone then. Poor cockless fool that he'll become.

He fed me these weeks without Ma. He aint all bad.

Toosey clenched shut his jaw. He turned to the boy. You ought to have stayed with your uncle, he said. Where you was safe.

I'm old enough to take life how it comes. No need for coddlin.

Toosey stopped then. He stared hard at his boy. He had on Toosey's old boot, inches too large for him and the toe caved and flattened and the laces dragging. He had on Toosey's old shirt. He had a sharpness to the brow, a shape to the chin, that Toosey also knew. He saw what he'd made of the boy and it needled him. A pair of villains we are, he said. A pair of no-hopers.

I should like to be on that boat, William said. And be gone for good.

So should I, lad.

The mountainous smoke above town had begun to lean in the breeze and in the blinding noon sun the bonfires burned invisibly. Smoke and ash blew, sheets of paper aflame in the updrafts. Toosey pulled his swollen arm against himself. Under the high sun their shadows gathered at their feet and they walked each in his own pool of black towards the hospital hill, towards the home of Brother Michael Payne, knife sharpener.

Be on that boat, he said after a while. But it's the money we'll need for it. That's the grit in the oyster.

How much did them fellows steal from the safe?

Never you mind.

That oriental should have shot em. Useless old pisser.

I should say he wasn't ready when they come back.

William looked at him. They never come back, he said.

Oh but they did, lad. Later on. And they took the lot.

No, William said. I was there all night. In the lane or watching you. No one come back. Not a single soul.

Toosey had taken a few paces before it struck him. He stopped. A moment of dizziness followed as the knowledge shuffled in his head and locked into place. He removed his hat and threw it on the ground. For the love of God and his holy fuckin mother, he said.

What?

Jesus, Mary and fuckin Joseph.

What?

You miserable whore-made lump of shit.

William frowned at him.

You won't out-think me, you yellow bastard, Toosey said. He fetched up his hat and replaced it. He began to walk once more with long strides, wincing with the pain of his arm. Come on, he said. We'll have our gold yet.

THE PARK

Caislin Flynn sat on a fallen tree watching the road. Not the smallest rain had fallen in months and the track through the hills had cauterised into a span of bedrock that showed two stone ruts where cartwheels had ploughed the winter mud. All night she'd waited for Fitheal Flynn to return, but by the daybreak light her father had not appeared. With the advance of morning she began slowly to change in her bearing. She dropped her head. Canted forward. Soon she was sobbing into her palms. The sun reared brightly over the forest and it was a queer heartsick sound that she made among the birdcall of dawn. Silence followed by a moaning release. As if she'd finally seen some sombre truth about the world.

In the heat of morning she gathered herself up. For a time staring dumbly at the camp, the sundries of billytin and bedroll and possum-skin blanket laid among the gum bark and bracken. She pulled on her hood and again all sound dimmed and the heat of her breath grew close. After a while she walked off and left. Cicadas hummed in the gums above and, elsewhere, the call of ravens. On a pasture cut from the forest, fleets of cockatoos foraged among the sheep. She passed by, and they raised their thousand eyes to her. Mid-morning she reached the market farms of King's Meadows. Here the track rejoined the main road and she saw that this road was filled with a good many folk decamping the town. They filed past laden with hessian sacks, roped-up bedding, dragging children like captives. A few came in gigs and others came that had very little or were barefoot, hatless, attended by lean dogs and clouds of flies. She adjusted the eyeholes of the hood to better see. She made for a menacing presence descending out of the scrub. She was starved, dirty and in despair, and the men and women on the road whispered to one another and gave her room.

She walked and, later, upon broaching a hill, she was given a view to the branching rivers and the rooves littered along the banks. Several columns of smoke stood centred above the town against the stainless sky and for a while she just stood staring at these frail towers. They grew tall and thin until at the head they swelled into the shapes of flowers, each a differing shade of lead. But as she pondered on them, on the character of them, the plain conclusion gradually revealed itself. A great violence had taken place in Launceston. She pushed on more quickly.

As she walked, her thoughts returned to her father and that calamitous day when their sky had darkened, standing at the railing fence with her sisters, Ashley and Brannah, just babes the two of them, and herself a child of nine, watching their mother drag a stillborn calf from the birthing yard on a spring morning so cold the rails had thistled with ice and when the heifer in the far corner turned and made towards their mother the children didn't see the danger, no one cried beware, and only when the heifer struck did they scream, but it was done in that moment and she was damned and the heifer crushed her against the mud and butted again and again and trampled her underfoot and their mother, making no sound at all, rolled limply with every blow and bled on the mud, and when after an age their father entered the yard and carried her out the younger girls were tearing their hair in anguish, screaming, screaming, but there was not a thing to be done and their father carried her to the house, slack and trailing blood, and he towelled the dirt from her wrecked face in silence and sat and stared at the wall equally in silence while the girls cried and Caislin fetched water and firewood but their mother was not breathing, not moving, and that was it and she was gone, gone, and their father seemed at first quite philosophical for after a while he stood and poured some tea, saying not a word, staring at the chipped cup, until on a sudden it fell from his fingers and he stalked into the thin daylight and after a while he returned carrying O'Malley's pistol and entered the birthing yard and he shot this heifer, this killer, clean through the eye and then he walked down paddock and shot another of the herd and another and Ashley and Brannah had not ceased crying and would not for days and all this was a long time ago, ten years at least, but on that morning years later when Caislin had appeared hooded in a flour sack from which she'd cut eyeholes hastily and jaggedly with a knife and told her father that for all he might fight and curse she would not let him set forth alone, she'd been met with the same deadly silence that prefaced his long-ago bout of slaughter and she knew then what he was about, what he meant for Toosey, and it left her in fear for them all.

Desolate civic streets. Smoke like a morning fog. Caislin walked, crunching over glass as she crossed the inner part of town through wide stone buildings, hovels of weather-aged scantling. The streets were strewn with wreckage. Furniture had been stacked and burned in pillage and the cinders smoked in the sun. She walked and she stared, murmuring to herself in disbelief. There was no good explanation for any of what she saw. Among the destruction wandered men and boys searching for bits and pieces of value and they eyed her across the road. She steered away from them. Soon she came to the police house, scorched by the flinging of blazing bottles, the tall palisade around it buckled, the gates wrenched out of true. A pair of territorial troopers sat their mounts before the

ruined building with their clubs drawn. As Caislin came by, her
gaze to the ground, the senior of them tapped his stick on the
rump of his horse and trotted it forward. Caislin stopped. He
was chewing something and he leaned and released a squirt of
dark liquor and sat upright once more. He wiped his considerable moustache.

That's close enough, he said.

She looked off along the road. She looked up at the trooper.

You aint seen an Irishman around? she said and her voice
was muffled. Funny old hat on him. Bout yay tall. She put her
arm out to indicate a height.

The trooper chewed. Lad, I saw near every bastard in town
this last night. Most of which was tryin to kill me.

He carries a stick.

They all had sticks, the senior man said.

Caislin lowered her head. She put her hands in her pockets.
If you do see such a fellow, tell him I'm lookin for him.

And who are you exactly?

Her head rotated inside the cowl. She was gazing up at the
senior man but the eyeholes stayed straight ahead. Jack Ketch,
she said.

On hearing this the senior man made a short laugh or a wet
sort of cough, she could not tell which. Well you look the part
at least, he said. The trooper was watching her closely. You
scared of the sun or somethin? he said.

No. It's not that.

Caislin pulled her hands from her pockets and let them
hang by her sides, fingering her untucked shirt. She seemed
about to speak but then she dropped her head again. The
horse huffed and the trooper leaned and spat. Caislin turned
away, wandering off she knew not where.

By noon of that day she found herself at the park. Spare
young gums stood like convict flogging posts. The lawn a

waterless brown. She walked beneath the arched entranceway and made towards the fountain where she might take a drink. In the centre of the park stood a Rechabite tent and men were bobbing under the guy-ropes as they came and went, bandaged and sutured, as bruised as carthorse fruit, and there were women in pinafores administering to them, wrapping limbs and feeding grown men from mugs. Caislin slipped up the hem of her sleeve and dipped her hand into the fountain and drank from it. She was studying the tent as she swallowed. She dried her hands on her shirt and approached.

There was a prim-looking woman with a small timepiece pinned on her apron and she saw Caislin coming. Her expression grew concerned. She put down the tray she was carrying and came over.

My blessed saint. What's happened to you?

What?

Your face. Are you burnt? She reached for her hood to lift it, but Caislin caught the nursing woman by the wrist.

Don't touch it, she said.

She looked at Caislin, looked into the ragged cut holes. Caislin lowered her eyes. There's an Irishman I'm tryin to find, she said.

Let go of my hand.

Have you seen any come through?

We've had a few Irish today, yes, the nursing woman said.

Was any of em old?

You're hurting me.

Was any of em old?

Well, I shouldn't wonder.

He's wearin a ratty sort of a suit. Walks with a stick. He has a way about him you wouldn't soon forget.

The woman was pulling at her hand. If he come through, she said, then I never saw him.

Others at the tent had begun to take notice and some

crouching men had stood and begun to approach. Caislin dropped the woman's wrist. A chap in his underflannels was crossing the grass and coming up behind the woman. He wore no hat but had a length of white gauze wrapped about his knuckles like a prizefighter. He drew up and he stood there. He began to laugh. It was loud and it sounded across the park and soon everyone turned to see what was going on. He held his belly and crowed.

Rodney, what's the matter with you? said the nursing woman.

The fellow, this Rodney, he wiped his eyes for the laughter. That is some piss-backwards company you are keepin, Maud, he said.

She scowled at him. He is looking for someone is all, she said.

Never in all my days, said Rodney and he laughed.

Other men were drawing around to see what had caused the fuss. No one offered a word as they formed up and studied this strange thin figure. Rodney, standing with his two feet spread, slapped these men on the shoulders and pointed at the hooded figure. Slowly their faces split with grins and they too fell to laughing.

What the devil is he wearing? one of them said.

He's as drunk as a wheelbarrow, Rodney said.

No I aint, Caislin said.

She was staring at this chap. Her breath sucked the cotton in and out. She reached her right hand around behind herself and paused in that stance before speaking.

It's how the lady said. I'm lookin for someone.

Rodney steadied himself, he straightened up. Lookin for who?

A man called Flynn.

Flynn?

Rodney scratched at his pestilent undershirt. Bristles of

chest hair poked where the fabric had frayed. He scratched and he turned to survey the group and the men at the tent, spreading his arms in mock showmanship. Don't see no one here called Flynn, he said.

I'm Flynn.

A fellow came forward from the group. His coat was torn full of holes and faded, his beard growing in fleecy tussocks from his chin. He looked to have lately unseated himself from a grog shop somewhere, or was otherwise just soft in the head. The snarl of hair about his mouth parted as he smiled.

Caislin shook her head. You aint him, she said.

But most of them had started guffawing and clouting this chap on the shoulders and the chap grinned.

I'm Flynn as well, said another one and they all howled at the grand joke.

There, said Rodney. Two Flynns for you.

He was watching Caislin closely. The nursing woman stepped in between them and she had her finger raised up, meaning to dress down this Rodney for the quarrel he had picked. She was big through the hips and carried herself in sure fashion but Rodney had no mind for it. He pushed her aside and came towards Caislin in a show of menace.

What have you got under there anyhow?

She backstepped.

A leprous nose? What?

Pull it off him, someone said.

There was a juncture where Caislin might have turned and made away, broken across the span of dead grass for the gate. But at the final second, fearful, her eyes pinched shut, she slipped the pistol out of her belt and brought it level with the centre of Rodney's forehead. Rodney flinched like he was whipped. He stumbled and slipped and fell to his knees. He's armed by Christ, he cried, he's armed.

Finding his feet in a hurry he bolted. They all bolted, to a man. Holding their hats they dashed for the few bits of cover in that sloped and featureless park. All bar the nursing woman who stood with her arms rigidly at her sides.

Best you put that away, she said.

Sorry missus, I really am. I never meant—

There's been enough of that this past night.

Yes, she said, yes. She looked up at the nursing woman, her dark eyes wreathed in white. What happened last night? she said.

Bloody drunken fools tearing up the town, the woman said. Angry about that levy they don't want to pay.

They did a job of it, Caislin said.

My word. And a job of each other.

She reset the hammer and lowered the gun and wedged it behind her back. At the tent where the wounded lay on cots many of the men had begun to cluster, to speak in conference, now and then one of them pointing at the hooded girl. Caislin did not like the look of it.

If you see an Irishman, she said, a chap carryin a walkin stick, a chap with a strange way about him. If you see such a man, would you tell him I'm lookin for him?

I will.

Thank you.

She started off towards the gate. Crossing the lawn she was met with a chorus of whistling and bitter howls from the men and she picked up her pace, ducking under an elm and scaring up galahs and other birds, whose noise momentarily drowned them out. At the gate she stopped and looked back. No one had followed. She was damp and the cowl stuck to her cheeks. She laid her forehead on the gate as she let her breath come back.

She moved on, towards the greasy river over the way. The cowl seemed to grow ever more suffocating. Her breath churned inside it. She passed the gasworks factory where the chimney stack cast a precise black stain upon the earth and she crossed the road and came to riverbanks dressed with grass and stands of reed. Ahead the river in its furrow carried a dead cat floating by. She sat in the grass rubbing her thighs and gazing along at the wooden bridge span. There were people moving on it, and police, darkly shaped against the shell-blue sky.

Where are you, Pa? she said to the river.

She buried her face in the crook of her arm.

After a while she slipped O'Malley's bulldog pistol out of her belt. It was British made and took a .44 calibre shell in the revolving barrel and it was loaded with all the rounds she had. She held it in her palms. She thumbed the cylinder around until the charge was aligned against the hammer. The finish on the trigger guard was worn where it had once sat in a holster, rendered back to bare metal. She reset the cylinder. Then she levelled the bore against her temple.

The river sloughed past bronze with a glaze of sun. On the bridge a horse cried out. She closed her eyes. A dull unending ache pulsed in the cave-dark of her innards. She pulled off the hood, tossed it on the bank, and let the breeze play upon her neck. Each crank of the mechanism as it turned ticked through her skull. The hammer clacked back and locked. She maintained the gun above her ear and soon the weight of it set her arm trembling. She would fall on the grass, her limbs made slack. Sink like a long sigh into nothing. A last breath then a long dreamless sleep. But at her innermost, lodged like a rifle ball in her heart, was a hardness. It would not crush nor would it dislodge. Her finger found the trigger. Settled there. For a long time she sat in the full sun watching that silty stretch of water. Wanting an end of pain.

But there were Ashley and Brannah alone and waiting.

At length she let the gun fall.

A pair of rats bellied from a hole in the reeds leaving an

outward flare of wake where they broke. She watched them swim downstream in the mud-brown river. After a time she stood and adjusted her pants, reseating the pistol at her back, and reached for the hood and yanked it on. Stepping out of the weeds she found the road, a sad and dusty gutter, and looked either way along it. She began to walk.

Jack Ketch

When Jane Hall reached St. John Street she was breathing hard. She stopped and leaned on her knees. She needed to find the hangman and she thought she knew where he might be but crossing through town was proving difficult. Away towards the church of St. John along a hundred yards of double-height stores and hotels a strange spectacle played out. Territorial police from other districts had begun to sweep through on horseback and they cantered up and circled and drew their great long batons. Hall sheltered in a yard and kneeled where she could see them pass. They rode big horses, the colour of sand; they seemed to dissolve inside the dust they made. Their mounts skipped sideways like cattle dogs, heading off men who broke. The constables atop held grimly to the reins and yelled. Soon they had assembled before them a group of cowering men and women. At length the crowd was turned and the territorials pushed them along the black iron pickets by Prince's Square and the crying and the calling began to fade.

She moved on through the central part of town. At Johnson's grocery the doors were kicked in and Johnson himself was squatting in the footpath. Looters carried off his barrels, his sacks and tins. He looked up at Hall and he seemed bewildered by these events. Blood from a broad red wound in his brow ran and dripped off his jaw. He sat in the dust. He lay over. In the year before he died, her father had bought her to Johnson's for a pair of boots with money in his pocket from the railways, and Johnson had slipped the boot over her wasted foot and laced it with a tender sort of embarrassment while her father stacked some coins onto the counter. They'd walked out and left her old shoes behind. Such a day, such an hour, as would never come again, walking the streets to the squeak of new leather, holding her lost father's hand.

But the town in which she'd lived her sixteen years of life now seemed outlandish. Mad scenes played everywhere. There was the druggist that was a charred hollow smoking in the sun. Hordes and hordes of people roaming unchallenged. Men with clubs, dogs, ropes. Women drinking in the roadside or laid out cold. The whole scene adorned by wreaths of black smoke and broken glass in the dust alight with sun. For a moment she could not place herself. She limped through an intersection and stopped and she stood for a time, unsure. When she looked back Johnson was lying as before, staring, and his eyes stood whitely from the red mask of his blood. She moved on.

From laneway to shadow she went along Brisbane Street where the fighting had been the worst. An unnatural quiet ruled here. The road mottled with the black pits of fires. She picked her way and when she reached the park at the end of the road she realised she'd been gritting her teeth the whole length of it. Her jaw felt locked shut. She entered the park near the fountain and the glass conservatory. The Rechabites had raised their gaudy tent that they might dole out soup to the drunk or wounded and recruit the worst of them and she crossed the crisp brown lawn to where she knew she would find John Bunyip propped inside probably holding a mug upon which he'd be blowing like a baby. She hobbled up and they all looked around, all the wounded and bandaged, and the attendant women. Sure as shit Bunyip was in the tent too. He sat tenderly up on his elbows when he saw her. He waved her inside.

Did you see him? she said. She was breathing fast.

Oh, he said and sat back. Here I was thinking you was worried.

I been talkin to Oran Brown, she said. He's tellin every bugger. Notice a hangman gettin about and you're likely to talk.

Bunyip had above his ear a gash where he had met with a sportive trooper early that morning. Brown had told her all this as well, told her how upon being struck Bunyip had folded to his knees and wailed. The lion was not half so fierce as he was painted.

So? Where did he go?

That lass there in green, Bunyip said and he gave a secret move of the eyes. Hall glanced around. There was a young woman bending over another fellow, putting a stitch through a cut in his arm.

What about her?

Tits on her like brandy jugs. I am working meself up to a fit. See if I can't get her leanin over me that way too.

Listen, you mouthy bugger. Where's this hangman if he's here?

You don't mind it when Finlay talks about tits.

She crouched beside him. I aint muckin about. Just tell us where he went.

Bunyip locked his long bare arms about his knees. He was set upon by that Georgetown Rodney when he presented here, he said. Took off out the river way.

The river? she said.

A penny says he is one of Rabbit's boys.

The nursing woman came past and Bunyip brightened up and smiled and held up his soup to her. When she had disappeared into the sunlight he put his mug aside and frowned.

Gawd what I would give, he said.

Behave yourself, Hall said and she started out of the tent.

What do you want him for anyways? Bunyip called after her. You're not still chasin them ten quids, are you?

She stopped and looked back. She came towards him and whispered. If some mongrel murdered me, she said, would you want to know?

What?

Murdered me. If I was murdered, would you want to know?

Course I would.

You aint just sayin that?

Bunyip patted her on the arm. Rabbit knows a few lively types, he said. Types as will run a blade where it's needed. Between us we'd see you revenged.

She blinked a few times. You mean it?

Course I mean it.

The matter is, she said and lowered her voice, the matter is one of Ketch's mates was done in.

Christ. Jesus.

I saw it.

Janey, he said. No.

What?

Don't go stickin your nose in.

Ketch will want to know.

Bunyip grabbed her wrist and pulled her close. It aint smart to stick your nose in, he said. You'll bloody lose it.

She huffed and looked about the tent and for a time was quiet. The sun had the canvas brightly aglow. Through the tent flaps the framed view of the town, the black-fleece smoke above. She looked at him. This fellow, she said. This Toosey. I been followin him. All night. All day. He did for Ketch's mate. You know, the tall one with the stick. The Irish.

I see, he said and dropped her wrist. I see. You've grown a conscience.

Bugger that, I'm talkin about what's likely.

Likely how?

Pay attention, she said. I told you how it was. This Toosey has money. A lot of it. Ketch's money. I show Ketch how to find him and I'll get a cut. Enough to see us clear. Enough to pay out Rabbit.

Janey, the hangman will kill him.

That won't happen. I won't let it.

Janey. No.

For ten quids I will risk it.

Bunyip dropped his head and looked away. They sat in silence. The canvas heaved and creaked.

You think Rabbit will just forget, she said. You think he'll let us off.

What can he do to you?

Burn Ma's place. Have her beaten. Have her shot. Have me in a brothel. Break me good leg. Break me—

All right, I hear you, I hear you.

You don't know Rabbit like I do.

There's easier ways to get ten quids, he said. That's what I think.

Not if I do this properly.

Bunyip grew agitated. Doin it properly means this Toosey gets shot through the heart.

That won't happen. I won't let it.

Jesus, he said. You are pigheaded. I fear you aint long for this world.

I'll come find you later. Don't tell no one about this. Not a soul.

I hear, he said. Get along and find your hangman, you bloody fool.

She moved in her odd gait down the narrow river esplanade. Happening the other way was a loaded stage coach, men on the running boards, men perched atop like vultures, cutting so close she could smell the horses. She stood by in the grass as it rolled through. The driver had a whip that was fully twelve feet of leather and the concussion when he cracked it caused her to flinch. The carriage rocked, the rear wheels kicked stones. But standing aside, breathing the dust it left, she had time to think. Bunyip was right. She would bring harm to Toosey and that was the fact of it. Her heart turned and skipped like a pebble but her mind remained hard-set. She'd seen him knife the Irishman. Ketch would want him for that. If it led her to money, then all the better. Yet when she stepped off the grass and walked into the wake of the coach her heart was tolling louder and louder. For there was the matter of Toosey's boy pressing on her mind. The way he followed his father always a pace behind, as if he was in awe, was the same way she had followed her own. She walked, and her blood beat a march, and the road seemed narrower than ever.

At the bridge municipal police stood a loose guard on the rail platform on the Invermay side of the river. It seemed they held some concern for the continued operation of the western line, for they had cordoned off the loco and were stationed along the Invermay road at intervals. A mixed troop of municipals and mounted territory riders, teams of them, holding their positions at the terminal, to a man befouled from the violence and missing bits of uniform, bandaged or sutured, their unshaven faces dark in the sunshine. They looked at her limping along and she looked calmly away. No good asking them. She went on. Near the brewery a line of men were conveying crates off a flat-bedded cart while the horse stood meekly in its tack. They had a fire burning beneath a huge copper brewpot that filled a corner of the yard. It was being tended by a chap with a long packing rod allowing him some room from the heat. He was blacked up and sweating. She came by the gate and called.

Here!

The brewer looked up from his work.

You aint seen a chap come by, have you? Has a sack on his head?

The brewer stuck one hand behind the bib of his leather

apron and with the other kept tending the coals. Did you say sack?

A sack. A hood.

I seen him, said the brewer. We all seen him.

You see which way he went?

He come along there from the bridge and down thataways, the brewer said and pointed the glowing red end of the packing rod downriver. We all seen him, he said. How could you not?

Hall surveyed the ships at wharf and the street that ran by. Dockers worked a hand-cranked swivel crane to put wool aboard a steamboat. Bales like coffins, long and square and wrapped in canvas, descended into the dark. The men waving them down from the hold. She began to limp out towards them. The brewer watching after her called, What's the matter with your leg?

Nothin, she said and kept limping.

The street was a strip of hard powder guttered its whole length where carts ran, pressed between the warehouse rows and the creeping river. She crossed the ruts towards the wooden dock at river's edge. Below, banks of mud rife with weed, the oozing river. The water sluiced past slow and thick. She paused here. She was looking around and turning. Something had caught her eye. She was considering likely routes out and what lay along them and paying little attention to the white shape arranged against the brewery's roofing-tin fence. She stared for a full minute at the figure bunched in filthy shirt and pants, bunched like a child, before she understood it. She took a few steps. Then she pursed her lips and whistled.

Ketch, she called.

The hooded figure gave a start.

Christ, she said as she came limping over, no one forgets a bloody hangman, do they.

He did not speak. He seemed to be hungry or faint in the

heat for he hardly moved. Hall crossed and sat on her haunches, back against the corrugated wall. The wort boiling in the brewery was rich and bready and she inhaled a lungful.

Get up, she said as she breathed out. Let's go.

The hooded man said nothing.

I have him. Your man Toosey.

He lifted his head and Hall saw now the eyes inside, the black of wet flagstone. I don't know where Flynn is, he said.

Across the esplanade the unrigged ships strained on the bowlines, lifting with the tide. Hall watched them jostle. There was a realisation that sent her skin itching.

You aint been told, she said.

The hooded man looked at her.

Oh you aint been told. Oh hell.

Told what?

Hall stood and stepped away. You're his mate, she said. I thought you would've known. I thought you would've heard.

The hooded man stared.

He's stabbed him, she said. Toosey.

The hooded man did not seem to comprehend. He stared, his head tipping slightly.

Murdered him. Your mate the Irish.

Beyond the brewery fence the ringing of bottles as crates were stacked. The hooded man gazed off down the alley. When he turned back his eyes were pinched shut. What? he said.

Hall limped out into the sun. I know where he's goin, she said. Get up. I'll take you. There aint much time.

But the hooded man could not answer. He had slumped forward and wrapped his arms about his head. She looked down at the fellow huddled among the mess of gorse and this-tle on the fence line.

Are you sick or somethin? she said.

Then the hooded man gave a long ugly wail. He began to

pull at the cowl as if it caused him pain. It spooked Hall and for a moment she merely stood watching. He was pulling and the wailing noise he made whirred inside her ribs, behind her eyes. It brought the hairs up on her arms. The sound of a man carved out, left hollow, now collapsed and caving in. She crouched beside him.

Come on there, she said. Come on. This won't do.

The wailing eased to a spasmodic sob that shook the whole of his frame. He lay a long while, wracked at intervals by his grief and covering his head and clenching his fists. After a spell the hooded man ceased this noise and lay quietly. The whole front of his mask was wet and the skin beneath was like an undershirt of muscle. He lay and did not move. Jane Hall reached and shook him by the shoulder but the hooded man made no response. The cowl looked suffocating. A forked stick lay at her feet, which she took up and placed in her teeth. It was sour and chalky and she sucked it anyway.

She sat for a time just watching the hooded man where he lay. He was gazing at some point in the middle distance and when he breathed in the cotton made the shape of his mouth. He must have been only young for his features seemed to have a fineness to them, through the cloth, that a grown man's would never have. Hall chewed the stick and waited. She wanted to speak but instead turned to stare along the street, at the roped masts standing above the dock, the low-tide banks of mud. The sun hammered down. Blowflies landed along her arms. She waited and watched.

At length the hooded man sat up in a strange movement, as stiffly as a corpse. He sat and stared ahead and said not a word. Hall chewed her stick and studied him and she saw how the eyes inside the hood were dissimilar in appearance, the right being ringed by white and unmarred skin, the left by hard red scabs. She stopped chewing. When she leaned to get a better look the hooded man switched his gaze onto her. Hall tossed the stick. She leaned close to him. Finally she grasped a corner of the hood and tugged at it.

Why don't you take this off?

It caused the hooded man to burst into life. He rolled to his feet and backed away to the fence where he drew the pistol and brought it up trim. Hall flinched. She raised her hands. The barrel was scored and weathered as if it had seen a lot of killing. She held her hands before the muzzle.

Sorry! she said. Sorry. I'm sorry.

The hooded man stood with the gun out. He was breathing heavily.

I come to help, Hall said. I know where he's going.

The hooded figure swayed as if he might fall. You can't help me, he said.

How about you put that away?

For a moment he didn't move. The gun remained steadily upon her. Then his shoulders slumped and it dropped. He reset the action and wedged it behind his back. There was a looseness to his movements as he stepped into the sun, the strength gone from him in full, and he moved into the sun and stood gazing around himself at the bushes of gorse, the scotch thistle that wore each a purple flower, and he lowered his head and walked forward along the lane that led from the river behind the tin fence of the brewery. Hall rose in a sequence of hops with her bad leg.

Oi, she called. Where you goin?

The hooded man kept on walking.

Oi!

She limped after him. She came alongside. Wait, she said. Listen. I know where he's lodged.

I don't care.

He's killed your mate and you don't care?

The hooded man shook his heavy white head.

Then where you goin? Hall said.

To find my father.

Forget visitin right now. You have a chance to settle with Toosey. A chance to get your money. I know where he'll be. I know how to do the deed.

I don't care.

So what? So he robs from you and kills your mate and you just let him? A hangman afraid of justice. What a story.

I'm not a hangman.

Well whatever you are, I'll tell you one thing. There must be plenty of food in your cupboard for you to turn your back on a sum of money like that.

The hooded man pulled up. His shoulders straightened and when he turned his head the eyeholes grew misaligned so that the eyes inside appeared to belong to some imprisoned thing peering through cracks in a wall. He took a long steadying breath and let it out loudly. There was the pealing of beer bottles, the cries and calls of dockmen, and these two staring at each other in silence. It was the hooded man who looked away first. He put his hands under his armpits like he was cold.

That man, he said and he stopped. His voice broke a little. That man, he said but he could not continue.

I know, Hall said. But here is your chance to settle with him.

I want to see my father.

Don't worry about your father right now. It's your money and your mate Flynn is what should concern you.

It happened then that a pair of police came by from the muster at Invermay and they saw Hall standing in the untenanted backlot beside the brewery and saw the curious figure beside her and they crossed the road from the river, walking with an easy calm like the world for them held no fear. The taller of the two leaned towards his companion to whisper before pointing out the shaved-headed girl limping about in the sun. They were locals and wore the municipal crest on their caps and carried on their belts long and heavy billyclubs. They stopped and briefly conferred there in the road and then one called out. A sudden booming sound.

I aint forgot about you, Hall.

She swung about and was startled. Constable Beatty, she said and tried not to frown. Yes sir. I know, sir.

Damn my livin soul if I aint.

I'm easily found, sir.

Found? Beatty said. They won't find you when I'm done. Not a chance. I will bury you so deep the devil will bump his horns on your arse.

Very well, sir.

Your miserable little body here, your arms and legs some-wheres else. You hear?

Yes sir.

Beatty leaned his head around. His hat was too large and it folded down the tops of his ears. He was staring behind Hall at the hooded man. At the sight of the two municipal men the hooded man had stiffened and reached one hand to his back in nervous fashion. Hall slapped the hooded man on the arm and shook her head.

Would you look at that, Beatty said and nudged his mate with the point of his elbow. Now that there's a sight for a new man like you.

Who's this fellow with you, sir? Hall said and grinned.

This is Constable Webster.

Afternoon, Webster said.

He'll be in charge of floggin the arse off you once I shift to sergeant.

Hall smiled at him a little too broadly. No one flogs quite like you, sir.

Shut your mouth.

Yes sir.

They both studied the hooded man.

What's on his head? Webster said.

Thinks he's Jack Ketch, sir.

Does he now.

But he's no bother, sir. None at all.

Beatty moved closer. Each pace he took set the billyclub swinging like the weight in a clock and he moved about and stood and stared hard at the hooded man. Is there somethin amiss with him? he said. In the brain, I mean.

The hooded man was poised with one arm cocked behind his back, his eyes flicking between the two municipals.

No sir, Hall said. Just drunk.

Drunk. Oh deary me.

And how is Mrs. Beatty, sir? Hall said.

What?

The missus, sir. How is she? I was two years under her tutelage at the rough school at St. Leonards if you remember.

Mention my wife again and you'll come in for a proper floggin. By Christ you will. A floggin from arsehole to breakfast.

Yes sir. Sorry, sir.

Beatty let his shrunken eyes hang on Hall. He had a hand on his club and was twisting it on the leather thong securing it to his belt. Course you could spare yourself, he said. If you know what I mean.

There's nothin I know worth tellin, sir, she said and held up her palms. Honest.

A fellow was killed, he said. Last night. In the troubles. Not far from the police house. Old cookin knife in him. What do you know about that?

Hall looked sidewards at the hooded man where he stood head bowed and round of shoulder.

You hear what I said, Hall?

Yes sir.

Know anythin about it?

No sir.

She's a good one for gabbing, he said to Webster.

I'll remember that, Webster said.

Give her a bit of stick. Makes her talkative.

I bet.

Beatty pointed his club at Hall in an offhand manner. You'll hear somethin, won't you? A smart young lass like yourself.

Hall licked her lips. Do you know his name? she said. This dead fellow?

No. He was quite elderly. Wearin a woman's gold ring too, so it wasn't no robbery.

You'll be first to know it, sir. When I hear who done it.

I better be. Or I'll flog bruises into you like tiger stripes. Won't I?

You will, sir. You're a gem for floggins, you are.

Beatty stared at her for a time. He twisted his billyclub. Then he clapped Webster on the shoulder and walked off along the esplanade with his arms crossed loosely behind him. Standing in the shade of the tall sheet-iron fence Hall watched them amble away and once they'd covered some distance she spat in their direction and dried her chin.

Wonderful how I tracts the bluebottles. Come round me like flies they do. Tract em wonderful. Even when I'm well behaved.

A long spell of quiet passed between them. When Hall turned again the hooded man had crouched among the thistles with his head pressed in the crook of his arm. He was squatting there, staring at nothing.

Hear them two just now? Hall said. You hear it? They don't know who killed your mate.

The hooded man looked up and his eyes were shot with blood.

Toosey will escape this, Hall said. He'll get clean away.

That seemed to put off the hooded man a little, for he dropped his head.

Don't you even care?

The hooded man could not answer. His head hung low between his arms.

If you won't go get your money off him, I'll tell Beatty. Tell him who killed Flynn. Tell him where to find the fiend.

No, the hooded man said. No police. We don't yield to the Crown. Not ever.

You what?

The hooded man was rubbing his arms. He stood and he pushed back his sleeves. Hall could see the foul scabbed scarring that ran to his right elbow and stained also the skin of that hand. You need to understand something, he said.

What? Understand what?

The hooded man took a breath. He lowered his head, grasped the point of his cowl, and drew it off.

Hall's eyes grew round with wonder. Jesus Lord fuck almighty, she said.

BATTEN STREET

B atten Street in the early afternoon. A lane of hovels in plain hardwood board, rooved some of them in slate, some in sheets of rusted iron. Set hard upon the footpath in the London manner was one lower and meaner than most. Toosey could feel his heart beating in his arm, a throb that slowed the mind and made him feeble. He stepped onto the verandah of this place and knocked at the door. He moved back. William came beside him, so close their shoulders touched. A child's face appeared in the window by the door and then another and they were boys, unwashed, their hair still rough from the bed. They watched him cautiously.

Who are you then? the first one said and his voice was stifled by the glass. He wouldn't have been more than eight and was missing his front teeth.

Is your father about? Toosey yelled.

The boy turned. Pa, someone's here, he called.

A reply came from deep in the house.

Chap with a bad arm, the boy called.

The reply, indistinct.

Like a bushman or somethin, the boy called.

There were more sounds, the thundering of boots, a wailing child. The door opened. It was Brother Payne standing in the hallway and he smiled when he saw Toosey and his son on the verandah, but Toosey did not return it. Payne stepped into the street and looked up and down and then he turned and took stock of Toosey, the crust of blood on his shirt, the black and lifeless arm.

You don't miss trouble, do you.

I've had kinds you've never heard of.

Found your boy though.

Was him as found me, Toosey said. Out by the Star.

Payne clapped William on the shoulder like an old friend.
Good man, he said. Your father needs some lookin after.

At the rear of the house was a square of ungrassed earth, an
outhouse standing open to the day. Either side each of the
neighbouring yards had such outhouses. You could see them
through the low paling fence that had in part been removed for
firewood. Payne led them along a side lane into the yard and
closed the gate. He was like a landed vulture with his craned
neck and his rounded hump pressing the cotton of his shirt
taut. In the yard his hawking cart rested on its shafts and
Toosey walked to the pool of shade it threw and crouched in it
fully. He removed his hat and tossed it. His arm hung mon-
strously at his chest, throbbing with an evil heat. Listen now,
he said. I need your pistol.

Oh I need your pistol he says. Just like that.

Toosey rubbed the perspiration from his neck. He
looked sick.

What in the name of buggery is goin on? Payne said.

Ask me where the money is.

Why? Where is it?

Lost.

You what?

All of it. The entire two hundred.

Oh my bleedin Lord.

She's under the care of a Chinaman. Hidden somewhere.

So you want me pistol to square him away?

The sun was drubbing down. Toosey dried his chin on his
sleeve. Well, he said, that will be a start.

Brother Payne closed his eyes, turned and walked off. After
a while he pulled his pipe from a pocket and tapped it out onto

his palm and ran his palm down the long drab stain on his pants produced by this habit. We are told to put back our swords, he said. For all who take the sword shall perish by the sword.

It's me or him.

No, Thomas. It will be the both of you.

Crouching there in the shade, swaying, sweat darkening the folds of his shirt, Toosey felt ready to fall. He could not look at Payne. William knelt beside him in the cart's slanted shadow and it was a comfort, just the heaven-sent sight of him. He rubbed the boy on the head and felt well.

I shouldn't need to tell you there is only one who bears a sword, Payne said. He does not bear it in vain.

A gate somewhere far off slammed. A dog started up.

Now you are meant for history, Payne said.

Toosey was grinning as he looked up, but it was a grin of pain. Even with one arm I'm twice what that Chinaman is. Show me your pistol and I'll give him hell.

So this is a dust-up now?

Brother, I either fight or I die. Aint no middle ground in this. Not no more. Here, Toosey held up his crook arm. This was not lightly earned, he said.

Payne put the empty pipe in his mouth. He chewed the stem.

Catch my drift? Toosey said.

If I aint replied, it's because my mind's at work on the problem of how you've lived this long.

I hear that a lot.

Don't reckon you'll live long enough to hear it again, so enjoy it.

Listen now, Toosey said. I know I'm a fool—

Worse than that.

I know. I hear you. But we have passage booked at four. The *Derwent*. Bound for Melbourne. We must have the sovereigns by then. Miss that boat and we're buried.

Payne crossed the yard in his bent hobble as if he was forever at the hilt of his cart and he stood beside Toosey, patted him on the shoulder, and he squinted, curious man that he was, squinted down at his brother-in-law, the creases of his eyes as deep as knife scars. It always worried me, he said. The way you revered the lad. Like it was only him making you whole in God's eyes.

It is.

Well, Payne said and the pipe bobbed up and down. It's led you to this. Your reverence. I hope you see that.

Toosey quietly stared at the dirt. He had no answer.

What do you say, young William? To your father's scheme?

William was fingering something from the mud and when it came loose it was a long splinter of iron broken off from a cart spring. A point at one end that would pass clean through you. He wiped it on his pants.

There's another fellow will give us a pistol, he said. If you won't.

Payne nodded. He chewed his pipe and looked first at Thomas Toosey and then, with a slow tilt of the head, his son. The apple aint fallen far, he said.

This is done that we might live, Toosey said.

Yes, live. But how? With him seein the world along the barrel of a gun?

We do it, or he's an orphan. That's a hell of a way to see the world.

Payne grunted. He shuffled over to his cart and bent and riffled through the loose and rusted implements in the tray, lifting things, setting them aside, and he pulled free a twisted bundle of cloth. It was yellow muslin used to boil puddings and he unwound the length of it around his knuckles and revealed at the centre an antique firelock pistol. The mechanism and the stock guard were ornamented in brass and a thick jade-green patina covered these parts. It was Scotch in design and had a flared crown-shaped butt fitted with a vent pick that formed the topmost jewel. He held it out to Toosey.

You won't be talked out of it, he said.

No.

Then put this under the Chinaman's nose. See what he thinks.

Toosey took the pistol. He turned it. Does it fire?

No. But there's safety in an appeal to lead and powder.

All right, Toosey said, looking the pistol over. All right. He stuck it in his pocket. It will have to do.

Besides which, the police are occupied. They will not hurry to help a Chinaman today.

He don't need them. He's armed.

Is he?

Bastard gives it fire at every chance too.

Well, Payne said. Better keep your head down.

Not this time. This time I've out-thought him.

Payne fished a stem-winding pocket watch from his trousers and snapped it open. I make it two, he said. You'll need time. An hour. That don't leave you long.

Both turned then to the boy. He was picking rust off the shard of iron. His head bent, the mop of his hair cast across his forehead. When he looked up his hair parted and he saw them staring at him and his face fell. He rose to his feet. What? he said.

I'll see him aboard the steamer, Payne said.

Now I aint asked you to do that, Toosey said.

But Payne just waved him away. Be sure and get that gold. I'll have him at the wharf when you come.

William's eyes jumped from one to the other. No, he said. I'm goin too. With Pa.

Stay with your uncle, Toosey said.

No. You promised. You said you would keep me near.

I know.

So I'm going with you.

No.

Pa. Please.

Come on now.

Please.

Come on. You saw what that Chinaman done last night. He's as likely to shoot the both of us.

Then don't go. We'll take another boat. We'll find somewhere to hide.

Toosey gave a gentle shake of the head. This put the boy all in a work and he clenched his fists and frowned. He turned away from his father.

You're my soldier, Toosey said. You're my fighter.

His boy folded his arms.

See this done and we're free. We're gone.

But his boy wouldn't look at him. Instead he walked away to the outhouse.

I'll have him there, Payne said.

Toosey glanced around the yard one last time. He raised his hat to Payne in a gesture of thanks and of brotherhood, and stuck it on his crown and pushed it. A dog yowled in a yard beyond. He wanted to say more to the boy. Promise more. What was it worth though? Air, spit, sentiment. Nothing. Worth nothing. What counted now was deed. The boy kicked a grass tuft with an outsized boot. The sense that he would never see the lad again struck so hard that he felt unsteady. He looked to the blue fullness of the sky and the distant smoke and his ears boomed with the gale-wind of his blood. No thought but the thought of that loss. A loss to crush him like a noon shadow into the pits of his boots. He breathed in, breathed out, and hoped to hell it would never be. He left along the lane.

At the corner he stopped and looked either way along Charles Street and adjusted the useless pistol. The sound of the dog cut through him. Men were coming and going from the troubles, young men with a perilous certainty of movement, some armed, some calling brashly as if they owned the street. He lowered his eyes. He hugged his arm to himself and set out. The weight of the gun tugged in his pocket. As he walked he trawled over the sorrowful acts of his life and he saw, like he always saw, how he'd never done well by anyone. He'd lied, killed, stolen. He watched the road ahead and ground his jaw. In making a man of himself he'd given up all other mantles. Other futures. But see his boy safe and well and that history was rethreaded through a new eyelet, to be pulled as he saw fit. That was the only sort of acquittal for which he could hope now. A gallows' reprieve. He mopped his forehead. He turned towards the Star of the North.

THE HOODED MAN

There was a glazier's scaffold set below the hotel windows, poles lashed up and braced with crossbeams and a running board slung between them. Perched upon it three Chinese boys at rest. They were dressed as white folk and ate from a cob loaf handed along the line as white labourers might and as Toosey came up the footpath past the head-height row of swinging legs one of the boys wished him a good afternoon in perfect English. Toosey kept his eyes away. At the steps to the hotel he stopped and looked back, all three watching him but saying nothing. The narrowness of their eyes like an insult. He scratched his balls through his pants. Exchanged stares with them. The first of the three said some words of Chinese and quiet laughter went between them.

He nodded and turned away. Not today, he said. Today the joke's on you. He disappeared inside the ruined double-doors.

The lobby was empty. He had his hand on the pistol in his pocket as he crossed the polished boards and fronted up at the reception counter. The lodgings book lay open. It was dim and he saw now that the gaslights were off. He drummed his fingers on the desk. There was an ornate brass bell on the varnished oak and he spun it around in place, studying the flowers engraved upon it, the Latin inscription. He had a smirk on his rimpled face when he raised the bell and rang it.

At that sound the clerk stepped from the side door. There were crumbs on his chin and he was chewing something. When he saw Toosey there grinning like a charlatan and holding Payne's rusted pistol he paused. Toosey merely waited and watched. The clerk's face fell. He called to Chung and crumbs flew.

Yeah, said Toosey. Get the maggot out here where I can see him.

The proprietor in his white gloves emerged from the same door. He saw Toosey and saw his gun and he backed away. The two men side by side, the lank Chinese wearing a frown and the clerk grave and stately in his tie and high collar, as upright as men on a flogging post. Toosey moved the pistol from one to the other. He wasn't smiling any more.

He needs a long spoon that eats with the devil, he said.

Pigfucker, said Chung. I shit on your ancestor. You pig-fucker.

Steady now.

Get out my hotel.

Not this time, said Toosey. I aint goin nowheres.

The two men eyed him nervously.

Now, Toosey said. Produce that gold for me without a fuss. Without no bloody municipals comin by. Without no pissin about.

Chung raised a long, gloved finger and pointed at him. No gold here, he said. Gold gone.

Toosey exhaled. He shook his head. That is a lie, he said.

No gold—

Shut your mouth, you cunt-eyed fuck.

Toosey walked towards him. He held the pistol close under the proprietor's chin. That is the last lie you ever speak to me, he said. The last. You hear?

The tall man's nostrils pumped and his lean mouth tightened. You go fuck pig's arsehole, he said.

Now, Toosey said. I am quite nettled. Understand? Quite nettled indeed. I'm as likely to give fire through your fuckin teeth. Split your cunt face clean apart. How would that be?

Chung ground his jaw.

Best you produce that gold, Toosey said. Right now. Fore I act the wild man.

A few instants passed where the Chinese stood facing that darkly visaged bushman. Toosey grinned at him, a grin of threat. His shirt spattered in blood, his armpits ringed with sweat, his hand a swollen grotesquery at his chest. The Chinaman's puckered brow flattened a little at what he saw.

You take gold you go, Chung said.

That's right. I go.

You no come back.

I'm as gone as the proverbial rat, old mate.

Chung gave a snort. He ran a white glove over his greased black hair. Then he knelt down and prised loose a false floorboard and buried his arm to shoulder inside the cavity. When he stood he had the bag of sovereigns cradled like a child at his breast. He dumped it on the desk making the books and calling bell all jump. Toosey was grinning even more. You almost had one past me, he said. I'll give you that. You almost had me believe it.

Neither of the men moved. They stared at Toosey and waited.

He pointed with the gun. Open her up, he said.

The Chinaman unknotted the throat.

Take out two bits.

Reaching inside, he retrieved a single immaculate coin. Even in the dull hotel interior it threw a light that winked off the walls in a gleam of fire. He lay the coin on the counter.

And another, said Toosey.

Chung pulled one more coin.

That's for the door. The window. The rest of it.

The Chinaman glared, his nostrils grew. He said nothing.

Now listen good, said Toosey and he shook the pistol. This is what will happen. I intend on retrieving me swag and other bits from me room. You have a palm gun somewhere. I know it. When I walk up them stairs I don't want you to send a bullet through me. So give me the gun here.

The Chinaman gave a snort.

I will shoot the man to pieces that betrays me. Be sure of that.

The clerk reached under the counter. He fished around. Chung was delivering a baleful glare but the clerk seemed unrepentant and after a moment he came up with the derringer and slid it butt first along the desk to Toosey.

Good, Toosey said. We are all friends now. No need for no one to shoot no one.

The derringer was loaded. Toosey laid down Payne's useless pistol and took the American gun in hand and cocked the hammer with his thumb. It was small and cold and solid-feeling. He looked it over. He pointed it at them. That old bitch weren't even primed, he said and he wanted to laugh. I bailed you up with her and she was as empty as a cup. That's a trick I learned off some lads out Liffey way.

The two men looked at each other and looked at Toosey and said not a word.

You can keep her now, he said. A parting gift.

He swept up the bag under his arm and rounded towards the stairs. As he walked away he glanced at them, pointed the pistol, unsure what they would do, what they would say, but he crossed the broad wood-panelled lobby with his boots falling heavily and they both remained still. Outside, the Chinese boys had taken to horseplaying along the platform and their shadows cast through the glassless holes like spectres, eerily silent. He crossed to the stairs and started upwards and there was only the squeal of boards as he ascended. Then he was gone into the murk of the landing.

In the first-floor hallway the gas lamps were out so he was presented with a den of perfect gloom. Toosey looked along its entirety left and right before advancing. At the door to his room he dropped the coin sack and dug the key from his pocket with his one good hand but when he bent to the lock he saw how the door was ajar. He straightened up. It swung slackly as he pushed it back. He fished out Chung's pistol. Stepping into the room he found it empty, his swag and other pieces still on the floor rug where he had placed them, the grand posted bed undisturbed. Likely the Chinaman had searched it for more gold. The greedy little coolie. He stowed the gun.

He was grinning to himself as he toed the coin sack over the threshold and knelt beside his swag. Grinning for his own sublime luck. He pinned the swag beneath his knee and yanked loose the knot. With his bad arm at his chest he chased the coin sack onto the unfurled canvas and he rolled it and secured the rope with a half hitch. He pulled the gun and placed it on the floor. Then he sat for a moment in silence. His mind seemed to ratchet over and lock, like a piece of clockwork, onto a single insistent thought. He'd done it. The boy was found. The gold. The liberty. Not since he'd shipped here, manacled as a child of fourteen, had he such hope of life. They'd board a boat, him and the boy, and by week's end be gone off the island for good. Starting in Melbourne with pockets full. Free of all concern. Some good could yet come of this vile business.

It was as he was sitting and considering his prospects that the door behind him creaked open.

He looked around. The door swung in and settled on the wall. Standing in the void was a tall thin figure cowled in stained cotton, fissures cut where its eyes were. The figure clutched a brown paper package under one arm and in the other hand was a gun and the gun was trained on Toosey. He frowned at it. The figure entered the room and pushed the door closed and then it just stood quietly. A forlorn and slipshod effigy of a man, breathing so hard he could hear it.

Jesus, Toosey said.

The hooded figure said nothing. Toosey looked at Chung's pistol but the figure kicked it away to a corner and that was it. He was done for.

What do you want? he said but in his deepest parts he already knew.

The figure inclined its head. The hood sagged over.

A modest amount of disquiet started to settle upon Toosey. It was an uncommon feeling for him. I expect, he said, I expect it's the money you want.

The figure was breathing fast.

Toosey pushed the swag forward. Here. Have it.

It aint the money, said the figure and its voice was quivering.

Then it reached up and with its gun hand gripped the roughly stitched hem and in one deft jerk removed the hood. Inside was a girl barely reckonable as human. A wide and raw-looking burn mantled the whole left part of her head, pocked and blistered and bleeding. The skin above the right eye had drooped and her ear was a dark nub plastered to her skull. She stood breathing hard and holding the pistol on him. With the black morass of her hair, the weeping sores, the scars. Toosey saw in that moment the whole of his failure. He'd been dragging her along like a shadow. A girl barely older than his own son, made pain-mad by his acts and spitting the taste of his name from her mouth. He was the belly-crawler and she was the fighter and these were God's own facts.

I never meant for that, he said.

Her eyes welled and ran but she never blinked.

It was an accident, he said. What I did.

The girl took a step towards him with the gun up. You killed me father, she said.

No.

Liar!

He come at me, Toosey said.

You killed him.

I warned him.

You killed him.

He give me no say.

Get down.

What?

Right where you are. Down flat.

Toosey was staring up at her, a sudden woe in his old creased eyes. What do you want, girl?

Blood. Blood is what I want.

Aint you lost enough?

She levered back the hammer and the sound of the barrel and the sound of the lock was huge in the small wood-walled apartment. What I lost is what you took, she said. You think I'm a frightened little girl. Think I won't do nothin against you. Well you thought wrong on that.

Toosey shook his head. He give me no say. There was nothin—

Shut your hole.

Look, he said and he held up his crook arm. See what he left me with. He come for me, girl, and you know it.

The girl had started crying and her face contorted into an outlandish ritual mask. We never done wrong by you, she said.

No. You never.

Look at me, she screamed.

Toosey stared.

What have you done? she screamed.

Please just put that piece away.

What have you done?

Girl, listen.

Get down. Down.

She clasped both hands on the butt and steadied the gun. Toosey did not move.

Down, she screamed.

This aint right.

There's five shots in here. Five. I can make you howl just how I howled. Make you plead for it to stop. Now if you want that, then keep playin me.

Hurtin you was never me intention. I give you a push. That's all.

Shut up.

Fire in here and half the town will come runnin.

Let them come, she said and the fervour of it was wholly convincing.

Slowly and with his eyes fixed on the gun Toosey began to stand.

Get down, she said.

But he did not. He moved onto one knee. He raised up and when he was halfway to standing she kicked out his leg. He tumbled sideways on the patterned rug, his arm in agony as he came down on it. Fuckin mother Mary, he said. He watched as she picked up the hood and threw it to him.

Put it on, she said.

He craned his neck to look up. Eh?

The girl leaned down and pressed the cold muzzle against his forehead. The breath wheezed through her ruined nose. Put it on, she hissed.

Please, he said. Not this way.

Still holding the gun on him, she tugged the stained and stinking rag over his head. The eyeholes were misaligned and all he saw was the inner darkness it contained. He felt his own damp vapour on his skin as if buried alive. He lay huffing inside the hood in a mounting fear as she stood above him bearing the big pistol in her fists like a leg of iron, levering back the mechanism with her thumb.

I want to know something, she said.

Toosey turned his head but there was nothing to see.

You killed your baby, she said. All them years ago. Killed it. Buried it.

No, he said. God no. I never. He was my boy.

Liar.

I swear it. Give me a bible. I'll swear.

I know you're lyin. They locked you up.

That false and murderous bitch sold me for it. She was the one. He was me little boy. He was the pulse of my heart.

Don't you dare say that. Don't you dare.

Wait, he said. It's the truth.

Put your head down. Down. Now!

Wait.

She pushed his head down with her boot.

Wait, he said. Tell me son.

He could hear the rattle of the hammer. She removed her boot.

Tell William that—

The first shot caught him in the throat. He jerked and clapped his palm over the wound and the blood burst through his fingers. His cry was full of fluid. He choked. She worked the hammer and fired a round that snapped back his head and punched a smoking hole in the hood that discharged in a gout. A pool formed that crept across the rug. He slouched over.

There was freckled blood on her knuckles, which she wiped again and again. The hooded man lay quietly, his head as lop-sided as a raggedy doll, his rope of hair hanging in the slick. She rubbed her fingers and she rubbed her arms but in those small acts she found no relief. She stood long looking down at the wash of gore inching outward, at the hood turning red. She looked away. For a time she just stared at the wall panelling, one hand over her skittering heart that she might slow it, the other gripping the hot smoking pistol. From his pool the hooded man surveyed the room in startlement.

She was standing thus, staring, when the noise from

downstairs started. Her head raised as if from a trance. The voices of men, their boot-thump in the lobby. There was a brown paper package under her arm and she dropped it on the floor. They would soon come and she knew it.

For a time she knelt on the floorboards looking at the package. She thought of her father and mother, gone from this life, into a cleft of godless earth and gone. There were her sisters though. Alone without her, unprotected, destitute. Given in care of a neighbour. Now, she was needed. Now, she could not be caught here, with him. A time might come when they found her but now she needed to see the money home. She lowered the gun. She opened the package.

Inside was the crude fringed overskirt Jane Hall had chased up, roughly constructed of cotton the colour of hay. Standing, she stripped to her boots and threaded on the dress. It felt alien after so long clothed as a man. Cold about the ankles. Stifling. She laced it at the front. Then she wrapped her old road clothes and the pistol and the gruesome hood in the sheet of paper and over her scabrous head she drew a bonnet. There was a floral handkerchief, which she knotted at her throat. As she was retying the package she saw Toosey's bedroll.

The banknotes. She unrolled the squalid bundle and a sack fell to the floor like a cannonball. She stood still, looking at the sack. Not banknotes but coins, some pounds of them. She was at a loss. She looked around the room. There was nothing else for it. In haste she rolled the dimpled sack among the clothes in the paper and retied the string. It was a poor sort of ruse that might fool the simple. Her heart ran at speed.

In the hallway she stood the door ajar and began towards the landing, the package pressed awkwardly under her arm. Someone was thundering up the stairs. She lowered her eyes. Slowed her breathing. Thought of her little sisters and the spread of Quamby land. A time would come, but not yet. Please not yet.

Two constables appeared then at the top of the stairs. They saw the girl hovering in the hall's dim void, hugging her package, head down, and they drew their sticks. She stopped. Two men she'd seen. One called Beatty. The other Webster. They nodded and touched their caps.

Beggin your pardon, marm, Beatty said.

She dared not look.

You better get along now, he said. There is a lout in here has fired off a gun.

I heard it, she said. In there.

Right. We'll have him out. Stand aside, marm.

She gave a faint curtsey and began to pass by.

Oh dear, he said. Your face. What's happened?

No, please sir. Don't look. Please. It's terrible.

She turned her head aside, but Beatty only leaned to get a better view. Well, he said. Yes. That must be painful.

Webster was staring at her. His mouth was wide open. She looked down at the floor and looked anywhere but at him. Her heart was so loud she thought they would hear it. Beatty was tapping his billystick in his palm. He gazed a long while at her. Her fingers shook. She closed her fists and stared at the floor. Beatty cleared his throat.

Excuse us, marm, he said. Best you move back.

She gave a dim smile, which was all the pain would allow, and made for the landing.

The municipals approached the door and Beatty bent and gave a rap on the wood, holding his ear by the panels. This is Beatty of the Launceston police house, he said. If you is in there come out peaceably.

Silence. He nodded at Webster and then he pushed back the door, standing aside from it. As the scene within was exhibited Beatty put his hand to his mouth and drew a sharp breath. He took a faltering step backward. What the devil, he said.

Caislin had started quickly down the stairs. She could hear

the constables entering the room and she did not look back. She held tight to the package that the coins would make no sound. At the foot of the bannister a group of Chinese boys stood talking amongst themselves. With them a Chinese porter kit up in a formal tailed coat and white gloves as well. When they saw the girl coming they shifted around and watched her. She gave them a sidelong glance. Going fast, hugging the package. The boys were wearing their faded hats inside and they removed them politely as she descended out into the room. She began towards the street.

Beatty called down from the landing. You have a mess up here. Bugger of a mess. Someone has done for your lout.

The Chinaman was studying her and studying the bundle under her arm and she could see the mechanism of his mind beginning to piece the elements presented there, see it registering with him. He started walking. At the pair of shattered doors she stopped and looked back. The Chinaman was wearing a snarl as he pushed through the boys towards her. She stepped out onto the street.

Stop! he called. Stop!

She bolted, holding her skirts up and revealing the road-worn boots beneath. She ran to the alley cutting beside the hotel and turned down it. Jane Hall was waiting there among the shadows. She came forward with her hand out.

Move yourself.

A tall paling gate opened into a shared lot and Hall kicked it and shoved Caislin through. They ran, the pair of them, around piles of unlaid bricks and footings dug for some unfinished place, the dirt turning under their feet, and Hall hiking her leg out wide in her odd hobble and they reached another fence over which Hall dove headfirst, hardly slowing. Caislin stopped. She hitched up her voluminous skirts and chucked her leg up. A cool wind blew about her uncovered nether parts. She dropped the package, jumped after it and she could hear in the distance the small cries of the hotel Chinaman as he sought them in the alley. Hall limped for the next fence and Caislin grubbed up the package and followed.

A braced gate led onto Cameron Street and there was a clothiers here and a druggist and some folk were at the business of boarding up their stores before the curfew when the gate walloped open. Emerging onto the footpath a shaved-headed girl lame in one leg and another with a face half torched beneath her bonnet. Rattled and guilty and awkward for it, the pair of them cut among the wary citizens and the mounted police venturing by. They made out for the river sliding by at street's end, the water rippling with sun, hand in hand, hearts a-thud.

The Queen's Wharf

In the hour they waited by the wharf, William watched and wished so hard for his father to appear that his legs began to tremble and his lip to quiver. Ships were docked along the pier, fat, rope-webbed sloops, screw steamers out of Port Melbourne, and they heaved with the pull of the tide on the mooring lines making them fast to the wharf and it was silent save for this creaking, save for the talk between Payne and a fellow off a whaler. The naked stands of masts tottered and William never moved. He folded his arms. He could see the town spread on the hill and he could see the people in the streets, the mounted police making little order, shadowed, the whole of it, below an apocalyptic smoke.

The man that Payne had struck conversation with was no regular man but a half-caste Tasmanian of the islands. They took up a place on a bale of wool. There were many such bales and crates and boxes on flatbed carts and no dockhands to load them, no crews to sail. The Tasmanian, whose name was Harrington, put to Payne a string of questions about the course of the riots, the nature of the fires, and the response of police. His shoulders as he spoke rose and fell inside his heavy seafaring woollens. His hands were hard as oak and painted in Indian ink with waves and curving designs. Payne knew him somehow. As a well-known bag of wind he knew everyone.

White goats, the Tasmanian said and he had a voice like the

sawing of timber. They bleat and they cry, he said, but there is no action. Men. Men would burn the town.

More louts than men most of em, Payne said.

This Harrington reached to his belt and there was a long low hiss followed by the ring of metal as he pulled a boat spade and held it to the side. He must have lately sharpened it for the rim gleamed in the late sun. Take the ears, he said. Take the fingers. That is the old way.

Not no more, Payne said. Now they take furniture.

I would burn the furniture.

I don't doubt that.

Harrington put the spade over his knee. He stared narrowly at the town.

Hard against the far end of the pier sat a mighty three-masted barquentine. This was the *Derwent* and she made for a very quiet sight. Square-rigged of foremast, rigged on the main, bobbing on her rope but giving forth neither steam nor coal smoke from her funnel and her deck, her gangway unattended by crew of any kind save fleets of seagulls. William looked at her and felt cold. She wasn't about to sail. Her crew must have been drunk and rioting with the rest. His father needed to know this. He was hazarding his life in service of making her four o'clock passage. Yet they sat, Payne and the other man, without any thought of leaving.

The start of it, Payne said, was removing your kind. Shot the worst. Exiled the rest. Then what? Then there's a country full of the clans of Europe. Living on land without law.

Let them eat each other, the Tasmanian said.

That we are. My word.

William could not listen anymore. He walked away along the edge staring at the far side of the river where, like a place split by an axe blow, it emptied from ruptured cliffs, foaming below the bridge spanning the gorge mouth. We ought to go find Pa, he said. If the boat won't sail.

Harrington tapped spade on his thigh. He turned his dark face along the hill where the town smoked quietly. Ho, he said and pointed. Someone comes.

They all turned. At the far end of the pier walked a pair of men in level stride past the customs booth where officers would sit in safer times than these and they were conversing together, their hands moving and gesturing, the wind carting away their voices.

I know that fellow, William said and he walked forward. Mr. Fisher, he said.

Of the two it was the smaller that looked up. He wore no hat and the bald part of his head had grown pink with the sun. He straightened his pince nez.

Oh it's you, he said. The nameless son of a nameless father. I warned you. You won't board without paying.

She aint sailin, William said and thrust his chin at the *Derwent*. Her fires aint even lit.

But George Fisher paid him no attention. He was watching the Tasmanian. That man has an axe, he said. Why does he have an axe?

It's a boat spade.

Harrington grinned and his beard crawled. Fisher looked alarmed. He waved his finger. Listen, I don't like threats. If this is—

I told you. It's a spade.

Kindly put that away, he called but Harrington grinned out of his great black beard and sat as he was.

The *Derwent*, William said. Is she sailin or not?

Fisher looked down at him. You want to board without paying, is that what?

No. I want to know if we have passage today. Cause it don't look that way.

Who is he?

Him? Harrington of Cape Barren.

How do, the Tasmanian said.

Do you mean a threat with that weapon, sir?

Answer the child's question, Harrington said. Or I just might.

Fisher turned away with a long exhaled breath, almost a hiss, and nodded at the gallant-looking gent he'd been speaking to earlier. The gent had on a white hat, which he removed and tucked very formally under his armpit. The brass buttons on his coat were full of the sun.

Captain, she's your ship, Fisher said. Your crew to control.

The captain drummed his fingers on his hat.

I expect the loss in refunding tickets will be deducted from your wages, Fisher said.

The captain eyebrow's reared up. They won't wring much from that stone, he said.

But wring they will. Find your crew and save them the bother.

How would I ever find the bastards up there? It's a shambles.

Whatever you say, Fisher said and turned down his mouth. It's not my money at hazard.

William stood a moment looking between them, to the captain, the black, and finally his uncle. The sun formed a resplendent band upon his face behind which his eyes at first soft began to harden and he turned on his toes, seized suddenly with purpose. He walked up the pier. Passing Payne, he snapped with his fingers and tossed his head as if to call him to heel. Payne rose gingerly. He slapped Harrington on the back in the way of good friends. When Payne followed the boy in his bent-backed trot along the pier raising gulls off the decking, their wind lifting his sparse hair, Harrington slung his spade and called after them, Take the ears! The ears! And like a chain-gang of two in single file, heads bowed for the sun, William and his uncle entered again the disorderly city.

*

In the late afternoon they formed up before the Star of the North Hotel where men were massed at the entrance and where backed to the doors was a cart drawn by a dirt-brown mare. The mare stood entirely still like it was no horse at all but a waxwork of one. In the shade it cast squatted a team of street children and they were watching the hotel doors, waiting for something, waiting all with bulbous eyes. Payne went among the men there putting questions to them and they would lift their hats, scratch, and then shake their heads or point him towards another fellow. When he looked back at William he was solemn, the creases of his eyes grown deep. He nodded once and turned away.

A broad oilcloth covered the bed of the cart, over the sideboards to the wheels, and it was not long until the constables came out of the smashed hotel doors carrying a body between them, grunting, sweating, and swung it up onto the cloth. They were men that William knew well, Beatty and the new man Webster who'd lately been at his side. They had on butcher's aprons over their uniforms and the blood showed like black grease, as they wiped their hands on the heavy leather bibs. Several in the crowd removed their hats, several averted their eyes. The children at the wheel of the cart wore looks of haggard fright.

William Toosey began to quiver as he stood watching it all. The dead man stared at the sky. The wound in his forehead big enough to take your thumb. Over the moments there settled upon William a thought so black and destructive, so shot through with heat, that it scalded his innermost parts. The dead man looked like his father. The constables wrapped him first crosswise in the sheet and tucked under the ends and they stood away with their backs to the cart, wiping their hands, eyeing the crowd. William felt dizzy.

Brother Payne came elbowing through the pack of men up

alongside the boy. He leaned and spoke into his ear. William could not hear what he said, such was the heartbeat in his ears, yet when Payne's hand fell heavily upon his shoulder he knew. It was the weight of helplessness. Payne caught him by the arms and turned him roughly and crouched before the boy. He held William's eyes a long time before he reached and cupped the back of his neck and pressed his own forehead gently upon the boy's and pressed their noses together.

Above the tufts of his whiskers his uncle's eyes were hard and dark. He bore the smell of sweat, a breath of coffee. William did not resist the embrace of this solitary man. As their noses touched it seemed he would take upon himself, this wanderer, the charge of grief that William had gathered in his days, bear it away as his own, if he could, but there was no host and there was no power to make it be. Even so, he held the boy nose to nose, brow to brow, and the forthright giving of his pity unnerved William, set his heart racing, and when Payne stood and stepped back and folded his arms William felt light.

You are young, he said as his gaze stayed long on the boy. Let your shadow fall behind you.

The crowd began to break up. William could only stare at him.

They were silent for a time. Payne fetched a gold cross from his shirt pocket, which he rubbed in his fingers. Between the folk at the cart they could see the shape of Thomas Toosey under his sheet.

His hair is so long, William said.

Long as a horse's tail, Payne said. Never saw the like of it.

They were silent a while.

Why wear it that way? William said. He looks a fool.

Payne worried his little cross. Out of shame, he said. Out of love. Cause he loved you and your ma. He was sorry to have lost you. Very sorry.

William lowered his eyes then. He remembered his father

leaving in the long ago, when his mother had thrown his bedroll into the street and thrown after it a handful of coins. He'd watched his old man bend like a clumsy infant and grub through the dust to find them. Beside him a bottle of rum. We don't want you here, she'd said. His father had fingered up with great care the bits of copper, bits of bronze, and fumbled them into his pocket. His hat had toppled off. His hair was short. Not no more, his mother had said, not like this.

Clear back, clear back, Beatty was calling.

The cart started forward. William could not look.

Clear back, Beatty called.

J ane Hall knew every ownerless tenancy in the shire of Launceston and it was to one such hovel that she led the outlaw Caislin Flynn. They passed rows of tenements little better than shanties on the western road out of town, each the same seasoned grey and skirted around by a growth of thistle. They passed river flats where brushy reeds wilted in the mud and the boats above the tideline sat shored by poles. They did not speak to the folk going by that often bid them good afternoon. Ahead the Esk River discharged out of a gorge of sheer-sided stone. They walked, holding hands, looking up at the bare cliffs rising out of the wild river, the gum in bloom and the crowning scrub of black wattle.

An outbuilding lay on the road to the bridge and Hall ducked through the rail fence into the yard before it. She entered the ruin through a hole in the wall and Caislin followed in a daze. The floor had mouldered and the old manure of birds was cast about and there were blankets and two rough chairs stashed away beneath the sloping sheet-iron. Jane Hall showed the girl a place where she might sit, a frayed cane chair. She fetched in a bowl full with water and placed it on the ground by her feet.

Better get that mess off you.

She removed the neckerchief and bonnet Caislin wore and rolled back the sleeves of her dress and lathered water over her arms to wash away the freckled blood. Caislin sat stunned and silent, watching the road towards the town through the wall hole.

Just get the money, Hall said. Didn't we agree? Just get it and go.

Caislin lifted her eyes. The balded skin above her ear was mottled by blisters. Some seeped pus, some had hardened.

Get the money. That was all. Then come out the back through the kitchen like I told you.

Her hands dripped into the bowl. She held them out.

Now the whole thing is dead in the nest, Hall said.

It don't matter.

That celestial saw you, Hall said. When you're hunted as a murderess it will soon enough matter.

She seemed to stare at the hills a moment through the unclad walls, the folds of dark towering rock and up high the stunted cliff-top scrub. She looked back at Hall.

Christ, Hall said. You never had to kill him. You never had to do that.

She took a scoop of water and splashed Caislin's face. The girl blinked.

We are royally in the shit I can tell you.

Then you should go, Caislin said. It aint safe with me.

My word it aint. I see that.

So you should go.

No.

They will hang you too.

No one's hangin no one, girl. Not by a long shot. The point of the matter is to get you away. Get you home. That's how we beat this. Not a chance they will find you there. Not in the Quamby.

Water dripped off the unmarred point of her chin. For an instant she was a plain-enough looking girl, the upturn of her nose, the white of her cheek, and then she turned to Hall with the whole of her face and it was abhorrent. Hall lay a hand on her forearm. She let it lie there calmly, through a few long breaths as she slowed her bolting mind.

Simple truth is I'm too wise for them, she said. While I'm around won't no one will hang.

With a lazy lift of the boot Caislin kicked forward the package she'd carried from the hotel. It rolled and propped up in the floor litter and being only crudely secured her road clothes poked through the paper and with them something else. A knotted sack. She gestured at it with the toe of her boot.

Take your ten, she said. Then get yourself away.

Hall scratched her neck. Squatting alongside the bundle she peeled back bits of butcher's paper and pulled the money bag from within. She gave a tilt of the head when she saw it. She felt the underside of the bag for the weight and dropped it and fought with the knot.

Sister, she said looking up, you are some hard study.

From the sack she counted ten sovereigns. In her grubby hands they were something fanciful, the riches of kings. Her bad leg was cocked to one side and she pushed herself up and stood before Caislin admiring the coins.

So this is what he stole from you.

Yes.

And your father wanted it settled?

He wanted Toosey dead.

What did you want?

Caislin pulled her handkerchief and cupped it under her nose and squeezed her eyes shut. Hall watched her. The chair on which she was perched creaked as she rocked gently, this frail soul who wore her wounds equally within and without. She spoke through the handkerchief.

I wanted to die, she said. My father said I should bear it till it broke my back. Bear it for him. If I died, he said he would soon follow. That's what he said. He would soon follow.

The creaking stopped. Her eyes crept open. I have nothing, she said. I have nothing.

Come on now.

The girl leaned against Hall and Hall held her.

He pushed me, that man. Into the hearth. Into the fire. He'd come for the banknotes and I fought for them but he pushed me like I was nothing.

Shhh, said Hall. Forget that. Just forget that.

She could feel the girl breaking apart. Each sob made her shoulders jump through her dress, through her thin skin, so that it was like a sparrow she held more than some young woman.

You have to keep up. Are you listening? You have to keep up.

I have no heart.

You can't give out. There is something else you have to do.

Caislin sank against her.

I reckon I know. Your father, I know where he might be.

She held this hollow-boned girl.

I'll show you.

CHARLES STREET GENERAL CEMETERY

A meagre sum of seven black-suited men and women had congregated at the grave hole of Thomas Toosey. They were expirees to a man, the hunchback Payne and his wife, and four bent and badly fared fellows who'd once shared a cell or a shearing shed or a district road with Toosey. Across the damp black pit the men passed a hip flask of sugared and watered whiskey, each man taking his pull before giving it on. The minister had his own bottle from which he swigged. He was a well-known drunk and because of it was favoured by the emancipist class for any service requiring a payment, often made in his case by home-cooked liquor. He roughly corked the quart bottle and slipped it inside his vestments. Then he stepped away to the shade of a willow to relieve himself, head tossed like a whore, groaning as he hosed the tree in full view.

William Toosey among them was the only sober soul. He had borrowed an ill-fitting morning coat that left his wrists exposed and he stood, strangely austere, staring into the depths of the grave at the rough coffin filling the bottom of the hole. Chalk marks where the planks had been sized and cut were all that dressed it. Someone had driven nails through the joints at all angles, each ringed with a bruise, and through the gaps in the wood could be seen the immaculate dark within, the final home of men. The minister came swaying in his faded cassock up before the hole. He fumbled open a bible tagged at the Book of Job with a strip of red ribbon. He coughed and spat.

Man born of woman, he said and coughed. Man born of woman is short-lived and glutted with agitation. Like a blossom he has come forth and is cut off. And he runs away like the shadow and does not keep existing. Who can produce some-one clean out of someone unclean? There is not one. Not one. An able-bodied man dies and lies vanquished and an earthling man expires and where is he? His sons get honoured but he does not know it. They become insignificant but he does not consider them. I say again, he said and looked up at that poorly lot of men. They become insignificant. Only his own flesh while upon him will keep aching and his own soul while within him will keep mourning.

Here the minister stopped. He blinked a few times. It seemed he had finished, for he nodded at the men and waved an unsteady hand and then he stepped away and produced his bottle and yanked the cork with his teeth.

The men seized up their shovels and sharing few words filled the pit from a pile of earth, passing in a circle, tossing arcs of dirt spread thin as chaff across a few feet and soon the coffin was covered under the sprays and soon it was gone. William Toosey stood there, head low, hearing pebbles drum on the coffin lid. There was something that needed saying and he thought hard about it. In the end he said, That's a piss-poor box.

Brother Payne reached to take his wife by the hand, and she, a stoic, tight-mouthed thing yet. He wouldn't care, he said. Your pa, God rest him, was harder than a ten-penny nail, made so by the meanness of life.

William studied him for a time. He could not tell if Payne admired this about his father or thought it a misery. Perhaps he admired the misery. William looked away. There was a shovel laying by, the handle worn to a shine, and he took it up and with a steadying breath drove it into the mound. He began now to pace the ground between pile and hole hauling the loaded shovel and flinging clods of earth over the coffin. Beside him the old hands circled likewise.

What kind of life is that? Payne said.

It's the one I have.

Payne then caught hold of William's forearm and kept him still, looking steadily into his face. Around them the shovels scratched. There is as much ruin comes from love as virtue, he said. That is a fact, you have seen it. But do not follow that fool into his hole. He wanted more for you. You need to want more for yourself.

William blinked and blinked.

Stay with us, Payne said.

No. You are good and kind. But I can worry about meself now.

Mrs. Payne was holding to her mouth a handkerchief in the manner of a gentlewoman, except when she spoke her grey teeth showed. Who will look after you?

No one, he said.

You need lookin after, she said. A boy your age.

William did not answer. He was sweating and the beads ran on his cheeks. He circled with the shovel.

If the police lay hold of you, they'll stick you in the invalid depot, she said. You know that?

As long as they hang that mongrel Chinaman, I don't care what they do to me.

Should think they will, Payne said. He's guilty as Judas.

Brother Payne fished his pipe from his pocket and put it to his mouth, and then in frustration pulled it and replaced it in his coat. The ex-government men had taken up a song in their labour, each one raising his whiskey-harsh voice until the whole of them like a mangy choir sang his own peculiar range and the tune was carried after a fashion and the song found shape. William scooped up dirt and rounded for the grave.

What would your old man think about you? Payne said.

William tossed his load of soil. I don't rightly know.

He'd think you a grand sight, I'd say. A grand sight.

Payne tugged on his cap and, with his fists in his pockets, walked away towards the vacant street beyond in his strange stooped gait, a wounded bear upright, dust smoking from his heels. His Aunt Minnie came and touched William once on the shoulder, held her hand there a moment, and turned and followed after her husband. The dry grass in the breeze hissing.

William Toosey bent and buried the shovel. The men sang their song, a labourer's ballad he'd never heard before that day. He lifted a pile of earth, all of them lifting earth, throwing it across the deeply shadowed pit, and he picked up the tune. After a while he picked up the words and when he mended his voice into theirs they looked around at him, and no one stopped but they looked at him as he shovelled and sang, this young man, for his voice was clean and sharp and beautiful, and so they all shovelled and sang and in this manner was the gravehole of Thomas Toosey filled.

There lingered also in this hillside cemetery two restive souls searching along the row of hard dry mounds where the newly dead were buried. Caislin Flynn in the covering shade of a blue gum stood with her head bowed, a neat black dress snapping in the wind, at her stomach a bunch of wildflowers of unmatched colours and lengths, and each one twitching. Jane Hall was uncomfortable in this place, for only of late had she buried her father here. She held Caislin's arm and squeezed it. As the boughs moved overhead the agitating shade below lapped at their feet like dark lake water. They walked quietly looking about. The rank of graves all bore a carven stone save one solitary pile at row's end that sat unmarked by any memorial. It was to this mound Caislin Flynn came. She stood looking down at it, looking around. Then she lowered to her knees and touched the crust. Beneath the surface a russet soil, rich and cool. The towering light of the sun, the unlit dark of her centre.

Is that him? Hall said.

It's him.

She glanced about at the graves of the oblivious dead. You sure of it?

Caislin took a handful of soil.

What if it aint?

Then who is it?

Who is it she says. Buggerin hell.

Caislin looked at the mound. She looked up.

You're a simple soul, Hall said. I swear.

It must be him, Caislin said.

Very well.

It is him.

Hall stuffed her hands in her pockets. Very well.

I should buy him a stone, Caislin said, so as we know.

No you won't.

Why?

No stones, no names, else Beatty will get peery. Jesus, you don't want that philistine about. He's as likely to pick up the tale and come askin about you.

Caislin lowered her eyes. You're right, she said.

Look, girl. He won't be forgot. Not by you, not by your sisters.

No.

You are his keepers now. Here he is and he aint leavin. Bring them out, bring them to see. That will have to do you.

Caislin touched the mound. She laid the wildflowers there to wither and dry. After a while she put her cheek on the cool dome and closed her eyes and in time she laid out beside it, with one arm over the hump as if she hoped also to sleep there. Dirt painted her black clothes brown, and there she lay.

Through the heat of the afternoon Jane Hall stood in the

shade of a nearby gum. The sun slipped lower and their shadows crept out like elongated horrors, but Caislin seemed hardly to notice. She lay as before, arm cast across the mound, silent and still. Hall began to wonder if she was not delirious and she called to Caislin and Caislin brought her dark eyes to bear and she saw that it was only pain, only pain. So she waited, cocking and resetting the pistol, plucking leaves, dozing off.

In time Jane dreamt of the cold dead in the earth far removed, and far above, among the mounds, hearts that beat hot like coals in a burning hearth and when the fire dies the ash collects, always more dust than ember, more death than life, for that is the way. And the chiefly gift of parent to child is this, to bed down the land with their ash and make a place where fire will breathe and be warm, and the debt is told in beads of white smoke, the furrowing heat. And the sound of love is to name those lost who lived for others.

She woke on dusk and looked about. Caislin had not moved. She went and took the girl's hand and at first she was averse to leaving and tried to pull away but Hall, whispering through the ruffles of her bonnet, not words but soothing sounds, gripped her arm, lifted her, whispering, and in time she stood. For all the history of her, nothing was like those seconds. Seeing this burnt girl's grief, a thing still hot and whole in her breastbone. The loss of her own father gone these months felt new in the presence of it. The kink in the chest, the closed-off throat. It came to Hall anew until their sorrow seemed jointed at a common root.

Let's see you home, she said.

She led Caislin through graves placed everywhere without system, brought her close and held her, together, out onto the street. It was growing dim in the late day and the few folk they saw, perhaps for fear of what these two appeared to be, averted their eyes. They leaned into each other as they stood by the road, arms locked. The town rooves below were hued in bronze under smoke and the steam of breweries. The long black train inched over its track beyond the town's edge. They stood considering the troughed road, Jane Hall holding the girl and whispering to her, holding her dirty fingers, and then, as one, they wandered forward. With a kink of her mouth, Hall whistled loud and waved her arm and a horse cart by the road-side kicked into life. The driver wore a wide-awake hat made of felt and wore gloves made of leather. He waved and when the cart pulled up he dismounted from the bench in a ginger sort of way and stood smiling at them.

Was you waiting long? Hall said.

Oh long, he said. Yes, a while I'd say. But don't fret. You pay well.

He lowered the gate of the dead cart. Sawdust covered the bed and he had thrown hessian sacks across the mess and a fold of canvas lay to one side, which he spread for them. Then he jumped onto the bed and held out his hand. Come on, he said.

Hall took hold and climbed and Caislin followed. They lay on the canvas, on their backs, where they could hide. For a fee he would smuggle them out of the city. They stared up at the late eastern sky. A spread of shapeless cloud. A faint stain of sun like fire. The driver doubled the canvas across their legs and he stood looking down at them. Won't no one will see you there, he said.

As far as Perth, Hall said. That's all we need. We can worry about the rest tomorrow.

I'll have you there soon enough, he said and turned away. He climbed onto the bench and chucked up the reins and the horse when it started forward jerked the cart and startled them. They held each other secretly beneath the canvas. The driver looked over his shoulder.

I never had no one breathin back there before, he said. No, it's the first time I'd say. To cart the livin.

But the girls did not hear him. The reddening sky scrolled past. The wind sang fine through all the cemetery gums. A sweet smell of sawdust and oiled canvas. They did not hear him for they were busy watching the descending sun.